Rogues of
San
Francisco

ROGUES OF SAN FRANCISCO

Short Story Anthology

Edited by

BILL LEE

GLB Publishers   San Francisco

Published in the United States by
GLB Publishers
P.O. Box 78212, San Francisco, CA 94107 USA

Number 3 of ROGUES Series

Cover Design by Timothy Lewis and W.L. Warner

Publisher's Cataloging in Publication
(Prepared by Quality Books Inc.)

Rogues of San Francisco / edited by Bill Lee.
    p. cm. --(Rogues series ; #3)
    ISBN 1-879194-15-5

    1. Gay men--Fiction. 2. Erotic stories, American.   I. Lee,
Bill. II. Series: Lee, Bill. Rogues series ; #3.

PS648.H57R6 1993   813'.54
                                QBI93-20844

First printing, July, 1993
10 9 8 7 6 5 4 3 2 1

This book is dedicated to all the great guys who came and went and lived and loved in San Francisco during the golden days of uninhibited gay libido. They played innocently among the double-helixed guts of a multi-faceted monster that later cut them down in droves.

I hear they have some pretty fair orgies in heaven...

PREFACE

To many gay men worldwide, San Francisco has become the epitome of "gay-dom", an icon for gay men of all walks of life. The place where gays can "live the life they love," once the theme reserved for New Orleans' Mardi Gras. Where gay men prided themselves on their versatility in the bedroom and orgy room while maintaining an identity that brooked no constraints.

San Franciscans plead guilty to the charge of chauvinism in regard to their love affair with The City, but insist it is justified. Even before Harvey Milk proclaimed it as the politically correct stance, "Come Out!" was the daily cry from Polk Street, the Castro, and perhaps most insistently, from South of Market. Even New York took a back seat to San Francisco inventiveness for ways and places to enjoy sexual freedom while still maintaining the stability to show up for work in a three-piece suit. Perhaps taking a cue from such notable earlier rebel denizens as Twain and Kerouac and Ginsberg, gay writers and publishers too have settled comfortably here, receiving inspiration gratuitously from the "ordinary" daily exposures to gay life in The City. The inception of *Drummer*, *The Advocate*, and *On Our Backs* (among many other gay publications) in San Francisco was no accident.

And so it seemed logical to collect a group of stories from that effervescent fountainhead, written by some of my friends and me, that we thought characterized the diversity and universality of San Francisco experience. There has been no calculated scheme for establishing balance of theme (sometimes imbalance is the best way to reveal true character), although I suppose my personal preference has played an unavoidable role in selection of the stories appearing here. They cover a myriad of personalities and situations, from the immigrant fresh from the farm in Kansas to the settled sophisticate who takes gay freedom for granted while pushing the frontier a little further out.

The writers of these stories are as varied as the plots that interested them. As with all good writers, their stories are close to their experiences lived, bringing unmistakable authenticity necessary for good fiction. The writers' ages also vary widely, so the stories cover multiple strata in the gay experience beginning well before AIDS introduced its obscene choke-hold, when condoms changed from kinky to king. The stories are not only urban, either, ranging from Santa Cruz to Santa Rosa, from the Berkeley hills to the San Francisco Financial District, and to the Pacific shores at Golden Gate Park via Polk Street gutters. But throughout the series, the indomitable assumptions of San Franciscans that the gay spirit is to be heeded, even followed to unexplored extremes, come through clearly because that's what San Francisco is all about.

TABLE OF CONTENTS

SAM AND ANDY

Bart Louis

The slanting attic ceiling produced grotesque shadows of the figure moving slowly toward the narrow bed. The street light shining through the dormer window at the end of the bedroom, the only illumination at this midnight hour, gave off typical silver glimmers when filtered through the fog shrouding Twin Peaks on that May night. Slowly, very slowly, the slender figure knelt by the side of his sleeping brother, a much bulkier figure under the thin coverlet. The long, slim fingers gently closed around the prominent bulge protruding upward from his brother's mid-section, a shape that seemed to pulse rhythmically about once per second.

It was thick and hard and hot, even through the coverlet. It seemed to lurch with his touch as though waiting for it, welcoming it. The hand trembled; the entire body seemed to shake convulsively at the contact so long dreamed of but never before realized. The muscular body on the bed moved restlessly but showed no signs of awakening. Sam was a heavy sleeper, and their parents never came up to the attic at night. Slowly, hesitantly, without relinquishing the prize, the figure drew down the coverlet inch by inch, gradually exposing the bulging pecs with their perky, brown tits, the copious curly black hair in the center of the massive chest, and then the taut waist and flat belly of the eighteen year old athlete. Still no evidence of awakening, even as the matted black hair of the groin slid into view.

Andy stopped, his trembling almost uncontrollable now. Dare he do the unthinkable, expose that rigid cock he had gazed at, had longed to touch, to hold against his cheek, to the dim, shifting glow from that ghostly streetlight? Sam striding from the shower, his thickly-muscled high school lineman's body rippling steamily and that huge cock swinging, swaying thickly between his hairy thighs; that same thick tool towering stiffly in sleep, only a few feet away in their shared bedroom in their private attic, now in his grasp but still isolated by the coverlet clasped around it—Andy had dwelled on, dreamed about his brother to his great chagrin and shame, but the allure was unavoidable. Dare he —

But the decision was made for him at that moment. Even in sleep the tension in his cock called for action. Sam moved suddenly to push down the remaining cover, and Andy pulled back quickly to avoid those clutching fingers. And there it was, at least ten inches of thick meat in his brother's calloused fist, the head swollen hugely, bulging almost free of the retreating foreskin and already moist from whatever dream Andy's exploration had given rise to. Sam gripped himself hard for a moment and then groaned, pulling back and leaving his rigid rod throbbing alone only inches from his brother's face.

It was Andy's turn to grip his own thrusting tool. There were few similarities between the brothers, Andy slim with lighter muscles built for speed rather than power that served him well on the tennis court, four years younger and more studious, but in cock length they were quite alike. Now Andy stroked his more slender nine inches as he marvelled at, embraced with his eyes, the virility recently in his grasp. He knew what he wanted, and he was now beyond his capability of resisting his true impulses. He leaned forward and took the throbbing spear in his mouth.

It was sweet, it was potent, it was the very essence of manhood—his brother's manhood. The prick stiffened even more in his mouth, oozing sweet pre-cum onto his tongue, and even though Andy was not prepared for a suicidal dive to the base, it seemed to seek its way deeper and deeper into his throat. He gratefully accepted the gesture, and for the first time noticed the heavy, hairy balls stirring restlessly in their sack just below. They seemed prepared to give up their richness if he would but worship their phallus as it warranted.

He thrilled to the enormity as the spongy cockhead found its way into his throat. He absorbed the maleness of his brother with the instincts of a courtesan, willing to take all, needing it all to match his limitless yearning, and it was only when his lungs screamed for breath that he backed off, moving up, only to move down again compulsively to engulf the totality. And then the instinctive rhythm began, the up and down that is the pattern of the universe, the in and out that has given rise to the human race as we know it.

"What the fuck —?"

Sam suddenly awoke and partially sat up, his eyes blinking unbelievingly at his brother sucking his cock. Andy stopped for a moment, their eyes meeting directly in their first real confrontation as men on a sexual level.

"What are you doing, Andy?" Sam gasped, starting to push him away. But Andy, high on a plane of nirvana, only increased his worship of that maleness; he couldn't stop now, even if Sam hated him for it.

He forced the prick all the way into his throat and Sam groaned, his entire body tensing as a bow. "Oh, shit—do it! Yeah—down again—do it!" Sam groaned and thrashed in his narrow bed. His heavy thighs caught his brother's head in an inescapable clamping action, and as his balls pulled up and danced impatiently, he shoved Andy's head down hard to receive his first bountiful harvest of male nectar. At the same time, Andy had his first spontaneous orgasm, untouched by human hands, on the floor.

Sam had barely recovered his breath when he looked up again and snarled at Andy, still impaled on the softening cock: "You dirty cocksucker! Get away from me! Get in your own bed where you belong!" Andy obeyed silently, but with a smile on his lips.

The brothers never openly discussed what had happened, what was now different between them, but both came to rely on their nightly joustings, looking forward to them with thickening cocks at odd times during the day. It was Sam's senior year in high school and he was hoping for a football scholarship, but at the moment the balls of primary interest were between his legs. He loved Andy's blow jobs, but soon Sam sought more and Andy was a willing subject, learning quickly to serve his brother's lust equally well in his ass. Sam frequently called him a "fuckin' cocksucker," but that was OK.

Sam grew to particularly enjoy the verbal abuse, mixing "cunt" and "ass" interchangeably in his guttural enthusiasm that sometimes became quite boisterous. His violent fucking was always accompanied by vicious taunts and curses, humiliating epithets that punctuated the most penetrating action. "Fuckin' tight asshole — suckin' me in — yeah, take my prick!" But frequently he gripped Andy's cock in his rough fist while he hammered away, and didn't complain of the sticky cum that flooded his hand when he emptied his balls into his brother's gut. At the early age of 14, Andy was learning that people don't always mean what they say, and to take his pleasure where he found it.

The night before Sam's graduation there was a senior party and Sam had his pick of the girls for the date because of his striking good looks and his athletic prowess. But his date was uncooperative, and Sam got more than a little drunk, and late that night, as was their custom, ended up plugged deeply into his brother. With his inhibitions flown from the alcohol and his increasing passion, he became more verbal than usual. "Fuckin' hot asshole — goin' to take my cum — stiff prick deep in your gut, Andy — take it!" And so it was that, just as he was filling Andy with his viscous load, the ceiling light was switched on and their father witnessed the entire finality, his eyes nearly bulging from their sockets.

There is no need to detail all the gruesome consequences of that night, but the father's anger and vituperation were enough to send Sam packing to whereabouts unknown. Apparently Mr. Forbes came to regret his decision, going into a depressed slump from the absence of his favorite son. A few nights later, Andy's father visited his remaining son late at night in the attic bedroom.

"Sam would never have done that if you hadn't tempted him into it, you bastard! He's a football star, all man! I can see now that you're a fuckin' sissy, playin' around on a tennis court, hangin' out with those book-worms from school. It's your fault!"

Andy shriveled under his father's accusations. Why had he these compulsions about men's bodies, men's cocks? He curled his nude body in a ball under the covers as his father railed at him, but that was an inadequate defence. His father tore the covers away and began to whip his bare ass with his belt, swearing and calling him a whore. Apparently Andy's red ass looked better and better as the punishment went on, and that night Mr. Forbes took up where Sam had left off.

*   *   *   *

I learned all of this as a psychologist who had the opportunity to see Andy years later in consultation. Apparently Andy had never been able to establish a solid relationship with his father as a child, and came to see sex with him as at least some evidence of love, of worthiness that his father had never shown in any other way. Andy was berated and beaten, with his father's hand or belt, before, during, and after being fucked. And Andy still wore a smile, although now it was secretly.

Sam seemed to be lost forever. There was no contact with him. But as soon as Andy finished high school, he left home to become a tennis pro, traveling extensively in the competitive circuits. He was consistently good, never brilliant, but a favorite of the younger set, and the management was pleased.

Of course there was no shortage of male sex partners for the tall, handsome, agile athlete with the long dick, the ravenous ass, and the sad eyes, especially when Andy grew more accomplished in finding what he sought. From time to time he encountered men who enjoyed punishing and humiliating him as they breathlessly used him, and these were his most satisfying relationships, though brief. But the tour management became less cooperative as time went on and the bruises began to appear too obvious in his scant tennis costumes and in the communal showers. Eventually the word got around that he was not to be depended on to show up for a match or to teach a lesson; sometimes he was still in bondage when game time arrived. And then his name disappeared from the roster of the bigger tournaments, and it was rumored that he was spending much of his time in leather bars and dark alleys in New York, Chicago, or New Orleans. Once a friend bailed him out of a southern jail and gave him a lift across the state line after he propositioned a plain clothes officer in one of the many police entrapments that were popular at the time.

I never learned exactly why Andy returned to San Francisco when he did. He said it was because he had been offered a job as bartender in a South of Market bar, but perhaps there was a deeper significance. At any rate, he quickly grew disillusioned by the "macho masters" who changed their minds and turned their asses up to be fucked when they fondled his big cock to stiffness; the alleys beckoned and the darkness seemed promising.

Ringold Alley was too dull. Frequently he met there the same pseudomasculinity that had turned him off bars and parties. Because he was tall and athletic, the shorter, more muscular men shied away, although those were the most attractive to Andy. Tall, heavy men seemed to be the most likely to turn bottoms up, in Andy's experience. He grew a mustache and let his hair grow long, but that didn't help either.

On one of his late night meanderings in the warehouse district, he glanced down an alley and spotted a figure moving into deep shadows. Fog curled around corners, partially obscuring even usually recognizable objects. Immediately he sauntered deliberately down the alley toward the spot where the figure had disappeared. Andy was very experienced in these trysts, and eventually his sharp eye discerned a darker shadow in a brick archway near some garbage cans. He could tell the man was bulky, probably muscular, probably a little shorter than he, and his balls tingled with what might be in store. He could smell seasoned leather, probably from the man's jacket, but being black it could not be seen. He moved closer, staying in the shadows.

The fog was clammy against his cheek.

"Nice night," Andy noted, his pulse beginning to speed.

"Yeah," the man intoned in a deep baritone, noncommittal as the rules of the game required.

"Looking for something special?" Andy knew this was dangerous but his need was great.

"Maybe," was the answer after a pause. The rough voice, although seeming possibly forced, brought back memories of other times when such a brute had brought him to pinnacles of passion. Unabashedly Andy reached out to fondle the area where he figured the crotch to be, although it was too dark to discern any detail. His instinct was infallible; the bulge was impressive.

"You a cock-sucker?" the man inquired gruffly, perhaps unnecessarily.

Andy's smile could not be seen but his voice showed it. "Yeah."

"Here?"

"Wherever you say."

Under his hand Andy could feel the lengthening, thickening response that was always his first thrill. He tightened his grip and the bulge throbbed strongly in return. He waited for some move, some evidence of refusal or resistance, but there was none. The bulge grew larger as Andy caressed it, but the man continued to lean against the brick wall behind him, neither resisting nor overtly reacting.

Andy began to fumble with his zipper, pleased that the man wore no shorts. Thick, wiry pubic hair greeted his fingers, and Andy had to dip low into the denim pants before he could clasp a huge, thick prick that throbbed to his touch. Still there was no reaction from the man.

Impatient now, Andy extracted the heavy fucktool and almost moaned at its size. He managed to bring out the balls also, heavy orbs in a hairy sack. Andy could not encircle the total, beautiful set, even with his long fingers. With his thumb he tested the moist opening, and was pleased as the broad head pushed further through the foreskin to become almost completely exposed.

He fell to his knees and worshipped the man's broad cockhead with his tongue, savoring the sweetness forming at the tip and caressing the huge balls lovingly. It was perfect, it seemed, fitting his concept of master meat to a T. Slowly he worked his way down, consuming the massive prick, apparently to the total disinterest of the stud who was obviously his master. Some might feel it humiliating to kneel in a dark alley, servicing a man who at least pretended to ignore him, but to Andy it was the ultimate experience.

"Use me," he whispered, looking up to the towering shadow. He crammed the entire length into his throat. At first there was no response, but then Andy heard a low groan, an almost strangled sound as if partially stifled. Then he felt his shoulders gripped in iron fists that pulled him strongly against his crotch. Andy's nose was buried in thick hair at the cock base and the full balls were crushed against his chin. Dimly, even through the haze that clouded his fevered brain, Andy noted the fresh, clean fragrance of man crotch, so different from the musty, raunchy odors of some other men he had serviced willingly in such locations.

The man began to thrust in and out, the massive fullness alternately strangling and depriving. Gratefully Andy wrapped his arms around the man and clutched his hard asscheeks—thick, muscular mounds of a thick, muscular man. An athlete, surely, perhaps even a football player. A Forty-Niner, perhaps?

"Fuckin' cocksucker —" the man grunted through his teeth.

Andy agreed silently.

"Boy cunt–face —"

Whatever you say, Andy thought.

The man was trembling almost as much as Andy now; both were borne aloft in some fantastic whirlwind that blocked all contact with the world; they were alone in a world delineated by that foggy alley.

The man gasped and suddenly drew back, pushing Andy away.

Andy groaned, looking up pleadingly, but could still see nothing of the man's face. He was clearly close to orgasm.

"Stand up!" was the order.

Reluctantly, somewhat awkwardly, Andy rose to face the darkness.

"Drop your pants and bend over!" The voice was strangled, almost desperate, it seemed, as if the acknowledgement of his need was a mortal wound. Andy was only dimly aware of these nuances at the time; the new command had switched his mind to his hungry ass, and he hastened to obey, to meet the challenge.

Almost immediately after he had assumed the position, he felt the rough finger at his asshole, and then two, pushing into him. He willed his ass to open obediently; he needed this man at this moment in this place. And then the fingers retreated and he felt the broad, velvet cockhead, still dripping with saliva, press against him and enter, slowly but forcefully, stiffly but yielding, spreading him broadly, pushing in further and further, deeper and deeper, stretching him widely —

His mind whirling, the thick prick entered him, setting up familiar associations long suppressed but always in the background. As the man began to thrust in and out, the huge balls swung against his ass and the wiry public hair grated against him deliciously. As the thrusts became more powerful, he gripped his knees and set his feet widely, stretching his Levi's around his ankles. It was important that it be good, be perfect for this paragon who mastered him so completely. His own balls were churning hotly, and his untouched cock jerked violently in the cool and foggy night air.

"Fuckin' tight asshole — suckin' me in — yeah, take my prick!"

Oh, yes, I'll take it — give it to me, Master — please!

"Fuckin' hot asshole — goin' to take my cum — stiff prick deep in your gut — take it!"

The man's hand reached around and captured Andy's cock in a steely, painful grip and then shoved once, twice, and flooded Andy's ass with boiling juices straight from those heavy, hairy balls. At the same moment, Andy's cock gushed over the hairy fist.

"Sam — Sam —!" Andy screamed, "I love you, Sam!"

"Andy — take my hot cum, Andy — I love you, Andy!"

Both were only half conscious of their words. The expressions were wrung from their souls, unbidden, uncontrolled, writhing upward from the subconscious to surface in that dirty alley that dark, fog-bound night.

The echo of their words seemed to reverberate around them, and as their spurting cocks began to sag, their minds began to function tenuously again. Their gasps froze in their throats and for a long moment there was total silence in the alley. Then Andy straightened, the softening cock slipping out of its soggy haven; he looked blankly straight ahead at the brick wall across the alley. Abruptly the man swung Andy around sharply, stepping out of the deep shadows, and they stared deeply into each others' eyes for the first time in many years.

I'm not quite sure why Andy came to me. Did he expect some sort of retribution from a total stranger? He wouldn't get that from me, certainly. Fortunately he was not really on a guilt trip. Was it the ageless taboo of incest that concerned him? Obviously not appropriate in this case. There didn't seem to be a problem in handling grief from the death of his father several years previously. He certainly did not want to be "cured" of homosexuality, even if it were possible or desirable. Nor was his need to be mastered a problem, as far as I was concerned, as long as his Master was a caring one, and that was certainly true in this case.

When I told him I wanted to write up this case, he seemed pleased. The brothers have lived together happily now for over eight years. All I could do is congratulate him and send him on his way.

THE CENTER OF THE MAZE

David May

I. BEGINNINGS

Gene was in his last year of college, and still naive in some ways. He was clean–shaven, almost handsome. Some men thought he was pretty, but he wasn't — at least not anymore — just goodlooking in a fair–haired, boyish sort of way.

Aaron was more than handsome: dark haired, bearded, with powerful shoulders and a lean torso, and hairy all over. He was wearing worn jeans, black boots and no shirt when Gene saw him at Mona's Gorilla Lounge.

"A regular Neanderthal," a friend whispered in Gene's ear. Gene pushed his friend aside and approached Aaron, who had matched his stare from the beginning.

"Wanna dance?" asked Gene.

"I'd rather make you dance."

"Pardon?"

"Let's go," said Aaron. He grabbed a black leather jacket from a bar stool and walked out the door without a second glance.

Gene followed.

When he got outside, Aaron was already on the bike. It had gotten chilly, and Gene needed the jacket he'd left in his car.

"Get on."

Gene obeyed wordlessly. The bike started and Gene clung to Aaron's body for warmth.

They headed not into town, as Gene expected, but away from it and up into the Santa Cruz mountains. The air grew warmer as they drove away from the ocean and Gene stopped shivering. They stopped at a house secluded by redwoods.

"The place belongs to a friend. I live in the City."

"Oh."

"What's your name, boy?"

Gene wasn't sure he liked being called "boy." "Gene. What's yours?"

"You can call me 'Sir'."

Gene laughed nervously.

Aaron opened the door and, with a firm hand on Gene's butt, led him into the house.

When he was bent over Aaron's lap and spanked with a gloved hand, Gene didn't resist. His heart raced and his cock hardened. He resisted the impulse to think about where he was and what was happening. If he thought about it, he knew, he would panic. Instead of thinking, he closed his eyes and breathed a deep, whispered "Thank you."

Aaron gave orders and Gene obeyed. Aaron bound Gene and beat him, tormented him in ways Gene had never imagined. In a few hours, overwhelmed with sensation, Gene was no longer able to respond to Aaron's ministrations. His body numb, his mind foggy, he felt only gratitude for what had been given him. "Thank you, Sir," he moaned again and again. "Thank you, thank you..."

So Aaron fucked him.

Gene was jolted, if not into reality, then from where he'd been. He threw his ass upward to meet Aaron's cock as it pushed its way against Gene's ass, and a contest of wills began: Each man sought to force the other to shoot first. To the winner went the power.

Aaron won.

Gene pushed his ass up against Aaron's cock as it sawed him in two. He screamed like a man dying. His hole clenched hard around Aaron's cock as Gene's own cock bounced into the air and shot, each spurt arching through the air like a rocket.

He screamed again as Aaron's final, insistent thrusts pounded the tender prostate. Then Aaron screamed, his body and face tightening into a single knot of pain. Gene felt Aaron's cock pulse inside him, felt the force of Aaron's orgasm as it shot against the walls of his guts.

It was good that Aaron had won the contest. If not, Aaron would not have consented to see Gene again. And Gene would have felt he held Aaron in his hand, and continued to be the pushy bottom he'd been becoming before he'd suddenly found himself Mastered.

Every day for the next two weeks, Gene went to the cabin in the redwoods. He had passed from pleasure/pain to pain/pleasure in a single night. Now he had only to explore the varieties of pain he might find pleasure in.

A week later, Gene was led, naked except for boots and wrist restraints, into the forest. Aaron told him to stand, feet wide apart, in a clearing between two trees. Each ankle was secured to the nearest trunk. His wrists were also secured so that he was made to stand spread–eagled in empty space. Aaron attached clamps to Gene's nipples, kissed him gently in the space between the shoulders and walked away. Gene heard the crunch of Aaron's footsteps on the forest floor, disappearing.

Gene was excited at first. Then he felt nervous, abandoned. Finally he was terrified at being left alone and so vulnerable for so long. He pulled at his restraints. His breathing was hard and heavy. He hyperventilated and slumped forward against his restraints, blacking out momentarily.

As he came to, Gene was aware of the tit clamps again. He cock was hard. He stood up straight, flexing as much of his body as he could. He found that if he flexed his shoulder and chest muscles, the chain attaching the two clamps together danced against his skin, tightening the clamps. He threw back his head and called out like a man having a vision. He flexed his whole body against the shackles, fucking the air with his hard dick.

He came.

His cum shot across the forest floor for several feet. His face twisted into a snarl that forced his eyes shut with each spurt of his juices. He screamed ecstasy to the canopy of trees on the last shot of punk. He felt his soul had been pulled through his cock and that he was left only with this now–depleted body, an empty shell.

He was lightheaded bordering on euphoric for some time. Then he felt something spreading in waves over his back and buttocks: something like water only firmer, like fire only softer. He recognized the feel of the whip's stinglike caress.

He moaned softly to himself.

"Oh, yes," he murmured. "Yes, yes. Thank you..."

The strength of the blows increased, forcing small, sharp cries from Gene. He closed his eyes and was at one with the rhythm of the whip, even at peace with it. He felt himself fall; felt the wind about him and heard the steady beat of the whip as it cracked against his skin.

His feet were no longer on solid ground and he wondered where he was, surrounded by darkness. He looked ahead of him with his eyes closed and saw he was in a maze, saw that he needed to turn one way or the other. He followed his intuition and turned left, then right, then left again. The whip snapped along his back with greater urgency. *Gene increased his speed as he made his way through the maze, turning one way, then the other. Gene screamed, ran, turned a final time to what he was sure would be the center of the maze—*

Aaron was holding him in his great hairy arms, kissing, spanking him, caressing him. He heard Aaron speak soothingly to him, speak with pride, assurance and (Gene hoped) love. Gene felt himself being released from his bonds, felt his stiff limbs being massaged, felt himself being carried off over Aaron's shoulder.

Gene felt uncertain, felt that something was still expected of him. He was groggy and wanted to sleep for a long time.

Aaron laid him down somewhere, lifted one leg over each shoulder, and fucked Gene's ass long and hard. Gene felt himself come around now; being fucked gave him the needed focus. He felt the huge cock rearrange his guts, push him inside out. He yelled out his joy again as the dickhead swelled and filled his hole with hot, sticky cream, then shot all over himself, like he had among the trees, without touching himself.

Aaron kissed him again. Gene felt the man's beard against his face, felt the man's sweat pour down on him. Gene raised his head to lick the sweat off Aaron's body.

"You made it."

"I'm sorry?"

"You got there. To the other side of pain."

"I guess."

Gene tried to get out of bed and fell back on the mattress, unable to move.

"Take it easy," said Aaron, handing Gene a mug of something hot. Gene accepted it with both hands.

"Thanks. Do I look as bad as I feel?"

Aaron caressed his cheek. "You look fine. Your backside's a mess, that's all. We even drew blood."

"Oh."

"You'll feel better once you start moving around, but you'll be sore for a while. And you'll remember it for more than a few days."

"Thank you — Sir."

Aaron kissed Gene softly on the lips.

"But I feel like I missed something... Like I didn't get there at all."

Aaron nodded. "You went as far as you can go and still come back."

Gene shook his head, not quite agreeing.

Aaron's stay in the house was over.

This did not surprise Gene. He had already reconciled himself to this eventuality. What he was uncertain of was his status in Aaron's life. Would Aaron allow Gene to follow him later?

"May I come and be your slave in the City?" asked Gene.

"Not right away. This is still new to you. You need to learn more about yourself, first. In five years, if you still want to be my slave, I'll be your Master."

Gene was still too young to see five years as anything less than an eternity. Aaron might as well have said five thousand. "Why so long?"

"Then you'll be as old as I am now. It seems a good age to me."

"But what if you find another slave before then?"

"What if you find another Master?"

There was a pause. Gene turned and looked at the welts and reddened flesh still healing across his back. He felt a rush of pride in the marks, then a kind of disappointment.

"I make no promises," Gene said. "But if I decide to be another man's slave, I'll let you know."

Aaron nodded.

"How will I find you?"

"It won't be hard. Now why don't you be a good boy and bend over so I can fuck you 'til you bleed, one last time."

Gene was glad to obey.

When Aaron left, Gene was several days into a beard. He decided to let it grow. It was his first beard. He saw another self emerging as the beard took shape.

II.   FINDING THE WAY

When Gene arrived in San Francisco, he learned he had the kind of look that was currently popular. With his new beard, he was suddenly handsome, even hot.

He came into a modest trust fund. He wasn't rich, but neither did he have to work very hard to live well. He took odd jobs, jobs that were short–term but interesting. His financial freedom allowed him to spend his nights exploring the maze of streets South of Market. Months could pass without Gene seeing a morning sky.

Sometimes he travelled.

Sometimes he saw Aaron.

The first few months in the City he lived in the Castro. Being naive, Gene assumed any man in leather would be willing and able to give him what Aaron had. After several disappointments (the last one of which he told off, saying, "You don't have the right to wear leather!") Gene decided that he belonged on Folsom Street.

He found a small flat on Rausch Street. It had been empty for months and was cluttered with the remnants of the last tenant. Cleaning out the attic and closets of his new home, he found odds and ends of black leather — including belts, boots, straps, unmatched gloves and a well–worn motorcycle jacket.

"A guy named Karl lived here," said Jim, Gene's new neighbor. "He spent less and less time at home, then disappeared without saying anything."

"What do you think happened?"

"There were rumors. But there always are, so why listen?"

Gene nodded, not quite agreeing.

"Does the jacket fit you?"

"No, it's too big."

"Then sell it."

"I think I'll keep it," said Gene. "He might come back."

Gene made friends in his new neighborhood. First he met Jim, who lived a few doors away from him. Through Jim he met Alan, whose Master was a cop. The youngest member of the group was Willy, whom Gene had met walking along Folsom Street after three o'clock one morning. They were a society of friends, tight–knit and watchful for each other. They met at the Eagle before the eleven o'clock crush, talked about the men they met, their jobs and roommates. Gene said little, confiding only in Jim, his closest friend and occasional fuck–buddy.

Saying little, Gene was a good listener and heard details of each man's life that no one else heard. He heard tales others would disbelieve and accepted them without judgment.

"It wasn't an accident," said Jim one rainy afternoon in Gene's apartment. "It happened because you wanted it to happen. Isn't that what you'd tell me?"

Gene handed him a mug of coffee. A neighbor's cat had come in out of the rain and lay sleeping on the radiator. Jim eyed the cat wearily.

Gene had told Jim about Aaron and the maze. Now he felt relieved and tired, like a Catholic after confession.

"I wondered what your story was," added Jim. "I was sure you had one."

Gene smiled, sipping his coffee. "I saw him last night on Dore Alley."

"Did he see you?"

"Yeah. He nodded. I went over to say hello. Instead I just licked his leather jacket."

"What happened?" Jim was excited by the story.

"He held me for a while, kissed me and sent me on my way."

"Did he say anything?"

"No. At least not with words."

Jim made a noise somewhere between a sigh and a snort that said he wasn't satisfied by the answer.

"Well, what did he say without words?"

"That he loved me."

They sat without speaking for a while.

"How much longer?"

"It's only been a year. Four more."

Jim sighed again. "I wouldn't do it," he said. "Life's too short to wait for love. Or for a Master, for that matter. Masters are men like us. And men like us change, Gene."

Gene nodded.

"This man waits, but not alone. Are you up to the Slot

tonight? I already reserved a room for us."

Alan's Master kicked Alan out.

Alan spent hours on the phone with Gene, while he hid himself away in a new apartment. After half a year, Alan reappeared on Folsom Street for a few months. He was aloof, though, almost unfriendly towards Gene and the others — especially Willy, who had taken Alan's place as Officer Jackson's slave. Strangely, it was Willy who kept insisting he'd seen Alan around the neighborhood at night when no one else had.

Then Alan disappeared altogether, leaving his apartment and belongings unclaimed. There were rumors, of course.

Jim dismissed it. Gene felt a chill run through him whenever he thought about it.

A year later, Gene was alone at the Caldron. He was leaning against a wall, naked except for his chaps and boots, watching two men fucking with a shared fury, slamming against each other, shooting off sparks of dissipating rage.

"Fuck you! Fuck you! Fuck you!" bellowed the topman with each slam into his partner's butt.

"Motherfucker!" screamed the bottom. "Motherfucking bastard!"

Gene watched the scene, his face expressionless while his heart raced with excitement. His cock got larger, filled with blood; but he didn't touch himself, not wanting to cum yet.

He felt a hand on his cock and turned to see whose it was. If he was hot, then Gene might let him continue. Gene liked what he saw; a curly-haired man-boy whose chin just reached Gene's shoulder.

The man-boy was dark; clean shaven, though the shadow of stubble was apparent even in the dim light of the Caldron. His chest and torso were covered with soft, curly hair that grew like some furry vegetation out of his undone jeans. His bright blue eyes asked the question, "May I?" even as his full lips reached up towards Gene's.

"I'm going to fuck that pretty mouth," Gene thought as their lips met. The next instant Gene's arms were around the man–boy, holding him close to Gene's body, holding him still as Gene's tongue fucked the man–boy's mouth. The man–boy returned Gene's embrace, succumbed to the assault without resistance, responded in kind.

The kiss lasted forever.

Gene closed his eyes. He was back in the maze.

The man–boy's mouth broke from Gene's and attached itself to Gene's armpits. Keeping his eyes closed, Gene wrapped an arm around the man–boy's head as the sweat pouring from Gene's body was lapped up from the twin hairy pools. After a time there, the man–boy's attention wandered to Gene's nipples, which were chewed and sucked.

Gene made soft, low moans that echoed into the maze. Keeping his eyes shut, Gene not so much saw as sensed light not far from where he was. He moved toward it.

He was kissing the man–boy again, penetrating the strange, soft throat with his tongue.

Further, Gene thought. Further. I can get there in time.

The man–boy licked the sweat from Gene's face and beard. Gene pushed him down to his knees where Gene's hard cock found the wet warmth of the stranger's mouth. Gene lost himself in the maze of delight as the man–boy's throat pulled and sucked at the stiff meat sliding between the two perfect lips.

Gene no longer ran through the maze. He flew. His urgency increased with the pace of their sex.

Gene's crotch slammed against the man–boy's face as he fucked "that pretty mouth." He felt two hands pull on his tits, increasing the urgency he felt inside of him, the urge to shoot (the urge to reach the center of the maze).

Gene's mouth hung open, panting like an excited animal. A third mouth joined his in a long, deliberate kiss.

Gene was almost there, he could see the light—

With the kiss, Gene cried out, pulled the man–boy's head tightly to his groin and shot his load down the man–boy's gagging throat.

He had come too soon. He was back in the Caldron, a crowd gathered around him.

"Shit," said one man.

"Hot fucker," said another.

"I wanna fuck that pretty face next," said a third.

Gene broke away from the kiss that had held him as he came. He opened his eyes. He'd been kissing Jim.

"All right!" said Jim.

The man–boy continued to suck on Gene's softening dick, licking up the last few drops oozing from the piss slit. Gene slowly pulled out of the stranger's mouth and lifted the man–boy back to his feet. They embraced, kissed deeply, if tenderly this time.

"He came on your leather," said Jim.

"He can lick it up later."

Gene and the man–boy kissed a long, deep kiss again. This time Gene tasted traces of his own salty cum.

"What's your name, cocksucker?"

"Erin. Sir."

Gene shook his head, not quite believing his ears.

"Hey, buddy, let me have a taste," said Jim, waving his hard-on in a gloved hand.

Gene nodded vaguely at Erin, who dropped to his knees and sucked Jim dry while he and Gene kissed.

"Fucking fantastic," said Jim a few minutes later as he tucked his dick back into his pants. "Say, pal, let me have a crack at his other hole after you've had it."

Jim kissed Gene with a smack on the butt.

"I'll call you tomorrow."

Gene nodded, his attention now fully focused on the precious man–boy standing before him, looking up into his face expectantly.

"Sir?"

Gene brought Erin home that night, tied him to the bed and whipped him soundly with the length of an English riding crop. The whipping was methodical, lacking sensuality or warmth. He whipped until he drew blood.

When Gene stood back to admire what he'd done to Erin's smooth flesh, he noticed that Erin was whimpering from the pain, wanting/needing comfort. Gene ignored him. Instead, Gene poured hot wax on the worst of the lacerations, stuffing Erin's mouth with a dirty sock to muffle the screaming. Finished and satisfied with his handiwork, Gene fucked/raped the man–boy's ass without bothering to lubricate cock or hole. Erin's muffled screams continued.

Gene's orgasm was fierce, shaking his entire body and covering them both with sweat. He lay on top of Erin for more than an hour, thinking. Finally, he got up and untied the shaking, frightened Erin, held him close, kissed him tenderly as he stroked the man–boy's cock to an impressive climax.

"You hurt me."

"You wanted me to hurt you."

"Yes, but..."

"But what?"

"Not like that."

"Like what?"

"So cruel."

"Love is cruel. And I love you very much."

They became lovers, almost to the exclusion of all other partners or friends. Erin moved in, went to work every day, and handed his paycheck to Gene every other Friday. Gene put a chain dog collar on Erin's neck and refused to remove it, even when Erin went to work.

Only Jim ever visited the flat. Every few days he came by to fuck Erin, or lay back and be serviced by that pair of perfect lips.

Erin and Gene lived for each other, for the power of their

kisses, for the physical torment and cruel sex that Gene insisted they continue. He tried to explain to Erin about the maze, about finding its center. Erin understood only the concept. He didn't understand how his scarred body aided Gene in his quest, or even why it was so important.

In the end, Gene went too far, sending Erin over the edge into unconsciousness. Badly frightened, Erin moved out the next day without a word.

Gene found Erin a week later.

"Don't touch me!"

"I won't. I just came to say I'm sorry. Here's the money from your paychecks. I don't need it and you do. I should never have done what I did. I never found the maze again while I was with you, not since that first night at the Caldron. I thought I would because I love you."

Erin took the money without looking at it. "I loved you, too."

Gene handed Erin the key to the collar still secured around his neck.

"You left," Gene said. "It's up to you to release yourself."

III. FOUND / A CONCLUSION

"Kink chic is a thing of the past," Jim was saying. "The clones have hung their leathers out at garage sales and retreated back to their ghetto."

"And left us to ourselves," added Gene.

It was late on a rainy Sunday night. Out of boredom, they'd decided to get drunk. Jim barely finished two beers, and Gene had drunk even less. This didn't matter, though, since the fun was in the intention to get drunk rather than in actually carrying it out.

Jim was the only one left, along with Gene, from their original quartet of friends. Their friendship had increased in intensity over the years in spite of quarrels and jealousies.

Erin stayed with Jim for a while, but Jim never offered to share him with Gene as they normally shared their lovers, slaves, and (occasionally) Masters.   Gene for his part was always solicitous of Erin, but never suggested they have sex again.

"Things have changed so much," Jim continued, waxing on as he did when he was with Gene. "Half the guys have shaved off their beards."

"What's become of the world?" laughed Gene. "Where are the standards of yesterday?"

They laughed together, even in their shared sadness. Their world had changed radically overnight, and they mourned for it as much older men might mourn for their youth. Bars and clubs closed. Folsom's character changed, at least superficially; straight clubs opened, along with trendy restaurants, condominiums and mainstream businesses. That they would eventually be forced out of their homes, their community fragmented by urban renewal, was inevitable.

"Five years ago the only people who'd look out of place at Hamburger Mary's were the hets slumming from the fern bars on Union Street," Jim complained. "Now it's full of them. Fucking yups."

Gene nodded his agreement, feeling the same anger as his friend.

Occasionally, late at night, when the one or two surviving leather bars had closed, Gene would walk along the streets and alleys he knew so well, and still feel something like he used to feel: a dark, warm intimacy that was at once cold and comforting, like the fog. But it was also like seeing an old friend again, and Gene would open his arms to embrace it, only to find the moment, and the feeling, gone.

There was less action now, but with few adaptations, Gene and Jim (who professed a secret and long–standing condom fetish) continued to live as they had before.

"Just as well we're losing Folsom, though," Jim said with some finality. "The whole neighborhood's built on swamp, you know.

They didn't fill it in right, and the buildings are sinking. Like yours. Ever notice how low the first basement step is? Let the breeders have it!"

"The question is, Jimbo, whether or not we're going to go down with it."

This was supposed to have been a joke to cheer Jim up. It had the opposite effect.

"Hell," said Jim. "Let's sink with it."

"Sure," Gene said. "We'll be another lost civilization."

Gene bottomed less and less. He was so experienced in the art of being a slave that he found few men worthy of the gift of his submission. Filling the void, he spent more and more of his time being dominant. He took special care in molding new slaves and novices, taking them step by step to the entrance of the maze. Those who were unsure of themselves became frightened and ran. Those who had at last found their life's destiny entered the maze without hesitation; these men Gene came to cherish, even love, as men cherish their children.

He realized the obvious about the maze: it was entered by letting go. He had tried to force the experience before, so only experienced it when he was caught off guard. Now he stayed in the maze for longer periods of time, hoping that by delaying the final twist of the journey, he'd at last see the center.

Without mentioning it, he brought other men to the maze through pain and pleasure, escorting them in, then letting them run wild in its shadows. But as he showed men this new and, to Gene, sacred place, he also observed that he alone wanted to see the center.

"The center?" he'd ask. "Don't you want to see the center of the maze?"

"See the center?" the men would respond. "How? There's no light in the maze to see it. Only darkness. It's as if the shadows have shadows."

"The dark doesn't scare you?"

"No. It feels safe, familiar — like Folsom Street after the bars close, but long before dawn."

Gene thought he understood.

Jim suggested they go to the leather dance after the Folsom Street Fair.

"When was the last time you danced in your leathers?"

"I don't remember the date, but I know I was with you. It was a Black Party, I think. Sylvester sang. We separated after two o'clock and you disappeared for a few weeks."

Jim smiled, remembering.

"It will be fun," said Gene.

"Maybe it will be like the old days..."

"Right, Jimbo. We'll do drugs, snort poppers and fuck strangers."

"That's not what I meant, Gene. I was talking about the music."

"Sure, Jimbo. Maybe they'll play the old stuff."

Gene went to the dance wearing a pair of leather shorts he'd bought in Amsterdam, the boots he'd gotten in London on the same trip, and fingerless gloves. Jim wore chaps with leather jock and uniform boots. Both were shirtless, wearing only arm bands over their biceps.

Jim had a new tattoo — an eagle landing over his left pec, the talons closing on Jim's pierced nipple — that he'd been showing off all day at the Street Fair. Gene envied Jim's courage in decorating his body as he chose. Gene was waiting for Aaron to decide how his body would be adorned.

They stayed together for a time, dancing, talking, watching sweaty men dance in clusters or pairs. Jim saw Erin stumbling drunk across the dance floor. A hot man wasted, Jim thought.

They stood together, but not together, each waiting for the other's signal to part company. A young man, neatly muscled and smooth–skinned, wearing only dungarees and sneakers, paused to glance at Jim. Jim looked back and decided the man was too young, hardly more than a boy and easily dismissed despite a shaggy–haired charm. But then the boy reached out to caress Jim's new tattoo. Jim grabbed the boy's hand, pulled him close, hoping the suddenness of his action would scare the boy off. Instead, the boy licked the sweat from Jim's body, starting with the tattoo, finding his way to Jim's leather jock, and finally his boots. He might have been too young to normally appeal to Jim, too smooth and precious, but the kid had style. Jim rearranged his crotch beneath the leather to keep his hard cock safe within its confines until he got the kid home.

Jim looked around and saw that Gene had already disappeared.

Just as the boy had approached Jim, Gene had seen Aaron standing in the shadowed corner on the edge of the dance floor. Now Gene was standing before the man, offering himself. He knelt, crawled on his stomach and kissed Aaron's boots.

Men on the dance floor stopped to watch.

Gene was licking Aaron's boots now, making his way up to his Master's knees.

"You're mine," Aaron shouted above the music.

"Yes, Master," Gene yelled in response. "Always."

"You shithead," Jim said a few days later over the phone. "You and your Daddy upstaged me and my boy!"

"And I wasn't even trying."

"Bastard."

"So who's the kid?"

"Name's Tim. From the River, he says. Before that from some hellhole near Tahoe. Used to hustle. Think I should put him on the streets for me?"

"Is that all he's good for? Can't he cook?"

"Don't know. Makes a handy footstool. In fact, that's what he's doing now."

"Talk about bastards."

"I try. So how about you? You're Aaron's now, right? You

moving in with him?"

"Soon. Right now I'm putting things in order. Then we're going to Europe. He says he wants to lead me on a leash down the streets of Amsterdam."

"Sounds romantic."

"Won't be the first time."

"Slut."

"I try, Jimbo. I try."

Being a slave, or at least Aaron's slave, was harder than Gene had anticipated. Not because Gene failed or refused to be submissive, but because they were so obviously equals — intellectually, spiritually and financially. While Aaron was a professional who could have easily supported them both, for instance, Gene neither desired nor needed that support and continued to work whenever he felt the need.

Since it was only in physical size and strength that Aaron was clearly Gene's superior, Gene's status as submissive was established and maintained by symbols that held more power for both Master and slave than chains or shackles: Gene always called Aaron "Master" or "Sir," even in public, and refrained from sitting on the furniture without permission when Aaron was present; Gene's right ear lobe and both nipples were pierced in a public ritual at the Cell; Aaron locked a dog's choke collar around Gene's neck and stored the key in a safe deposit box. More important to both of them, though, Aaron made certain that always healing somewhere on Gene's body was a welt or bruise inflicted by Aaron's own hand to remind Gene of his slavehood.

Gene had kept a journal since his first encounters with Aaron. Now he spent hours reading and re-reading it, searching for clues to the maze. He spent even more time writing in the journal, recalling again and again the events that led him to where he was, and speculated on what he would find when, and if, he found the center of the maze. In some ways he feared it.

Aaron wanted to know more about the maze, listened carefully to the words Gene used to describe the experience, and soon he was in the maze with Gene, and like Gene, looking for its center.

Their intimacy increased. Gene saw his friends only while Aaron worked or was out of town. And each night they spent together they made the journey: Gene was bound, gagged, chained, beaten, and tortured until his balls exploded cum across the room, and each time they both felt closer to the center.

Before leaving for Europe, Aaron was away on business and Gene spent an evening with Jim and Jim's new boy. Keeping his slave collar on, as he did at all times, Gene fucked Timmy-boy (as Jim called him) repeatedly.

"You're less than a slave," Gene told him, "being fucked by another slave."

Jim laughed. "Tell him, Gene buddy! Tell the dog what he is!"

When Gene felt himself ready to cum up Tim's butthole, he slapped the boy's asscheeks as hard as he could. The hole tightened around his shooting cock. Gene screamed and emptied his balls into the rubber.

When he pulled out a moment later, Gene tied the used condom into a knot and tossed it to Tim.

"Something to remember me by."

When they were done using him, Timmy-boy was sent to another room while his Master and Gene talked, as they always did, about everything and nothing. Mostly they laughed.

"I notice you let the cats on the furniture, but not the boy," observed Gene.

"Cats can't be owned and ordered about. Only dogs. Dogs are born to be ruled, and Tim's a dog, he does what he's told. That much he understands."

They both laughed long and hard.

"I'll miss you, Gene. How long will you be gone?"

"A couple months. I'll write. I'll bring you something back from Europe. They've got some nasty leathers in Holland that you'll love."

Jim sighed. "I'll miss you, babe," he said. "Be careful for me, okay? Timmy-boy and I will be here when you get back."

Gene had been to Europe before and thought he knew Amsterdam well: its bars, boy brothels and leather stores. But Aaron had other connections, knew where the black rooms were and how to access them.

Gene was impressed. Impressed to be shackled by iron chains to an ancient stone wall. Impressed to be blindfolded and left to the care of strangers, strangers who whispered and spoke only in Dutch when they were in Gene's hearing. Impressed to have spent a night in continual sexual subservience to a pack of men who barked orders and laughed at his humiliation. Impressed to be given a sack of used condoms in the morning, symbolic reminders of his status as Fuckhole.

After that he'd been brought to the dungeon and allowed to sleep on a bare cot for what seemed too short a time. Gene hadn't seen Aaron since the night before. He imagined his Master fucking and whipping some Dutch boy, slamming the too–pale skin with all his dark fury. Gene's cock hardened, thinking about such a scene, and only hoped Aaron had saved some of that delicious rage for him.

A fire burned nearby in the narrow room and Gene felt its warmth flickering on his bare skin. He put his face to the stone wall and felt its coolness, smelled the city's pervading dampness. He pulled on the chains. Relieved at the hopelessness of escape, his cock stayed hard.

He turned and saw that he was in the maze, a place where four paths met. He turned slowly in a circle and chose the path: there. That one. Where the darkness was the deepest, where the shadows had shadows...

Gene felt the feathery touch of a gloved hand softly stroke the smoothness of his taut skin. He knew Aaron's touch at once.

"I bought a new whip."

"Thank you, Sir."

The whipping began.

He turned and saw Aaron next to him. Together they found their way through the blackness, seeing the walls, doors and windows of the maze with their minds.

Gene felt flowers of fire blossoming over his back, shoulders and buttocks — felt them turn to ice, then back to fire — over and over again, flowers that never stopped blooming.

He heard himself cry out.

They held back this time, refusing to hurry. Almost touching, but never quite.

Aaron's cock, engorged and fat with blood and cum, swung free, ready. Aaron felt the sweat drip from his body. He was exhausted. He was afraid to pause, though. They might lose their way. He concentrated on Gene's body as it writhed in its steel shackles; he watched it, heard its moans, then its screams.

Someone said something to Aaron. The voice was concerned. Aaron heard the question and raised the whip to strike Gene's battered body again as his only response.

Gene's cock was hard. He felt it fuck the air as they flew through space, felt the universe suck it with a warm, wet throat. "Yes," he said. "Show it to us, and we'll give it to you. But show us the Center first." He followed his cock as it soared across the sky, turned and saw Aaron beside him, flying on the power of his own enormous member, dripping sweetness.

Aaron's hand never stopped beating Gene's body with methodical calm. His face was a blank, broken only by a small smile when he whipped Gene's hard dick.

They were still together now, almost touching but not quite. Almost there but not quite.

The last moment before orgasm is anguish. It lasts forever.

They were there, in the darkness. They touched, joined. Both men screamed, feeling cum gush from their dicks, cum springing not just from their balls, but from their guts as well, from the center of the solar plexus. They were there together, joined for an eternity. They saw the center, at last. Together.

The light was blinding.

First they heard their own breathing. Then each was able to separate the sound of his own breathing from the other's. Then they heard concerned voices speaking loudly, words Gene didn't understand.

Gene felt many hands lift him, carry him away, bathe him, caress him, put him to bed.

After he'd slept for most of a day, Gene lifted his head from the pillow just long enough to see Aaron nearby, staring into space, saying nothing. Curling himself into a ball, as an animal does to keep warm, Gene fell back to sleep until the next morning.

Gene came home alone.

Aaron went south to Crete.

"Amsterdam is best for leather clothes and toys. And SM porno. But London is better for boots and whips."

"Is that where you got that one?" asked Jim, pointing to a whip that hung over the mantel like an icon.

"I think that's where Aaron got it," said Gene. "I wasn't with him then. I was only there for its inauguration."

There was a comfortable pause as Jim admired himself again in the leather uniform shirt Gene had brought him from Europe.

"Gene, where's Aaron?"

"He's staying in Europe for a while."

"You're not wearing your collar."

"No, I'm not. What about Timmy-boy?"

"Gone. Disappeared one day."

They returned to their comfortable silence.

THE BRONZE BOY

Jay Markham

This story starts in a bar, but it isn't about a one night stand. It's about something that lasted for four and a half years, until last November. That was when his bike slid out from under him on a freeway curve on his way back to the city one rainy night. Back to me. The police said he hadn't been drinking, speeding maybe, but it was the diesel oil-slick that had brought him down. If he had to go, I'm glad that was the way it happened, speeding home alone on that big machine he loved to ride so much. If he hadn't gone down I wouldn't be telling my tale now. There'd be no need.

The bar was crowded when I walked in, but when I saw him it might as well have been deserted. He was leaning back against the counter sipping a beer, tall and square–built in a well–worn bike jacket. He was looking at the movie projected onto the back wall, a blurred tangle of pink and brown bodies in perpetual motion. He looked completely at ease, not bored, not expectant, just out on his own and comfortable, which is not easy to do in a bar. He wasn't young, somewhere around forty-five, I guessed, with symmetrical, chiselled features that signalled a lot of willpower. His black jacket and jeans looked lived in. It was Saturday night but he didn't look prettied up for a weekend scene. He wasn't displaying chains or handcuffs or even a handkerchief like many of the other men in the place. I didn't need any paraphernalia to tell me what he was.

Although the bar was packed, there was space around him, as if no-one wanted to crowd him. I'd seen that before, how some men, usually older ones, can impose themselves on the space they're in. It's the lack of effort that's impressive, the sense of power held in reserve.

I registered all this in a single glance from the other end of the bar, by the door. And I knew instantly that I would have to try to penetrate that force-field that surrounded him.

I left the beer I'd ordered on the counter, untasted, and stubbed out the cigarette I'd lit automatically when I came in. They would look too easygoing. I maneuvered through the crowd until I was among the group of leather-clad men around him. I swallowed hard and took two steps forward through the line. It was like passing through a doorway into a vast silent space that held only the two of us. The noise of the bar at my back seemed to have vanished.

I stood an arm's length away from him, to one side, my arms at my sides, and just waited. He was even taller than he'd looked across the room, about six-three and rock–solid. I kept my eyes at the level of his chest. After a while he shifted his weight against the bar and I could sense that I was being looked at.

It was a slow inspection but I held myself steady and said nothing. Eventually he stood at full height and took a long pull of beer, then handed the bottle to me.

"Finish this and come with me."

By the time I had gulped it down he was halfway out of the bar, and I had to charge through the crowd to catch up.

He led the way out and down the block to a big old Chevy pickup, the kind a builder or construction worker would use. (Any clue to his identity was going to be useful.) I climbed into the high cab and kept my eyes straight ahead as he made a couple of turns and headed for the Great Highway, heading north. He settled back, turned on a tape which sounded like Ellington or maybe Basie, and lit up a long thin cigar. He blew out a stream of smoke in my direction.

"There's a bag under the seat. Put your clothes in it."

His voice was deep, slightly hoarse. I glanced across at him but he was watching the road, his head nodding to the music. I reached down and pulled out a big military duffle bag, which was neatly folded and very clean. I began unlacing my boots, fumbling in the dark, wondering wildly if I'd heard him right, if he'd been joking perhaps. When my boots were off I struggled awkwardly out of my jeans, pulled my t-shirt over my head, and stuffed everything into the bag.

A few moments later he turned off the highway and pulled up facing a wide expanse of deserted beach. He turned off the engine and leaned over to open the door on my side.

"Tide's going out now, there'll be driftwood all around out there. Go fetch me some pieces, anything that looks interesting between about two and four feet long."

I climbed down onto dry cool sand. There was no wind and the air was unusually warm, something I wouldn't have noticed if I'd been dressed. A line of foam was shining out ahead some twenty yards away. There was no moon and no other lights were visible along the shoreline, which stretched out into darkness on either side. I glanced back at the truck, which looked as big as a tank, and set off down the beach. My eyes were getting used to the dark and I saw the driftwood scattered about, strangely light-colored. As my eyes adjusted, the air around me seemed to be growing brighter, the wood appearing almost phosphorescent. I picked out two smaller pieces whose shapes appealed to me and ran back to the truck. He was standing against it with his arms folded. I felt curiously excited as I held them out to him in my arms.

"Look, Sir, aren't they beautiful? What do you think?"

He took them from me and ran his big fingers over them slowly, exploring their shape with his hands. What could he want them for?

"They are good pieces," he said, in a voice that now seemed slightly accented. "Go fetch more, some bigger ones this time."

I ran off eagerly along the beach, searching for larger pieces of wood. Not just my eyes but all my other senses seemed to have become more acute. I sniffed at the salty air, breathing it in deeply. The slushing foam and grating pebbles at the tideline were loud in my ears. As I moved, I felt the air curl around my skin, every inch of it now exposed to the night. My cock and balls swung awkwardly between my legs as I hurried from one piece of wood to another, trying to pick out the ones he would like best. Without noticing, I had become very hard. The warm night air, my nakedness, the task he had set me and his invisible presence in the truck had worked a kind of sexual magic. I felt excited and happy in an almost childlike way, and I enjoyed the heavy feeling in my balls without really thinking about it. I had the image of a dog dashing joyfully about the sand, sniffing at interesting objects, picking up a stick and racing back to lay it at its Master's feet.

I found four large driftwood logs and carried them back to the truck two at a time, my bare feet sinking in the soft sand as I bore them up the beach and set them down in front of him. There was no way to hide my erection.

He inspected them carefully and nodded. "That is enough for tonight."

When I had stowed the wood in the back of the truck and brushed most of the sand off my body, we set off again. I felt strangely closer to him, as if he had shared something important with me, though without explaining what it was. I still had no idea where he lived or what he did. I could imagine him in an old cabin in the woods. But we turned east to cross the City, and in half an hour we were driving through the warehouse section, deserted at this time of night. I began to realize that some time soon when we got wherever he was going, I would have to climb naked out of the cab.

We were on a broad street lined with warehouses when he turned suddenly off Folsom into a narrow alleyway. He pulled up to a double garage door, which lifted up automatically, and drove inside. I climbed down clutching the duffle bag, relieved that he hadn't had to park in the street. I felt rough concrete under my feet. We seemed to be in a huge warehouse. The light was dim, but I could see several long work-tables with tools on them and a dozen or so large irregularly-shaped forms, six feet or more in height, set around the floor. Some were solid like great boulders, some formed of twisted rods like leafless trees or the skeletons of gigantic animals. These looming enigmatic forms gave off a menacing energy that made me shiver.

He was beginning to unload the wood, but as I went to help he pointed away.

"Go up those stairs there in the corner. The door at the top is open. There is beer in the kitchen: put it on the table by the couch." As I went off he was cradling a large piece of wood in one arm and running his thumb along the grain.

The door at the top of the stairs opened into another large dimly lit space. I paused to get my bearings. I suppose I had been expecting something pretty basic, something that went with the old pickup. This was something quite different, an industrial loft that had been reconstructed and decorated by someone with a powerful sense of style who could obviously afford to gratify his tastes.

The room was at least thirty feet long but was decorated and furnished to seem spacious without being barnlike. Several large standing lamps gave off a soft light. One wall was entirely covered with books from floor to ceiling. On the others hung some very large canvasses of what appeared to be geometrical abstractions. A big brick fireplace was set into the wall opposite me, and facing it a long L-shaped couch. The floor was of dark polished boards that felt smooth under my bare feet. In one corner I noticed a tall branching driftwood log set upright on a marble base, and on the other side of the room a bronze statuette of a nude figure, apparently a boy, holding up a vase or goblet. On the wall near the fireplace hung a tall mirror as big as a door.

I had collected several bottles of beer from the kitchen and was setting them out on the low table beside the couch when he came in. I knelt down in front of him. He drank down the first bottle thirstily, opened another and sipped on it slowly with my face poised about six inches from his bulky crotch. It wasn't easy to keep still. At the end of his second beer he moved past me, brushing his denimed thigh roughly across my cheek.

"Come," he said, without looking back, snapping his fingers

at his side, and walked across to the bronze statuette I had noticed when I entered the room. I began to get to my feet, then hesitated. Something about his gesture and curt command made me stay down, and I crawled over to him on my hands and knees. He stood contemplating the figure.

"This is mine," he said. "I made it, years ago, in another country."

The statuette was about four feet high, representing a slender naked boy standing holding up a drinking bowl in both hands, as if offering it to someone. It was naturalistic, finely detailed, and its polished surface gleamed softly in the light. The entire body was completely smooth, and around the slim neck was fitted a small chain, like an ornamental collar. I looked up intently at the gravely beautiful young face.

"He was mine; he died still young."

He rested his hand lightly on the small bronze head and turned away.

He snapped his fingers again and I hurried after him the length of the room and down a corridor. He led the way to a spacious white-tiled room containing a wide sunken bath and a free-standing shower with the heads mounted on a ring at the top of a steel column. Facing me he unbuckled his belt and hauled out his cock. Still apparently soft, it was about as thick as my wrist, with length to match. He stroked it out, making the huge balls swing close to my face. I watched the great dark sex begin to swell as he cradled it in his massive hand, expecting it at any moment to plunge into my mouth. But something about my position displeased him. He ordered me into a half–squat with my head up and my ass stuck out in a tense, awkward posture.

"I am full," he said in a low husky voice. "And you are ready to be filled."

His cockhead was inches from my mouth. I opened my lips in expectation, and suddenly a hot stream was gushing into my throat. I held my mouth carefully in place, swallowing thirstily. It tasted sweet and musky, and I wanted to suck it all down without spilling a single drop. Then, abruptly, it shut off. He moved behind me and inserted his big dickhead into my hole. I winced, softened and pressed back against him, and in seconds he was thrusting deep inside me. Then the stream came again, flooding me, and my distended gut swelled even further. The pressure quickly built up into a pain that seemed to permeate my entire body. Just as I was feeling that I could take no more without bursting, he pulled out his cock and replaced it with a plug that rapidly forced me open and then sealed me again with its splayed end.

He stood over me, shook himself and buttoned up his jeans.

"Let that work in you for a while and you'll be ready to be rinsed out. I like a boy clean and empty."

I held my position in that terrible half crouch like a trapped animal while he looked down at me with his arms folded.

My ass and belly felt grotesquely distended, and now my cock was beginning to swell up painfully. In my fantasy I'd seduced him with my trim build and charming looks, and here I was crouched and bloated like a pregnant girl, barely able to control myself. I realized that I had no idea what he actually wanted from me.

What I wanted above all was for him to leave before I was forced to relieve myself. How could he possibly want me after he'd seen that? Just as my control was giving way he stepped behind me. He turned on the shower full blast and extracted the plug from my ass. It was like being melted down, liquified. Totally enclosed in a hot stream of water, my body opened up and his piss gushed from my cock and my ass together. I shook and shuddered uncontrollably as I was being emptied out, while he stood there watching. Finally he handed me a bar of soap and I washed myself thoroughly all over.

When I was done, he pointed to the wall where two steel rings were set high up about three feet apart, with handcuffs attached. I backed up and he locked my wrists high above my head. From a nearby shelf he took up a can of shaving foam and an old-fashioned straight razor. I flinched at the sight of the gleaming blade. He reached out and rubbed my chest firmly with the flat of his hand, moving down over my stomach to my groin, drawing my curly body-hair between his fingers.

"Be still," he said.

I felt calmed by the sound of him, the way a horse is steadied by its rider's voice. He covered me thickly with cream from my shoulders to my thighs, working it in around my cock and balls and between my spread legs back to my asshole, which he opened with the tips of his fingers. Then he applied the razor, moving down my chest with careful, confident strokes. The blade was so sharp and he used it so skillfully that it seemed to glide over my skin. The absence of pain took me by surprise, but my anxiety increased as he worked down my belly. When he grasped my cock, now very soft, and pulled it towards him while he applied the steel to my shaft and then to the balls, I was too scared to move a muscle, which was just as well. When he had finished in front he released my wrists, bent me over with spread cheeks, and removed the hair around my hole. He turned on the shower again and pushed me under it, then told me to follow him, just as I was.

He led the way back to the huge living-room and positioned me facing the wall.

"Raise your eyes."

I lifted my head and stared with astonishment at the image in the tall mirror in front of me. It was like looking at a stranger, the transformation shocking beyond anything I had expected. The slim hairless figure in the glass looked utterly defenseless, the cock and balls, stripped smooth of their protective fur, seeming somehow alien and fragile. I don't know how long he made me stand there contemplating what he had made of me. I really had no sense of time passing, but at length (very slowly it seemed) I came to acknowledge the reflection as myself. I was, now, that image framed in the glass. He had rinsed me and stripped me as smooth as the driftwood brought in on the tide. Suddenly he was behind me, overshadowing me in his black leather. I saw how my body tensed warily. I was utterly exposed to him. "Raise your arms."

I lifted them up high, standing taut and nervous.

"Ever seen a whipping?" he asked.

"No, Sir," I said, trying to control a shake in my voice.

"Now you'll get your chance," he said. "Keep your eyes on the mirror."

He reappeared behind me holding a thin leather crop and half turned. I saw his arm lift and stared fixedly at my body held at full stretch. His arm swung quickly down and I jerked forward under the shock of the blow. It stung sharply, but not as painfully as I had feared. I settled my weight on my feet again, more confidently this time.

"Do you not know how to count," he said harshly.

For an moment I was baffled, then his meaning flashed on my mind.

"One, Sir," I called out, and immediately received a second stroke.

"Two, Sir." The second was worse, and I realized how wrong I had been.

"Three, Sir... Four, Sir..."

Each cut of the whip intensified the one before, defining it more sharply, prolonging it until the next stroke, which sharpened it again. And with each stab of pain I had to count it off for him. Having to keep the count, proclaiming it aloud as if it were being done to someone else, disoriented me further. And in addition I had to keep my eyes fixed on the mirror, observing as I stiffened and jerked under the crop, still hardly recognizing the thin denuded body as my own. Unconfined by any shackles, I did my utmost to hold my position, straining upward towards the shadowy ceiling. At last, when my legs were shaking uncontrollably and I could hardly stand upright any longer, the blows ceased to fall. He stood directly behind me, spreading his broad hands over my raw, reddened skin. His palms felt rough as sandpaper, but I found myself panting with relief as he massaged my buttocks.

"Thank you, Sir," I blurted out, overwhelmingly grateful, but not knowing whether it was for the whipping or for the ending of it, or for both together. Under his touch I relaxed; the pain was still acute but I was accepting it, letting it flow through me. I felt my asshole beginning to pulse and throb.

He pushed me down until I fell on all fours, then moved off. I crawled quickly after him across the hardwood floor, down another corridor and into a darkened room. He lit several large candles, which revealed plain white walls, a large bed covered in deep crimson and a sling suspended on chains from the ceiling some six feet from the foot of the bed. He motioned me to climb up into it and, pulling my arms and legs high and wide apart, fastened them to the hanging chains. From a small flask he poured some clear thick oil over my cock and balls which seeped slowly down into the crack of my ass. Standing between my splayed legs he unbuckled his belt and unhurriedly removed his clothes. I gazed up as he gradually revealed his massive, black–haired chest and then the great dark sex which I had drunk from before. But now it was hugely erect, jutting over me with supreme arrogance.

I began to squirm in the sling, pressing towards him, trying desperately to stretch my legs higher and wider, making the suspending chains jangle loudly. My hole was oiled and hot; it had been hidden from the whip and now it was opening up. He reached down and took my balls in his hand, gripping them tight between his thumb and forefinger at the root. I saw them glistening, round and smooth as eggs. With a firm insistent pressure he pulled me towards him, forcing me to lift up my ass. Then the great bulbous head of his tool was at my hole demanding entry and with a single thrust he had buried himself inside me. It was like a fist driving deeper and deeper through my flesh, delving and probing. My body opened and gripped on him in helpless, pulsing motions. He lunged at me, lifting me on his column higher and higher, pulling me again and again towards him by my balls, my cock protruding stiffly from his hand, until with a growling roar he began to shoot with an explosive force that made me cry out repeatedly as he surged into me. At length, when he was fully satisfied, he pulled out with a deep bear–like grunt, and, just as before, instantly refilled my hole with a tight plug, sealing his juices inside me. This time it seemed larger and heavier.

He unlocked the shackles and I climbed down from the sling, turning at his direction to the wall where another full-length mirror was mounted. He turned me sideways and once again I confronted my reflection, hesitantly. My cock and smooth balls stuck out stiffly, shining with oil, and from my ass curved a thick tail of black leather thongs that hung halfway down the back of my legs. He towered above me, dark-skinned, statuesque, contemplative. He lifted the thongs and shook them, making them swing from side to side, and involuntarily my cheeks closed tighter around the plug from which they hung, gripping it more firmly inside me. He drew his other hand lightly over my balls and down my swollen shaft. I saw the tail lift and swing behind me, and watched his hand move just outside the reach of my sex.

I stared at the reflection of my need in the glass, appalled and fascinated. I knew with complete certainty that he wanted me to remain just as I was, aroused and unfulfilled, and that he wanted to imprint this image of myself deep in my mind. I realized at that moment how he would control me: my deepest submission would lie in displaying my desire, which I would not be able to conceal, without being permitted to bring it to fulfillment. This was a Master who liked to see his slave hard and craving.

He ran his rough hand very slowly over my hair and down my back in a way that both soothed and fiercely aroused me. Then he turned me to face him and held up a collar. It was broad and black, with an elaborate pattern of steel studs that gleamed in the candlelight. He was so close that the tip of my swollen cock brushed against his leg. I lifted my eyes to his, for the first time. They were wide–set and very dark.

He seemed to be waiting for a response. I realized that for the first time since we had met he was requiring me to choose; and I dimly sensed that this decision could be, in some way, my last. I knew that I need not speak. I bent my head and kissed the black leather, and remained with my neck exposed. He fitted it on and I heard the click of a padlock.

He went to the bed and sat down. I knelt quietly at his feet and raised my eyes slowly up the pillars of his legs to his sex which stood out thickly from a bush of dark brown hair. I put my face close, without touching, inhaling deeply the hot musky smell that came off his skin, a rich fusion of his scent and mine. He laid his hand on my head and kept it there for a moment as if asserting his possession.

"I will sleep now," he said. "Stay there until the morning."

When he had got under the covers and turned away, I curled up on the soft carpet, laying my head on my arm. I felt warm and at peace. The black tail draped over my thigh, while the plug that anchored it filled my ass without pain. My cock was heavy, and I lay there feeling it throbbing stiffly against the strange smoothness of my belly. He had filled me and left me full, and I would remain so for I did not know how long. I felt that at last I had found where I belonged, and as I drifted off to sleep I thought of the little statue standing out there so still in the darkness.

And now, after five years, when my eyes rest on the bronze boy, I think of the first evening I met his maker. The slim attentive figure, mutely offering himself, speaks to me always of the Master who fashioned us both.

UNDERCOVER

Bill Lee

Something moved in the shadows. I tensed, a part of me wishing that the moon would clear of cloud cover but knowing that it would increase the danger if it did. This operation had to remain in the dark.

I heard the rustling sound again, nearer this time, and my gaze snapped to the right. This might be it. Surely there was a figure creeping closer to the two shadowy forms that had merged a few moments before. I had to get closer to the action.

The warm, sultry breeze ruffled the hair on my bare legs and chest as I moved slowly, keeping in the shadow of the giant willow. Naturally I had to dress like the other players, which meant I could not carry a gun or even a communicator. So far it seemed that I was invisible to the third figure who seemed to be homing on the couple in a tight embrace. We were forming a triangle, it seemed, and I was able to move almost as close to the figures as my suspect who was off to my right a few yards.

The fog wasn't as low as usual that night. The hilly park in the middle of The City was illuminated by a surreal glow of distant streetlights reflecting from the fog cover above us. It was enough to see shapes, but not those very far away.

Again I wished that there were some way I could carry a weapon, but attire in anything more than cut-offs and sneakers would have drawn too much attention. The sergeant had been pretty dubious about this idea when I proposed it, but I had insisted.

I was close enough now to make out some details and to hear voices, and the suspect obviously was, also.

"That's a beautiful dick," the taller one whispered. He was extra-broad shouldered with dark hair. There was a dark smudge on his shadowed face that apparently was a thick mustache.

"So's that!" The shorter one was stockier and I could tell that his hair was a mass of curls, probably dark blond. His hands were working in the crotch of the taller figure.

The taller one groaned softly. "Oh, yeah, ugh—you got great hands—ugh—I bet you got a great mouth, too —"

"Let me show you," the blond whispered, and sank to his knees. I moved a few feet closer, keeping my eye on the suspect who was also moving closer to the couple but remaining in deep shadow. There was no sign that I had been detected.

The taller figure, apparently tanned darkly, was wearing white shorts that had slid half-way down his spread thighs. From the dark blotch of pubic hair in his crotch reared a thick, white pole that was partly engulfed in the blond's mouth. As I watched, the blond pulled back all the way to the head and then dove all the way down, nearly swallowing that gigantic tool. I knew I had to devote my attention to the suspect, but it wasn't easy to tear my gaze away from the thrusting pair.

The solitary figure crouched low, leaving the minimal shape to form a shadow. I could see that his shorts were brown or perhaps khaki, and they hugged his trim ass tightly in that position. He moved closer to the couple, nearly in my line of sight. While this effectively put me behind him and therefor less likely to be spotted, it also made it impossible for me to see what he was doing with his hands that were both in front of him.

"Fuckin' hot mouth," the tall figure gritted, clutching the curly head to his crotch. He began to thrust back and forth, his stiff dick plunging deeply into the throat of his willing victim, and I thought briefly of the previous night, my date with Carole. Sex with her was always very controlled, even boring, I had to admit. But as I watched this masculine coupling in the public park, my shorts were growing tighter, it seemed.

The cock-sucker and -suckee pair were not my targets, of course. This park had been the scene of numerous stabbings in the last few weeks. All the victims had been young gay men, all with their pants down and dongs hanging loose, and many of them had sperm in their mouths according to the Medical

Examiner. No, it was the *voyeur*, the hiding witness, whom I was looking for, and maybe I had him at last. Was that a knife the solitary figure was clutching in front of him?

"Oh, yeah, guy, yeah — you're goin' to get it — oh, man, fuck, yeah —" the tall dark man moaned, forgetting to whisper. The curly head pressed hard to his crotch, twisting and turning with that big prick in his throat; I figured it must have been paradise for the suckee, although I had never buried my entire shaft into a hot mouth like that —

"Aghhhh!" His cry was agonizing, and for a moment I thought maybe the murderer had struck again, right at the critical moment, but no—it was just his understandable reaction to shooting his wad into that gulping throat. And at just that moment the solitary figure straightened up and seemed to be tensing to spring. I dragged my attention back to my job; it was time for action.

With three giant steps I was behind my target and pulled both his arms back, clasping his wrists together tightly behind his back. There wasn't a knife in either hand.

"What the fuck—?" he yelled. "I'm cuming!" As I pulled him back against me, I could see over his shoulder his long, thick cock spraying cum to the wind. I gripped his struggling form hard against my chest, and could feel my own hard cock extending down the leg of my shorts and into his ass crack.

I lost track of the couple who had started all this. When they heard us struggling in the bushes nearby, they split, dashing across the clearing and toward the parking lot.

I had to take him in. You can't sneak up on a guy from behind and put him in a choke hold while his dick sprays the underbrush with thick, white juice and not take an official position. Besides, maybe he could add something to the meager file I already had on this caper. But sitting across from him at the interrogation table, all I could see was soft brown eyes and lips that trembled sometimes when I snarled more than usual.

There was also a stubborn defiance that I didn't even try to crack, one apparently born of repeated justification for his sexual tastes over the years. It gave him more dignity than I was used to seeing in a prisoner.

"Look, Jim, I'm not out to get you or the other guys playing around in the park. I'm after a murdering son-of-a-bitch who stabs guys like you and leaves them dead in the bushes of that park. Haven't you seen anything in previous visits that might be of help?"

His eyes were suspicious of my motives, it was clear, but as they roved over my chest still bare, in my "street-clothes" attire, they were not completely hostile.

"What makes you think I know so much about that park?" he retorted defensively.

I referred to the file at my elbow, picking out a column from the printout. I recited one of the numbers and watched his eyes admit defeat. "That's your license number, right? It has been observed in that parking lot by roving patrols four nights in the past three weeks, after dark, of course. Are you saying you had never been there before, cruising like tonight?"

He suddenly rose from his hard-backed chair and strode to the grated window, his fists clenched at his sides. I wasn't ready for this sudden move, but immediately recognized that he wasn't going anywhere, and he wasn't the type to try to take me on. As I stared at his back, hunched in defeat, I realized that he would probably be popular among the gay set; his shoulders were broad and muscled and his legs were sturdy pillars, nearly as muscular and hairy as mine. His brown hair was cut short and crisp, and I could imagine him in a business suit carrying a briefcase in the financial district or, just as easily, in full leather on a motorcycle. I already mentioned that trim butt that had felt my boner in the park—why did I get a hard-on like that, watching two guys making out in the darkness? Or was it the excitement of the chase, anticipation for making an important bust? That's what it must have been. But as I studied him in the harsh fluorescent light, my dick stirred again.

The door opened noisily and the Sergeant burst in. "Ready to book this faggot, Mike?" he snarled characteristically. Jim swung around, the tension returning in his shoulders, and his biceps bulged as if ready to fight it out with the new invader. The belligerent scowl on the Sergeant's face didn't do much to ease the situation.

"Naw, I can't charge him because he didn't do any-thing—unless you think it makes sense invoking that ancient ordinance about being in a park after dark?"

The Sergeant's dark blue uniform, immaculately pressed as usual, certainly set him apart from Jim and me, only half dressed as we had been in the park. I suppose it was especially impressive to Jim, because it gave the older man that badge of authority that I lacked. I could see the Sergeant's ire rising, so I interrupted what I knew would be a blast of hot air. I had already heard about a hundred times the Sergeant's bragging tales of the many arrests he had made when he was on the vice squad. They had crouched behind peek holes and pounced on guys having sex in public johns, until the courts started taking a dim view of such actions. "I want to check something else out. Give me a few more minutes, huh, Sarge?"

The Sergeant frowned even more, but then looked me over pointedly. "You going to get some clothes on, or is this a new uniform I haven't heard about?" His eyes roved over my bare chest and legs, hesitating a moment at my crotch that might have been bulging more than usual from my earlier thoughts. There were some out-gays in the San Francisco Police Department, but the Sergeant obviously was not one of them. Neither was I.

"Uh, yeah, sure, I mean I'll get dressed, but it's almost end of shift," I said flushing. "I just have a few more questions for this — guy." I had almost said fag, but for some reason it didn't seem right to use our usual queer term for Jim, now that I was beginning to know him. The Sergeant gave me another skeptical look. "Lock the fuckin' fag up and be done with it," he growled and stamped out.

I walked over to Jim, for some reason pleased to see him relax a little. I noticed him glance at my crotch, too, but I supposed that was just habit for him.

"Look, Jim, maybe we can make a deal. You know your way around that park and that — action — better than I do. What about teaming up with me on this thing—unofficially, you know? I'm pretty much out on a limb on this one. The Sergeant isn't really convinced that this undercover approach is going to work, so he won't give me any backup. But it looks like we're not going to find this sicko if we don't catch him in the act. You could be of help if we could lure him into an attack, you and me." I shrugged, all at once not so sure this was a good idea. Obviously I had to explain what he might be getting into. "It could be dangerous, of course, but forearmed – forewarned and that kind of bullshit, you know?"

Jim studied my face for several minutes, it seemed. If he didn't look like he could take care of himself, I wouldn't have suggested it. He still didn't trust me, but when I appealed to his sense of duty and loyalty to his own kind, he finally accepted the idea. I was pleased when he agreed, more than I really expected I would be.

The next night when I drove my unmarked car into the parking lot, I saw Jim's car already there, along side a few others. I casually wandered into the dense trees, but didn't see any sign of life for a while. Then suddenly Jim was beside me and I almost yelled when he materialized from the shadow of an old oak. This time he was wearing low-slung Levi cutoffs and sneakers. As my eyes adjusted to the gloom, I could see a widening band of curly hair trailing from his belly button to the waist band. For some reason that seemed awful sexy, and I had to look away. Jim took charge.

"Let's walk together further back where the shadows are deeper," he whispered. "That's where most of the action is." He didn't wait for my answer but started walking, and I followed closely. It was obvious he knew where he was going, avoiding gullies and downed tree trunks that I probably would have stumbled over. I couldn't help noticing how the Levi shorts hugged his muscular ass when he walked, and how the crease at the junction of his legs and ass smoothed out when he strode purposely, deeper into the woods. Soon he stopped in the shadow of a clump of trees and motioned for me to come closer.

"There are two guys over there, probably getting it on, and there are two more singles — there — " he nodded in one direction "— and there," nodding to the right. I couldn't see them at all until he pointed them out. Jim knew what he was doing.

"That guy is watching the couple there, but the other one—maybe we can get him interested in us and find out more about him."

"Uh—how do we do that?"

For the first time, Jim looked a little flustered. "Well, we have to make out a little—or pretend to, at least. Some of these guys are more voyeurs than cock-suckers, and that probably includes the guy you're after."

I guess I hadn't realized that it would come to this—actually pretending to make out with a guy—but when I felt Jim's hand feeling my crotch, tracing the outline of my cock down my shorts leg, I didn't really feel the revulsion I might have expected. But when my cock lurched and grew, getting stiff and throbbing, I didn't know what to do. Jim's eyes bored into mine, seeming to probe my inner mind, and I could see, even in the night blackness, a guarded yearning that still left the decision to me.

Trying to keep my mind on business, I glanced around and could tell that we had attracted the second single; he was homing in on us, sneaking closer in the shadows. Jim had been right about that. I looked back at him uncertainly.

"Now what?" I whispered hoarsely.

"You're supposed to do the same."

He was right, of course. I guess it wouldn't do to have it all one-way, for our voyeur, I mean. Hesitantly I reached out and almost immediately encountered a rigid boner in his shorts. I reached a little lower and was startled — I had touched his bare cock—the thick, bulbous head extending below his shorts leg, and it gave a little jerk as my fingertips made contact. In turn I jerked back and began to sweat. This wasn't what I had had in mind.

Jim momentarily turned his head a little to check our voyeur. "He stopped, still watching but waiting until we get it on."

"Hey, now, Jim" — I stammered — "I mean, we can't take this too far —"

"You want to catch your murderer?"

"Yeah, but —"

His experienced fingers had my fly open in a moment and I could do nothing but allow it to happen. Before I knew it my shorts were dropping down my thighs and he had my stiff cock in his hand. We both gasped, I from the shock and pleasure of that pressure and he — I didn't know why he gasped. My knees began to tremble for some reason — probably the tension of the moment, knowing that we were the object of scrutiny of a possible murderer.

His hand began to move, slipping the full length of my dick, and I stiffened, rooted to the spot. When his hand covered my cockhead and rotated around it, I could feel that I had seeped a lot of pre-cum, making his massage the closest thing to a pussy I had even felt. Certainly better than my own hand. Still his eyes held mine, the intensity of his gaze deepening, and I had all I could do to keep from cuming in his fist.

"Watch him," he whispered, his head tilting toward the observer. "Don't take your eyes off him." I tore my gaze from his and focused on the lurking shadow, but the guy, whoever he was, hadn't drawn any closer, at least not yet. I could tell he had his cock in his hand, intent on our activities. Then he started moving closer.

Just then I felt my cockhead enveloped in a hot, liquid embrace; Jim's mouth quickly engulfed all of me, taking almost my entire shaft, his tongue twisting, his lips clasping avidly. A tingle started in my feet, rising swiftly. Never before had an orgasm threatened this quickly, certainly not with Carole. I had to wrench my gaze from the prey and looked down; although his mouth was stuffed with my prick, Jim was looking up at me with those liquid brown eyes that spoke volumes — what were they saying? And then he tilted his head back, taking the rest of me into his throat, his eyes closing, and I couldn't take any more.

"AAAAaaahhhhhh!" I howled. Nobody, but nobody could have experienced that surge, that convulsive shudder that racked my frame without shouting his joy. As soon as I heard my own voice, I thought of our voyeur, but when I could turn my head, when I could focus again through my blurred haze, I saw he had stiffened against the trunk of a tree and was shooting his wad over the landscape. That didn't quiet any of my excitement, and I gushed heavily into Jim's gulping throat.

When I looked again, the voyeur was gone, and so were the other three. I guess I scared them off. And when Jim rose and leaned his head against my shoulder, I didn't even push him away. What a fucked-up undercover cop I was turning out to be!

I was in a fog all the next day. When the Sergeant asked me about the case, I just mumbled, and he grunted, "Well, I'm glad you're off that kick. It was a stupid idea, anyway. Now maybe we can get some real work done around here." I didn't say anything, just shrugged. "Let 'em kill each other off — all the better for the rest of us." Not exactly a law officer's mission, I thought, but I wasn't going to argue. He hadn't forbade me to continue on the case, I reasoned.

That night I met Jim again in the park. He seemed the same as usual, but I wasn't. We silently strolled into the depths of the woods, and my more educated eye could spot several figures moving in the shadows, generally going in the same direction. Finally we stopped at the same place as before, where several tree trunks crossed to make a dark circle on the ground. Some of the other figures continued to move further back in the woods.

"Mike," Jim began hesitantly after we had spotted the others in our company, "we didn't talk about last night. I hope — " I just shook my head to caution quiet. I didn't want to talk about it.

We stood closely together as Jim had taught me, and his eyes sought mine in that intense way he had. This time I started the usual procedure, reaching for his crotch and grasping his thick tube that grew rigid in my hand. This time I unbuttoned his shorts and pulled them part way down until his cock bounced up rigidly from his hairy crotch. I realized that I was hard, too, but that didn't matter.

All day my brain had been circling, revolving, wondering what I would do when this moment arrived. But there was only one honest answer, and I knew it.

"It's my turn," I murmured quietly. I didn't dare look at his face as I sank to the ground, leaned my back against the tree, and pulled him toward me roughly. His cock pointed straight at me, the swollen head that I had touched the previous night practically smiling at me, drooling at me its clear message of masculinity. Apparently he was as excited as I was in spite of being watched by anonymous witnesses. Jim's legs were rigid in my hands, but when I took his cockhead in my mouth they began to tremble. It was sweet velvet, swelling even larger as I tongued the ridge and sipped the sap from the slit.

But there was more, eight or nine inches more, and so I proceeded down the thick, pulsing shaft, taking more and more until I knew another inch would bring that make-or-break moment when I would either involuntarily gag or swallow him whole —

"Arggg!" I couldn't tell where the sound had come from, but Jim pulled back abruptly and swung sharply to the side, his cock jerking from my mouth. His arm came down in a karate chop and a dark shape crumpled to the ground beside us.

Quickly Jim, his cock still rigid and bobbing, straddled the fallen form. "Grab his arm, Mike! He's got a knife!" My befuddled brain finally reacted and I sprang to help, receiving a glancing slash from a long hunting knife in our would-be murderer's hand before pinning him securely. I stared down at the snarling face of our attacker.

"Sergeant!"

He was still in his uniform with all the metal removed. The dark blue was perfect for night prowling, making him practically invisible there in the shadows. But Jim had caught a glimpse of him through the tree trunks, just before he lunged and in time to save us both.

It was late when we finished making our report, a report that fudged the truth a little but was close enough. The Captain alternated between astonishment and anger, that one of his own, a true-blue trusted officer, could be a serial killer. The more I thought about it, the less surprised I was.

Jim hesitated at the door as I prepared to leave. "Well, I guess that wraps it up — " he said with a cautious smile.

I pushed him out the door and then pulled him around to face me. I put on my police face.

"Hey, man, where do you think you're going? We're not through yet!" His eyes widened and filled with questions — yes, and maybe hope. "But no more dark parks and anonymous voyeurs — this time, it'll be in bed!"

BRIDGES

Dixon Stalward

Jimmie had this romance goin' with bridges. He knew about all of them—well, the big ones, anyway—all around the world. Pictures of bridges covered the walls of the little shack he and his grandpa shared out on rural route 18.

"In the whole world," Jimmie said to me on that day when I first met him, "my favorites are only maybe three hundred miles from here. They're the Golden Gate and the San Francisco-Oakland Bay bridges out there in California."

I'd been in love with the little fella—he was just under five-four and cute as a box of buttons—ever since I sucked him off a week or so later on a Friday mornin' while were sittin' out front in my beat-up old pickup waitin' on the mailman. There were some crows makin' a hell of a racket in a dead tree across the road, and the flat, white Nevada sky looked like it was, most likely, gonna last forever. I was in one of them bleak moods where I know I ain't.

Jimmie was flopped down in a country sprawl, one foot up on the dashboard and the other across his knee. With his blond hair and green eyes he had the natural and common beauty of the American heritage thrown to the wind. His jeans were stretched tight across his thighs and butt makin' those sexy lookin' rolls and tucks around the crotch and fly.

I was watchin' him watch the dust blow across the road.

"You a virgin, Jimmie?"

"No."

"How long's it been since you ain't?"

"Oh, about two years."

I leaned back in the seat, my hat comin' down low on my eyes. "So when'd you last get a piece?"

"Aw, shit, Makon..."

"C'mon, tell me."

"It was at that Grange auction over at Carson Creek."

"Hell, that was almost three months ago! Right after you graduated high school."

"Well, you doin' any better?"

"A little." I made a little laugh. "I bet you beat off a lot durin' these long dry spells."

"Yeah, some. So what of it?"

"Nothin'. 'Course there ain't no real need for it, is all."

I could sense a tightenin' in his mood, sorta like he was waitin' for somethin' to happen that he knew to be truly needed and that he, even without words, wanted. He dropped his feet to the floor, crossin' his arms as if he meant to wait on it forever.

"Your dick of a good size?" I said, lookin' right at him.

"Well... yeah."

"And I bet you're horny right now."

"Kinda."

I put my hand on his knee, runnin' it a little way up his thigh. "And I bet you're a pistol when you get somethin' hot workin' on that meat. Somethin' wet and hot and real smooth."

His thigh tensed, then relaxed as he went lower on the seat, his legs wider. I put down a solid, encouragin' squeeze and that brought up a definite surge in his jeans.

"Oh yes, you're hot, boy," I said. "I can see that."

"Yeah, I guess so."

"You know I can help you out, don'tcha?"

"Yeah?"

"Why, sure."

Movin' in nimble authority my fingers opened his belt, popped the buttons of his jeans and laid open the fly. In the gathered bunchiness of white boxer shorts I could see the cock bein' held tight in curved restraint. I worked at findin' the gap.

"Raise up your hips," I whispered.

When he made that short effort I moved fast to pull jeans and shorts past his butt to mid-thigh. His cock sprung up in the fleshy grandeur of an indolent prince, the head glowin' from pink to peach as it emerged from its private seclusion beneath the satiny ruff of a luxuriant foreskin. Smirkin' in a red sass, the slit seeped those silvery drops so intricate in the design of this ever compellin' enterprise. Always eager I was summoned once again to the suck. Takin' his balls in hand, their soft, limited mobility warm with promise, I moved onto the curvin' knob, its sleek form well fitted to the reception to be found in my mouth.

"Oh, for the balls of Christ," Jimmie whispered, "that feels good."

Gently provoked by the clamor bein' heated in that penis, I sent my tongue in a flat curl around the head, plyin' the tender nut with wet caresses and bouncy punches that rolled into long, slick licks. Then sealin' my lips around the thick shaft, I made tight turns in the downward movement as I went to the root of the cock that was connectin' me to this wonderful, so very American boy.

"Oh, Makon," he groaned, his body turnin' in small twists against the tension he was feelin' that I was helpin' to build. "Makon! Oh, fuckin' Jesus!"

The organ was fattenin' toward a threatenin' response so I came off it but kept the beat goin' with the steady grip of my hand. My mouth, forever at a hunger with new ideas, went to his nuts to lick, nuzzle, lap, kiss and suck. High between his thighs and just beyond the folded corridor lay the anal rose, furled tight, its aroma reachin' my nostrils pressed low into the healthy sag of his scrotum.

"God, Makon, I'm gonna shoot in just a minute."

I pulled back and looked up into his angelic face, now full with the enthusiasm of a young man runnin' at a stiff pace with his very natural body. "So then, you like this okay?"

"Shit, man, it's like bein' pissed on... by God."

Well, I thought in a silky gloat, we do have definite possibilities residin' here in this boy.

Feelin' affirmed in expectation and with flowers of the future bloomin' in my mind, I returned to the comfortable suck where

I made a channel of my lips and tongue and went down on his stiff meat with the dedication of a philanderer ordained in sleaze, the fancy getup bein' a robe trimmed out in a deep shade of lavender which draped nicely across my shoulders. So, wheelin' away on that dick I called on all my able abilities in cocksuckin' to haul him up to the threshold of the jump. Well-timed and consistent, those efforts grew steadily in tempo as Jimmie, so keen for the slot, entered into the slidin' exchange. Pushin' and turnin' his hips in the ancient, liquid quest, he brought the organ once again close to its angry state of spit, the head gettin' ready to launch its sticky drench into my mouth. Prepared, then, for that slap of jizz, I felt a hand fumblin' with the tight, strainin' bulge in my jeans.

"Shit! I gotta see your dick, man."

Obligin', I flipped the buttons and pushed open the fly. Bein' as I ain't given to the fashion of underwear, my cock, a giant thing hung with nuts of courageous size, bounded into the arena with all its flags fully strung up and flyin' with the giddy optimism found in a robust libido. I was flooded with warm confidence in havin' such a manly presence, and when Jimmie's hand, cool and hesitant, closed on the burnin' staff, that warmth coursed into my belly, through my legs and spun in my asshole. My balls turned in a simple-minded joy.

"Jesus," Jimmie murmured, "ain't even a horse got that."

His hand moved on it, took it into a staggerin' pump that moved fast toward the clutch of possession. His cock was deep in my throat, poised there in arrested motion as I awaited the ascension of the hellish essence. For that moment the crest denied, I came up to torture the slit in a mean, between-the-legs kinda love; my urge was now growin' in the prickly garden of greed. In that angular place, high limbs hung with heavy, slick seeds, I licked my fingers and went between his buttocks. Findin' the spot, its round, cushy bow prim in oblivion, I pushed in, goin' fast for the plunder to be found in surprise. His cock jumped into a paroxysm of witless frenzy. I moved quickly to quell that jerkin' with deep plunges of steady, serious suckin' while my finger persisted in its turnin' in the earthy hole.

"Oh, goddammit." A moan came from deep within Jimmie's body, thrown up from his soul. "I'm gonna fuckin' come!"

Saturated with the licentious, bent into the lewd, I adored the thick, loose chains of jizz delivered out of his cock, turgid spurt by turgid spurt, into my mouth. Collectin' on my tongue, drippin' from my lips, the mess seeped back into my throat forcin' me into a gulpin' swallow. Shit, man, I was in the deepest swill of joy!

"Oh, boy, oh, boy," Jimmie said softly, spread low and spent.

"Okay, kiddo," I said, "now jack me off." My voice was perfunctory in the simplicity of the demand for I stood, in a certain regal decadence, on the very summit of the most sublime of destructions. His hands, ambitious in a double clutch, moved into the labor and in a sprint of immediate seconds a great, awesome—even to me after all this time—pitch of jizz sailed out of my cock in a flight toward the dusty, saggin' headliner of the pickup. Two salvos hit it, a third smacked against the radio and those followin', in the customary ooze, sank back on the staff, drippin' down, fallin' away like the jewels of a broken diadem.

"Jesus," Jimmie said softly, dreamily, caught up in our filmy ruse, "I ain't never see nothin' like that before."

"Does it every time," I said. "Yeah, it really pops off if there's somebody—well, like you—fuckin' me up the ass."

"Yeah?"

"That's right."

Jimmie looked at me with lascivious interest, a wicked leer washin' across his Sunday school face. "Would that be somethin' regular?"

"Could be."

He grinned as if he'd heard God lay out a long, loud fart.

"Hey! Hey, there! Hey, you guys in that pickup. That you, Jimmie?"

Jimmie rose up and looked out toward the totterin' bank of mailboxes. "It's Carl, and he's got my package, sure enough. Oh, boy!" Pullin' his pants together he hopped out of pickup to go collect his package from Carl the mailman.

Well, what could I expect? A confession of love, of undyin' devotion? Dammit, he was young. He was lookin' for a damned package and it came. Shit, he'd already had what he could get from me—at least for the time bein' and that only in the beginnin' ways. He'd be back.

Well, I didn't set out to get a romance and that's just what I didn't get. But I got a friendship with a handsome young man who, like me, was of limited education but in possession of a inquirin' and open mind. His sexual ardor didn't burn with the same hot coals that I stoked in mine, and his kinks weren't always as deep or bent in the same direction, but he never seemed to find, or needed to find, anythin' about me that wasn't okay enough to accept in a friend. I was happy with the way things went and he seemed so, too.

A little later on, not too long after Labor Day, there was a fire at Jimmie's place. His grandpa had left the hot plate on under an empty tea kettle. Most of the shack went up, and the old man was found in his chair in a corner by the radio. He'd been caught by the smoke.

I drove out there that afternoon after the burial.

"I hate this fuckin' place," Jimmie said. He'd built himself a lean-to across the unburnt part of the shack. If the winter winds came up from the south, which they don't, it might've been all right.

I stood leanin' against the pickup. I nodded at some boxes, bound up with wire, stacked in the back. "I'm pullin' out."

"Yeah? Where to?"

"San Francisco."

"Oh, man! No shit?"

"No shit," I replied. I saw, as I'd expected, a shinin' hope in his eyes, and then that followed by a quiet desperation. I put my hand on his shoulder. "C'mon, Jimmie, and go with me."

"Aw, shit, I ain't got nothin'..."

"That's true all right. There ain't one fuckin' thing here."

He smiled, possibility growin' toward reality in the simplicity of those given to faith. "If I only could, though. God, at last I'd see the bridges."

"And there's others, too, besides them."

"Well, maybe, but of all those I know of in the whole world..."

"Yeah, I know, they're in San Francisco." I paused. "C'mon and go with me, Jimmie. I can take care of things for us. There ain't much we need."

"You really sure?"

"I wouldn't ask if I wasn't."

So, abidin' by an American tradition spannin' four centuries, we just picked up and moved on. But it wasn't as precarious as it sounds. Though battered, the pickup was recently tuned-up and ran well, the tires were in good shape and I had insurance at an adequate coverage. So? Also, I had a little money, my health, several decades of expectation and, probably for a little while at least, Jimmie. So? Also, I'd been to San Francisco before. I knew my way around—somewhat—and, perhaps, some people. So? So we took off.

When Jimmie first saw the bridges I thought he was gonna cry. God, I never saw a boy with such open-hearted dedication to somethin' that wouldn't give back even if it could. He was put into a near-epiphany when we actually drove over the Bay Bridge with the Golden Gate in full view and serenely majestic in banks of movin' fog.

"Jesus, Makon," he said, "I can't believe I'm really here where people live every day in the presence of these heavenly beauties, these heavenly, earthbound beauties."

So, our days in San Francisco got off to a good start. We got us a motel, found a few places to eat at that had decent food for affordable prices, and started layin' down, day by day, the foundations for a new life. I got a job drivin' a truck for a big printin' outfit. It was kinda hard at first bein' that the city'd changed some, but with a map I got along okay. I bought us a few things, a VCR and clothes and such, to sorta put a home together. When we were pretty well set up—I don't like to just blow into town and call someone—I decided it was time to get in touch with Will Brubaker.

"Yeah," I said on the phone. "Yeah! Right here in San Francisco. Oh, I don't know, just a few weeks. Sure. Tomorrow night? Sure. I'll bring Jimmie. Sure. You'll like him. Same place? Yeah. 'Bye."

That evenin' when I was finishin' up in the shower, Jimmie came in lookin' happy and pleased as if he'd just scored a hot deal on moon property. He was takin' well to the hustle and bustle of city life bein' as he was of a nature basically optimistic. He looked very fetchin' standin' there in a pair of tan trousers and a brown gaucho I'd picked up for him. He was watchin' me in the mirror.

"Guess what," he said.

"I guess."

"No. Guess."

"I guess you want to go back home."

"No! I got a job."

"Well, that's great, Jimmie. What sort of job?"

"I'm gonna help put up billboard signs all over the city. Big ones."

"Well, pal, I'm proud of you. Dammit, I'm really proud."

He stepped up behind me keepin' his eyes on mine. His hands went across my chest, down my belly to my crotch. His fingers worked small tickles against my cock and balls.

"Makon, I owe you more'n anythin' I could ever say."

"You don't owe me nothin', Jimmie."

"Well, I'll just take somethin' for myself then." He went to his knees. "Turn around. I'm gonna suck you off."

Already in an agitated state, my cock fairly leaped to a full erection as that candid young fella took my balls in one hand and, with the other far back on the shaft, began suckin' on the head. Though as yet unseasoned in nuance, he was direct and resolute in those tight and not always gentle turns and twists as he set into motion a blowjob that was as unadorned as any staged in the raunchiest of toilets. Spreadin' my feet in the stance of the days of Hong Kong trade I leaned back to let the boy show his stuff as the ever-envelopin' arms of that fatuous goddess workin' the game took over and led me once again into the convoluted, curious miracle. Jimmie's suckin' was good, his devotion to it evidence of yet another life to be laid at that maligned altar where I, in my draggy duds as an elder, began helpin' the worship along with sharp thrusts forward. And soon enough the pinpricks announcin' the comin' celebration danced down through my dick to my nuts. My asshole, so often a throne to seat a visitin' dignitary, lay coiled in alerted expectation. When a thumb, hooked back, made its probin' entrance the coil loosed itself and pounced.

"Oh, Jesus," I moaned, "yeah, baby, thumb-fuck me."

Now suckin' with the exalted of all history, Jimmie ran the turns on me. His thumb, growin' slick with the juices it made flow, was joined by a finger, and the two were hitched into the race ridin' in a neat little buggy of sweet pain. Bein' yanked up tighter and tighter toward the finish I moved to a shallow squat, hot on the fuckin' line.

"It's comin', honey!"

He looked up and flashed me a lewd, knowin' glance. The healthy openness of his handsome face then a-drippin' with the wettest of slapped-down-on-the-concrete-floor passion pulled the trip line in my nuts.

I groaned. "You got it, baby."

The stuff, the grease, the gall and gang of it, came up from that black well, spinnin' in the mighty, magical curse to slam into his fabulously perfect mouth. He took it solid and still, and then moved in a soothin' sway while the jerkin' and pushin' were laid away into history. Pullin' his fingers out he moved back to sit on his haunches.

"God," he said, grinnin', "the thing always shoots like a cannon no matter where you aim it."

I laughed. "C'mon, hot stuff, I'll wash your back."

"You know," he said when he stood, "I'm gonna get fucked by that thing, and it's gonna be soon."

"Okay, and believe me I'm lookin' forward to it, but now let's see you in the shower."

While I got the water adjusted he stripped down. Turnin' to me, his dick swingin' in stiff, waitin' arcs, I was overwhelmed by a need to succor him in sex but also to nurture and protect him. In the need of the immediate matter I directed him into the shower and followed.

Soapin' his body under the gentle spray, my hands sailed on his shoulders, down his arms, and worked across his chest feelin' the pecs shaped like smooth tropical fruits growin' slowly ripe. Then movin' down over the belly to his penis and scrotum, I went between his thighs to the crease. Tucked in it, the asshole was wet, slick and nicely tight, and now made even more tantalizin' by the challenge of an imminent, if indefinite, gratification. Returnin' to the cock strainin' at its leash of pent up energy, I began a steady, relentless, controlled and slow jack-off as if I'd been sent as a heavenly torturer. Lickin', kissin' and puttin' small bites on his neck and shoulders I rolled his body, young and firm, vital and trustin', against mine, a muscular haven fully capable of a crush of love.

"Jesus, Makon," he whispered, "the bird's gonna fly."

"Let it fly, baby."

My cock, once again erected, danced in lewd grandeur near its prize—seekin' just the lightest passin' kiss—as the shimmerin' young fella in my arms stiffened and let fly a wad of spit from the bird I held caged in my hand.

I was lyin' on our tank of a motel bed when he came out of the bathroom lookin' like the cleanest of all queens' consorts. He sat down and kissed me on the belly.

"Well, now," I said, "I've got somethin' to tell you. We're goin' out to dinner tomorrow night, and I don't mean no cheap cafe.

We're gonna have dinner with Will Brubaker."

His eyes clouded as if perceivin' a threat. "Who's Will Brubaker?"

"Oh, Will and I go back a few years to the days of... Oh, hell, he's an old friend livin' right here in San Francisco. I called him up and he asked us to come over for dinner."

"I ain't gonna be in the way, am I?"

"Oh, hell, no. You're gonna love him. He's a great guy."

"Okay."

"And you can see the bridges as you never seen them before. His house is way up there on Telegraph hill."

History is writ, but if I hadn't been such a wanderer, I suppose Will and I could have made somethin' together. I don't know. But the real truth was that while I was livin' my nomadic life from palm tree to icy hill, Will was puttin' in eighteen–hour days and seven–day weeks buildin' his importin' business known as GeeGaw Collections International. But, you know, he never seemed to resent my poppin' up every now and then, and stayin' a while and then... hell, who doesn't know the pattern. And here I was about to do it again, but this time I felt a different man, and that in so many different ways.

So the next evenin' we walked up the steep, narrow walk to the old Victorian house that, when I actually saw it, I remembered in greater detail than I'd expected. The paint maybe seemed in better condition or the plants better cared for–it was all just prettier–and the place, somehow, didn't look so imposin' or seem so important in the ways that had always been so far beyond me. I rang the bell.

"Nice house," Jimmie said nervously.

"Big."

"Yeah."

"That you, Makon?" The voice came from above. I stepped back and looked up. It was Will.

"Yes, by God," he exclaimed, "it is you!"

"Yep, it's me all right."

"Don't move! I'll be right down."

Soon enough the tall door glided open and Will Brubaker stood there grinnin' in the widest welcome in the world. He'd gone grey some, but the sturdy, steady man of strong commitment stood there in the lanky posture I'd always found so attractive.

"Makon! Goddammit, it's so good to see you!" His dark eyes gleamed with pleasure.

"Jesus, Will, it's so damned good to see you. You look great!"

"Well..."

Our embrace was brief but in no way superficial or awkward, and then I introduced Jimmie and Will. They shook hands and we moved on into the house. As it always had been – and now even more so in times of growin' sophistication – it was a show-stopper of taste and elegance.

Jimmie went immediately to the wide windows overlookin' the city and the bay. The bridges glowed in the last of the settin' sun, their towers magnificent in permanence and purpose. Glancing at me, Will approached the window and stood at Jimmie's side, the two in a silent gaze upon the might wrought by the hands of men. In a placid greetin', Will's arm went around the young fellow's shoulder. Jimmie looked up smilin' in a satisfied calm.

"God, those bridges are beautiful," he said softly.

"Do you like San Francisco, Jimmie?" Will asked.

"Oh, yes, sir," he replied, "I sure do even though it's only a few weeks we been here."

"Think you'll stay?"

"Oh, yes. I'll never get tired of lookin' at those bridges."

The view was as commandin' as it ever was, but now it's perspective seemed less narrow. "Jimmie can tell you more about those bridges, and a hundred others, than any man anywhere."

"Is that so?" He stood away, his benignly handsome face glowin' softly as he gazed on Jimmie's flushed countenance.

"That's right," I said, "he's an expert."

"Aw, God, Makon."

"The hell!"

"Well," Will said, "let's sit down for a while. Dinner's in the oven."

Jimmie sat in a luxurious Scandinavian chair and looked around in frank interest. In a little while the conversation was goin' along at a comfortable clip with Jimmie helpin' in the passin' of soft drinks and small edibles. Pretty soon, though, we heard a bell ringin' from the kitchen.

"It's ready," Will said. "We've got meat and potatoes, plus a few other oddball things."

And it was a fine meal. The roast beef was put out with an overflowin' of the freshest vegetables I'd seen since departin' for the romance of desert livin'. Jimmie's eyes were as big as his plate. There were assortments of imported specialties and condiments, and that famous San Francisco bread with sweet butter. Followin' was a cake and two kinds of pie, and ice cream rich enough to float.

Afterward we sat around the table for a long time just talkin'. We touched on old times, the new times, the future and tragedy. We felt happy, sad, angry and glad that we were alive and could share that life in health and relative wealth. Jimmie and Will gradually fell into a banterin' and easy goin' friendship.

Along about eleven I started the wheels rollin' for our departure. "Well," I said, "Jimmie's startin' his new job tomorrow."

"Is that so?" Will said. "Where?"

"At Outdoor Festival Signs," he replied.

"Oh, I know that," Will said. "My office is just two blocks away."

"Over by those big tanks near the airport?" Jimmie asked.

"That's it." Will fiddled a little with the clutter on the table. "Why don't you guys stay over. We'll all see to it Jimmie gets to work on time."

Jimmie looked at Will then at me. "Do you want to, Makon?"

"Do you?"

"Yes."

"Then just why not!"

In a big bedroom at the head of the stairs, Will set about gettin' things ready. He put out towels, tooth brushes and pajamas. Turnin' down the bed, he fluffed up that luxurious beddin' I'd forgotten he had such an self-indulgent preference for. I was workin' slowly at the buttons of my shirt watchin' the man's confident movements, so characteristic of his gentle, purposeful disposition. Memories of peaceful nights—and many ridden with hot passion—moved those bawdy impulses I always carry in my pants.

"God, Makon," he said, "it's so nice to see you in this house again."

"I'm glad I called."

"I am, too. You and Jimmie will always be welcomed here."

Jimmie came out of the bathroom with his white boxers hangin' low at his slim hips in a way that wrapped that hard little body in a licentious invitation. I followed Will's gaze, calm in discreet desire, as it followed the young man as he circled the bed and then jumped onto it. Settlin' in, he crossin' his legs like he was quite willin' to sit there and wait—and for as long as necessary, too—on any new developments that might be comin' his way.

"Well, it looks like to me," he said, "that you guys belonged together."

"We did have certain rapport," Will murmured, lookin' at me. "And I still have a big piece of it."

"And," I replied, "I'd be lyin' if I said I didn't."

"Well, what the hell," Jimmie said. "C'mon, then. Jesus, I'm excited as hell!"

Throwin' off his shirt and droppin' his pants, Will's reserve hit the carpet just as fast his clothes did. His slender body slid onto the bed where he lay waitin' in poised expectation, sleek and firm from the years of methodical attention, while I made short work of doffin' my own duds.

"Jesus Christ," Jimmie exclaimed, "I gotta be the luckiest guy in this whole city. Just look, I got me two tall, good-lookin' men without knowin' how, and, to boot, I don't even know what's gonna happen."

I lay down beside him. "Ain't nothin' gonna happen that no one wants. That right, Will?"

"That's right."

Jimmie, bein' master of his own ship, seemed satisfied with that and went right away to a crouch before Will. The man's trim pale-blue designer underwear were at a listin' bulge, the marvelous sag goin' off down his leg. With Jimmie's slightest tug the frail elastic gave way and the enormous cock reared up into his face. The head, circumcised, had the comely countenance of a creature well aware of the depth of its beauty and, jerkin' in humpin' spasms of greetin', its mouth oozed with the silvery, slippery slop. Jimmie toyed with it in indolent decadence, thumb, forefinger and glans in a tight ballet that drew small groans of pleasure from Will.

"I always liked the look of this stuff," Jimmie said softly. "I never did know if anybody had it besides me."

"We've all got it, Jimmie," Will said.

"Yeah, I know that now."

Then the fair fella, yet new in the ancient endeavor, put his mouth on that dilly of a dong and began the suckin' plunges, one after another in the very finest form of our cocksuckin' elite. That put his ass out there for the mountin' of another neat perversion, so I, also in a crouch, moved down intent on the suckin' of asshole. I pushed the cheeks apart with my fingers and entered the crease. The rubbery goodness met me with a prim pucker and a sweet wink as my tongue, wide and lovin'ly wet, launched another fine vessel into these fascinatin' seas of debauchery. Suckin' his asshole, knowin' that he was suckin' the dick I'd sucked many a time in pits of passion and flights of love, I was twisted into a wonderful desire for all of everythin' for everyone. I came up on my haunches with my dick thrust out in its impudent status of excess.

With it in my hand, I looked upon the compact body before me and said, "I'm gonna be fuckin' you, Jimmie."

"Oh, Jesus," Will murmured.

"I'm gonna fuck you, Jimmie-boy. You hear?"

He came up from Will's cock. "I heard, and it ain't none too soon neither."

After layin' a thick spread of grease on Jimmie's bung, Will handed me the tube, then opened his own legs wide to give Jimmie all possible comfort in his suckin' as we moved toward the rack of the masculine torture that was comin' up. With a hand on Jimmie's shoulder, I laid my dick, greasy and grand, at the portal of the consumin' desire that is born of no less than the push of life itself. The knob a greedy, horny red at a fully gross distention, I pushed against the tight clutch, at once exhilarated and damned: the exhilaration seated in the sharin', the damnation lyin' in its brevity. The rubbery ring, so simple and so marvelous, resisted for a few heavy seconds only and then—flexibility numberin' among its charms—it lay itself open in submissive glory and then began suckin' in the tube by fractional inches. Jimmie's bobbin' head had slowed down to a near stop.

"Hurt, honey?" I said.

His head then came up. "God, like I'm bein' crucified by a Mack truck."

"Well put," Will observed.

"Wanna stop?"

"No!"

With most of possible alarm now at bay but caution still the watchword, I pushed on, findin' the old thrill ever new as the tight constrictions of this sweet anus worked slowly down the long shaft until my thighs kissed at his. Puttin' my hand under his belly I found the prod there hard, heavy and meaty and seekin' somethin' dandy—and handy—for itself.

"How you doin', Will?" I asked.

"Hell, I'm close to a shoot right now!"

"Hold on there, old buddy. In just a little bit now, we'll get

Jimmie into you, and then we'll all go for a nice ride."

"You bet. I'm right with you."

Its authority soon established in the lovely labor at hand, my meat, that probin' blood-filled prong of diligent effort, moved into a round of long, steady strokes of serene confidence. The bond of trust we had in place was now extended in those heavenly movements—the symphony of cornholin'—into the indefinite future. I was the guy of guys—yeah, all gay guys everywhere—gifted in the givin' and gettin' of the magic that this manly and very exclusive pursuit bestows.

"Are you okay, Jimmie?" Will asked.

The boy came up on his elbows. "Oh God, I'm bein' pushed into heaven without even havin' to ask." He looked over his shoulder at me and winked, and then back at Will. "Kiss me, Will."

Movin' to their knees, my two friends—so different and yet so the same—fell into a long and fervent kiss, their very simpatico embrace bein' fueled by the rugged work of my cock. And in that work I was granted power of the most approachable kind in a world rife with its distorted perception: I was granted the power of love in all its frustratin' and edgy—and lovely—confusions. My asshole sang madrigals of sly lust and happy, peekaboo deceptions of warm summer evenin's.

At the endin' of their kiss, Will brushed a light caress on my cheek and bent into the fuckable crouch in front of Jimmie. His butt, boyish and yet slung with the baggage of survival, called loud and clear for an invasion of the anus that winked its coy leave between the fleshy mounds. No clown, Jimmie saw the invitation and we, in an ad-libbed shuffle, moved toward the waitin' Will and his well-greased asshole. With me in full penetration, Jimmie sank into Will with the acolytic radiance of an innocent stridin' manfully into his own inevitable future. Grapplin' for a moment with the timin', soon enough he had the wheel of the fuck well in hand and moved at a rapid pace into the refined world of the double fuck.

"Man, oh, man!" he exclaimed hoarsely. "Ain't this just the fuckin' fuck of heaven!" He giggled. "And with all manner of holy hosts lookin' on, by Christ!"

"Oh, Jimmie, baby," Will crooned. "Oh, my God, you sweet young creature, fuck me!"

So we rolled along, we three, bound up in the peachy chains of lust that clinked with wonderful sounds as we dragged them behind us in a carpet of flowers. Jimmy was exemplary in the cadence maintained, Will was his steady, reliable self handsomely spread out with his asshole hostin' the star of this willin'ly wicked constellation of gay fellas and I, well I, vain enough in pride to take credit for the sizable cock bein' thrust into Jimmie and the main engine in this petite extravaganza of lust, felt the poetry of the outrageous, the common and the quaint spinnin' in my head. My cock was givin' me those superlative servin's of vanilla ice cream hung heavy with butterscotch sauce, whipped toppin', crushed mixed nuts and sweet red cherries saturated in sugar. God!

"Oh, shit, Makon," Jimmie said softly. "I'm gonna come."

"Come, honey," I said.

"Yes, honey," sweet Will said, "come if you want."

"Shit, I can't not!"

The boy was in control of himself, admirably so, right up to the explosion, and then some real verbal shit hit the fan. Oh, God, he let fly with a litany of obscenity that did more justice to scatological literature than anythin' we were actually doin', but it sure was nice to hear as the foxy fella worked himself down to the wire on the double fuck.

"Nastyboy low ball Jesus pimps Holy Ghost fuckin' pigs! Lay the bastard deep go for a hot drip in ass fuckin' cheap bellhop slut! Piss shit up his nose! Pus in the preacher, Gonna reacher, Hot cold cocker, Better knocker! Up the fuckin' ass!"

He was slammin' into Will and pushin' back onto me, back and forth into a hellish seesaw of screamin', jizz-pullin', shit-kickin', suckin'-ass cacophony.

"O, God's mother, Pregnant by a fish, Ain't that caviar, Don't she wish. Sit on a pole, Roll up a joint, Ain't but a soul, Got no point."

Makin' one last whoppin' turn he made the magnificent heave.

"Hey! It's the fuckin' drip of heaven comin' right up!"

Then, vain, profane, lovely, human and funny, he slumped down on Will's back, a boy hugely spent and breathin' hard. My cock rose in him like an unyieldin' bird of gentle predation.

"Okay, Will," I said, "now come fuck me so's we can put these hot deposits where they belong."

Pullin' away from Jimmie's cock—out with a lewd smack—Will came around behind me and, without a whole lot of ceremony, plugged in while I went on hoppin' hard in Jimmie who was now an exalted pawn in the steamy matter of two guys workin' together to get their rocks off. After some nice strokes in masterful form, it wasn't much longer before Will opened his final barrage on me and, bearin' down hard on the little doodad mechanisms inside that make all this shit worthwhile, popped his nuts. In a silky hell of heaven I worshiped at the altar of Jimmie's sensational ass while Will, still slopped in the abundance of love, pulled out and, low on his hands and knees, threw sucks and licks at my asshole while I delivered into Jimmie a mighty spew of jizzycum, the sticky stuff that sometimes helps glue driftin' lives together.

We lay there for many minutes—the flow of time caught in the kinks of the postcoital enigma—collectin' ourselves and the new awareness of each other that this unique—well, maybe not so unique—swing of perversion had brought to us. We were no longer just the congenial group of men who had climbed those stairs together. And even if nothin' ever went any further than this sloppy, steamy, wet moment, we were all forever changed both individually and in our perceptions of each other: the fella who tosses the salad ain't the same fella who tosses in the sheets.

Rollin' off the bed to his feet, Will bent to kiss Jimmie, then me, and padded away to the john. Jimmie came up close to me, pushed his marvelous arrangement of muscles against my ribs and breathed hot against my ear. I put my arm around his shoulder.

"Do you think," he said softly, "all this might happen again?"

"I don't see why not."

"Good. I sometimes need reassurance." He laughed and jumped from the bed, and then turned back. "But it's true, I do."

I got up and we followed Will into the bath.

He stood at the long window runnin' the length of the narrow space. The bridges, silently constant in another night of the thousands, held high their lights of endurin' promise.

"I see them every day," Will said, "and I still sometimes forget how important they are."

Jimmie rolled a soft grab across Will's butt. "Well, come down to it, y'know, they ain't nothin' but cold iron put together from a plan."

Will pulled away from the window.

"And," Jimmie said with his bright-eyed optimism, "what we got right here is a hell of a lot more'n that."

Will looked at me smiling and shaking his head.

"Get in the shower, kiddo," I said. "We'll show you some iron. Hot iron!"

"And you," Will said, "can take that for a promise."

THE MONASTERY

Robert Burdette Sweet

The Greek god Eros was the patron god of pederasty.

The Aztec god Xochipili was the patron god of male homosexuality.

The rules of our order forbade us to speak, but his face spoke to me, his bearing spoke to me, his silence talked. — Saint Aelred of Rievauix in the 12th century referring to Simon when he first entered the Cistercian monastery. — *from* John Boswell, *Christianity, Social Tolerance, and Homosexuality*, 1980.

Because he became one, Mike has to struggle to view clearly the tribe of fantasy men who at night come to the long block of warehouses which have been altered to accommodate their needs. Warehouses that rot under the sleek pyramidal towers of the city's businessmen, hustlers in their own right, many who cross the fine line to traverse the ageless, bleak and treeless street, through broken glass, and enter portals with brutal names: Stud, Ramrod, Brig, Slot. Places where salesmen–hunters and doctor–medicine men and poet–shamans and plebes all merge, drink from loins and otherwise cannibalize the flesh. Here they perform the ceremony glorifying the ancient lust to never be alone, never separate.

Inside the grey, sweating walls of the Slot, Mike stumbles with other men down dark halls and over stairways. He passes cells with doors ajar where anchorites meditate on their backs or stomachs, eyes closed, soliciting a father, a son, a holy ghost to deliver them.

At the end of the hall, Mike mounts, expectant, another tier of worn, splintered stairs, aware of his own fall from safety more than the silent push of men. He senses that they are all fated to crawl these steps at least in dreams that recall the descent into the savannah, the bonding herd, and hard thighs entwined for warmth against the fear.

Mike slides his hand along the worn railing and knows many families had lived there. The warehouse was thrown up around a tenement to be used for the storing of merchandise and now is utilized for the press of wandering bodies. He can smell the original families' pasts and hear their ghosts soughing around the haloes cast by orange lights.

Mike enters a small room, possibly once a bedroom, its walls deeply shadowed, ending in a closet where to ease his body is to encounter bits and pieces of life. There is a cock shoved in Mike's hand, stiff and lightly greased, attached to no body discernible in the dark. In that black closet there must once have dangled wilted clothes, a torn suitcase tied with rope on the floor, a baby's broken doll collapsed in a corner.

Mike politely passes his fingers around the warmth shoved into his hand, lets go and rejoins the circulating, nameless, voiceless wraiths he can't quite see and for whom he doesn't exist as a specific entity. Love me, love me, they plead with each gesture, though nobody ever has or will for this, especially those they seek who dread the mirror that every identically–dressed man is for them. Mike has come to suspect that the worst homophobe is gay.

Mike flows with others up a last flight of stairs to the topmost room in whose center swings a man tied in a sling by someone cooperative, someone who understood. A frail light, pale as dawn, leaks down onto the man's trussed beauty as he sways in the leather straps held by chains to the ceiling. He is commanding in his helplessness, naked and confessing with his amber-lit ass thrust forward.

Mike stares as he would in an old church at this saint in a reliquary, poised to inspire or prepared to be ruined by that chance fist that might rip his gut. All martyrs are webbed spiders, waiting. Not even a sigh comes from the bones that have lived all their lives, all week, for the leathered seraphim Mike watches stalk toward him, who stops, unzips his fly, leans forward, rubs spit on his love and enters, black shining pants angled down, iron studs in his hat glimmering, serving slavishly he who controlled from his cerements, demanding worship. And getting it.

An exit leads out to a porch and more wood stairs that feel soft, shrinking to Mike's feet as he descends into a courtyard. A tall yucca tree with spiked, umber leaves punches the peeling paint of the building rising on four sides to form walls for the cloister. Mike pauses, looks around and then up at the oblong sky with its few stars in a scud of fog. There is relief here. In the garden.

Young men and old pass strolling, heads lowered in awe of their contemplation of the lingam of all peoples and ages, the same respect given the crippled, the ugly and the ideal, every man shaded in his purposeful twilight. Mike joins them where they congregate and crowd the steps that lead off the edge of the garden into the muted glow of what could be the sacristy, heavy beams marking this entrance that has no door.

Mike pushes through to see over their heads. In one corner of the large room he makes out a smaller room, unfinished, bare timber, no plaster, glowing in a faint light that seems to come from nowhere. Within it shines a narrow table or raised bed wrapped in a formica sheen within whose simulated folds must hide a grail.

"Fuck me, fuck me," whimpers a novitiate leaning against the wood but not daring to walk through what Mike now realizes are bars of iron, like a jail, stretching from ceiling to floor parallel to the boards. Now many men lean against the iron, arms folded across chests or touching some man near, yet none will move through the bars and present himself upon the altar to acknowledge what might be there.

They huddle close. They are gentle, stroking thighs and beards. Hands touch Mike. He moves aside, not ready yet. The hands are gone without protest as Mike steps over three men trundled together on the floor. He can feel the crush of their trinity inside his head.

Mike looks up. In a dim alcove he discerns a bathtub, apparently an original to the place, with lion feet, wide and deep, where children now grown and dead from age must have sailed boats and sunk navies of rubber sailors. In front of the tub a blond young man, his jacket heaped about his ankles, peels free his T-shirt, slowly pulling it over this tousled head. For a moment his face is turned to the side, his profile sculpted, neat and clean, a parent's pride, but not if they knew, he being a member of the only minority cast out by those who give them birth. Now, as recompense, he is the satyr-sphinx in rapt concern over the ridding of his body of obstacles. He slides down his pants, faded jeans, seeming not to be aware or caring that anyone watches. And no one is, except Mike. The ritual is too usual. Stripped, he pauses, head bowed, chin near his chest, a supplicant. Then languidly his muscled hams move glowing into the light. Bending over he touches, tentatively, the cracked rim of the tub, his fingers long and searching. He dares, and nestles within the cold and arid zinc, adjusting his strong body to the confines, curled and mute.

"Go piss on him." A voice close to Mike's ear.

"No one would."

"Oh, they will. He wants it. We all get what we want."

"I could never do that," Mike says.

"I think you don't know why you're here," the voice mutters. "Here . . . everything is . . . real. Know what I mean?"

Yes, Mike thought he might: our species' sacrifice to its overproductive richness, Michelangelos and bar-lonelies, Tchaikovskies and drones.

One of the three who had tossed together on the floor comes

forward from behind Mike. Casually, he enters the light near the tub, takes out the Priapus honored here and beatifies the holy Francis of the rich blond hair. Who yowls in exultation, "God, God. My God!"

STAFF OF THE SHEPHERD

Ray Boatwright

With a last burst of energy he rounded the crest of the hill, his muscled thighs and buttocks working like pistons. It was all down hill from here and soon this little deer path would merge with a proper trail that would eventually take him back to the Berkeley campus. The descending path was narrow and rugged, so he slowed his pace and adjusted his gait to accommodate to the terrain. He always took time to tape his feet and ankles carefully before these runs just for this kind of surface.

As the path began to level, he saw the makeshift wire fence and the sign warning that it was electrically charged. Beyond it, goats were feeding intently, barely noticing the young blond student running by in a lather like a race horse. Although he had never seen the shepherd, the goats were familiar from previous runs. It was a project to help control the wild fires that could plague the brown California hills. The goats, with their voracious appetites, were moved to various locations in the park and valley to graze on the underbrush that was so instrumental in feeding wild fires. Further up the hill he saw the 4-wheel-drive truck with the tall camper shell that always accompanied the goats.

Something, perhaps a sound, made him turn his head to the left. On the embankment a man stood looking down at him, a border collie at his feet. Apparently it was the shepherd. After the initial start at the unexpected encounter, the runner was struck with the beauty of the man. In a second's time, before returning his gaze to the trail, he took in the shepherd's sturdy build, his soft, curly black hair, thick moustache, the smile on his lips, and his eyes as dark as night. Just before the trail bent sharply, he glanced back over his shoulder. The dark man still watched him, his intense eyes seeming to stare into the secret, unrevealed heart of the runner.

Later in the shower, with the communal bathroom door of

the frat house carefully locked, he soaped up his rising cock and imagined the shepherd there with him, naked, looking at him with those dark, insolent eyes and smiling. The shepherd's rough hands stroked down his broad chest, over his belly, and gripped the root of his cock.

"Go ahead, feel me," the image said. He imagined stroking down the shepherd's chest, his fingers tangling in his body hair, measuring the size and shape of his cock.

"Go ahead, suck me." And he imagined what it would feel like to have the man's cock in his mouth, taste his cum as it spurted. . . Before he knew it he was shooting his own load through the pouring water and onto the tiled floor, unaware of his groans forced between his clenched teeth.

These jerk-off fantasies used to be a torture to David. He would try to imagine a girl, a slut, a porn queen, any female, but she would always turn into some hot guy before he came. He had sex with some girls — they loved the soft blond hairs on his belly and his gentleness — but he always felt like an imposter, rutting away with his eyes closed. After a lifetime of denial, he acknowledged to himself that he was homosexual, but just to himself, for this was not something he could tell his frat brothers, and certainly not his father.

David was the third son of Walter Morel, a successful and powerful corporation lawyer in the San Diego area. And just as his two older brothers had done, David was expected to follow in his father's footsteps, get his law degree from U.C. Berkeley, pledge his father's fraternity, graduate with honors, and marry a society girl. And then become a partner in Morel, Morel, Morel . . . and Morel. Of the three sons, David was the smartest, best looking, and most athletic. Generations of careful society breeding were reflected in his bearing. But from childhood David had troubled his father with his rebelliousness, independence, and some other foreign quality Mr. Morel couldn't quite figure.

As a boy, David loved animals with a passion. He would spend summers at the family ranch, following at the heels of

Simon, the caretaker, hanging on his every word about the nature and care of the farm animals. Simon recognized that David had a special talent or "Shining" with the creatures and mentioned this to his father. Mr. Morel was not interested in hearing this from the caretaker. Simon, he felt, was an unhealthy influence on David, so he was fired. David was in a sullen rage. The few weeks that remained of their stay at the family ranch were a battle ground. David would sneak from his room at night to sleep in the barn which, when discovered, enraged Mr. Morel. He abruptly canceled the stay and returned to their San Diego estate. Later that fall, Mr. Morel put the ranch on the market.

David remained a cog out of sync with his father's dream. As a high school student, his appearance and ideas didn't reflect well on the son of one of the most successful corporation lawyers on the west coast. In his senior year David announced that he was applying to U.C. Davis for pre-veterinarian school, not law school at Berkeley. A war raged in the Morel household. His mother scolded him, his brothers shamed him, and his father had a stroke. The fact that Mr. Morel was a workaholic who drank and smoked to extreme didn't seem to matter.

"Look what you did to your father," they all seemed to say. When David saw him in the hospital bed in a tangle of tubes and hoses, he broke down and cried like a child.

"I'm sorry, Daddy," he sobbed.

And so David entered U.C. Berkeley and fell into the traditional ways of the Morel men. As a freshman, he moved into the fraternity house and took up the beer-swilling and carousing that is often characteristic of young fraternity men. He partied with a fervor that left his fraternity brothers in the dust and earned him quite a reputation. But despite his best efforts, he remained unhappy and dissatisfied. In his sophomore year, he started having nightmares and insomnia. Although he didn't dislike his frat brothers, he had little in common with them and his growing awareness of his homosexuality made him more guarded. He was attracted to the more radical and bohemian segments of the college crowd, but he was quickly rebuffed when they found he was a frat boy from a privileged, W.A.S.P. background.

He started running to get back in shape but the runs soon became an obsession. He would start from the frat house on the edge of campus and run up the streets to Strawberry Canyon and to the trails that would lead him into the hills. Over the ridge and into La Morinda valley was a myriad of small paths that grew more isolated as they wandered. Fearful of the consequences of choosing a new life, his young manhood, his essence, was frozen. But on these lone marathon runs, David would tear along for hours, the anger and regret pouring from him like sweat, his blue eyes glazed and focused on something far away. In the extreme fatigue he felt on his return, he found a temporary peace and a sleep-filled night.

One Thursday night he returned from the library and, after exchanging some small talk with his frat brothers, went upstairs. In the quietness of his room his father's voice played on the answering machine.

"Hi. It's a school night, hope you're not out drinking with the boys. You've really got to buckle down and pick up those grades. Neither of your brothers had this problem, and neither did I. I had a 3.95 average. Don't let me down, son."

This was followed by a message from his older brother who sounded tired and irritable.

"It's me. Hear you're still having problems at school. Saw someone at the country club, he heard you don't like hanging out with your fraternity brothers these days. And you're not even dating. Why no girlfriend? Gotta go. By the way, Dad's having some more problems and will be in the hospital a few days next week for some tests. 'Bye."

The messages just provoked David's already troubled soul, causing him to toss through another sleepless night. When day broke he was up and putting on his running shoes and shorts. He was confronted by a soft, unseasonal rain falling when he stepped outside. The damp and fog seemed to match his own mood as he started running up the streets and into the hills. By the time he crested the ridge and descended into La Morinda valley, he was running at a steam heat. As he ran, his face was a scowl and he was muttering make believe dialogue. He cursed his life and his family and he hated himself for not standing up to them, for being afraid to express his sex, for being afraid just to "fucking live" for himself. The anger seemed to pound out of him with every stride as he pushed himself to the limit, running along small muddy ruts, tearing through brush and branches, unmindful of the mud, cuts, and scratches.

He jumped a small creek of flowing water and started chugging up a steep hillside. He was so preoccupied when he had set off this morning, he had forgotten the ritual of taping his feet and ankles, so when his left foot dipped and twisted into a rainwashed rut, he heard a loud crackle. The pain wrenched up his leg, causing him to fall on his back. He gritted his teeth and yelled once. It echoed in the distance through the fog and rain. When he was finally able to catch his breath, he tried to stand. The slightest weight on his left foot caused the pain to sear. As he assessed the situation, at worst he had broken his ankle, at best a tendon was torn. Either way, he only had use of one foot to find his way back. He was miles from nowhere and the only sound was the muted rain. He remembered the creek he had crossed at the bottom of the hill. Perhaps if he followed the creek, he thought, it would lead to a road.

Going down the hill was slow and painful. He slipped and tumbled, causing deep and bleeding abrasions on his elbow and hip. When he finally reached the creek bed he was shaking uncontrollably and his heart was racing. Slowly he followed the creek downhill, grabbing onto branches when he could, sitting down and scooting along on his butt when he had to. Eventually the creek bed leveled off and opened up, the banks spreading up to groves of small laurel trees. Following the creek, he thought he was hallucinating when he saw a wire fence and the rusted sign indicating it was electrically charged. Beyond the corral, goats stood staring at him like a spectral presence. Then the truck with the camper shell came into view, backed into a flat, open area.

He stood looking at the welcome scene slack-jawed, as if it were a dream come true. A dog sat under the bed of the truck, leisurely scratching an ear, keeping dry. His temporary trance was broken when the little border collie saw him and set up a ruckus of barking, running forward and stopping midway to display it's impressive canines.

A figure appeared, almost filling the open camper door — the shepherd, dressed in a open flannel shirt and jeans, holding a shotgun. At first he peered fiercely across the distance at David, blinking his eyes, then dropped the gun, leaped from the truck, and galloped to him. David stood frozen in confusion and fear until the shepherd was at his side, putting his arm around his shoulders, helping him through the fence, supporting and carrying him to the truck.

"I'm sorry, I didn't mean to trespass," he said deliriously.

The big shepherd grunted and hefted him into the camper. David continued mumbling apologies. "Shhh," the shepherd said, and touched David's face as he sat him on the edge of the narrow bed. He removed David's muddy running shoes, then pulled his soggy and torn tank top off, and tossed it out the open door.

"Lift up," he ordered. "You need to get out of these wet clothes." David raised his hips from the bed and the shepherd's big hands yanked the trunks off in one swoop. He took a towel and started rubbing him vigorously, starting with the top of his soaked head. Shivers ran in waves down David's naked, muscled shape. His pale flesh responded to the rub down, turning warm and rosey. If the shepherd noticed David's naked flesh, he didn't show it. After drying him, the shepherd wrapped a thick, wool blanket around his trembling frame. "Here, take these," he urged, handing him two aspirin and holding a tall glass of water to his mouth. When the shivers stopped, the man served him a bowl of left-over dinner stew and bread which David ate greedily.

David finally found his tongue. "I was running and hurt my ankle — I heard it crunch. I might have broken it." As he told him his story, the dark, silent man served him some coffee in a large mug. He had mixed the coffee with boiled milk and much sugar. David sipped at the sweet, thick mixture, trying not to burn his tongue. It left a milky film above his lip which the shepherd wiped away with his finger. The bold but intimate gesture made David blush.

The shepherd knelt before him and examined the ankle, which was swollen and slightly blue.

"Relax your legs and feet," he grunted. "I can do this with a lame goat, but I've never tried it with a lame man."

David watched as he grasped his right foot and rotated it, then switched to the left and gently did the same, comparing the two.

"What's your name?" David asked curiously.

"Raul," he answered without looking up. "Raul Davila. We're gypsy. My family has been goat herders for generations. We live in Oregon but this contract was too good not to travel to. We finish up tomorrow. Hopefully we get the job next year, too." His voice was low and husky with the suggestion of a European accent.

"You said 'we', is somebody else here with you?"

Raul's dark eyes twinkled up into the boy's blue ones, grinning. "No, I meant me and the goats. All my brothers and their families are up in Oregon. I'll join them later."

The left foot definitely flapped more loosely. "You did not break your ankle," Raul said authoritatively. "Probably torn or stretched tendons. I'll tape it up for you and you can see the doctor tomorrow." He reached beneath the bed and pulled out a tin full of first aid supplies and got a roll of tape.

David sat still for the shepherd's ministrations and, as the striking man bandaged his ankle, glanced around the camper. Although modestly appointed, the truck was very clean and compactly arranged. The dim light came through the open door, giving the interior a warm glow. David watched the big hands, the thick fingers, expertly work the tape around his ankle, and he stole glances at Raul himself. His thick, collar-length hair was so deep black there were blue highlights in it. He had thick, course eye brows over deep-set dark eyes, but long lashes gave his rugged features a mysteriously delicate effect. Full lips were partially hidden by a thick black moustache. Beard stubble was appearing along his jaw and chin. David realized with embarrassment that he had a painfully large hard-on hidden beneath the folds of the blanket.

"There, that should do 'til you can see a doctor," he said as he moved back and squatted on a stool. He looked at David with a warm smile. "I've seen you running through these hills many times before. You always seemed so driven, like you were being chased. I half expected to see a posse with blood hounds following behind you," he said with a chuckle.

David felt himself blush again under the man's hearty, almost brazen appraisal. Raul's attention fell on the bruised elbow. He reached into the tin and pulled out a tube of ointment. "Let me put some of this on that elbow," he said and sat close beside him as he gently began applying the ointment to the wound. His shirt was hanging open and David's eyes were drawn to the smooth, dusky skin of his chest, the pattern of black hair extending down over his belly. Sitting this close, he could feel the heat from the man's body. David wrapped the blanket tighter around himself to hide his erection.

"What about that scrape on your hip?" he remembered, and abruptly yanked open the blanket. David's rigid dick sprang into view before he could respond.

Raul paused, arched one dark eyebrow and smiled. "Don't be embarrassed," he said; "See, the same thing happens to me." He took David's hand and placed it on his lap. Beneath the loose jeans, David felt the man's large cock pushing upward. It was warm and seemed to quiver with his touch.

David swallowed hard. His shower fantasy flashed to his

mind, but he dared not speak of it now. It was his first time to feel another man's cock. His tongue felt clumsy and awkward. He gripped the huge rod firmly.

Raul looked up with a smile on his face. "Does that feel good?"

"I've never done this with a man," was all he could say.

Raul was smiling gently, and a fire seemed to glow in his eyes. "Would you like to do more?"

Sitting naked now, all of David's senses had grown uncommonly acute. With his hand still on the shepherd's hidden cock, the rain drumming on the metal roof of the camper surged in his ears; he could see a vein throb in the dark man's throat, and smell his warm, musky odor.

"Yes," he said.

Raul rose from the bed and let the soft flannel slide off his shoulders, then undid the loose fitting jeans and shucked them off. Davis stared up at the figure, his eyes worshiping the brawny, male flesh. Raul stood proudly with his hands on his hips, like a king before a subject. His broad chest was smooth except for a few curly hairs around each dark nipple. Across his stomach a pattern of black hair swirled down to his patch of pubics and further to his broad, thick thighs. He had large, heavy balls above which his cock jutted upward. The shaft was thick and heavily veined to the foreskin which was stretched over half of the bulbous head. A single drop of pre-cum glistened at the piss slit like an ornament. He stroked the skin back with his blunt fingers to expose the whole cockhead, and the drop spooled in slow motion to the floor.

David sat transfixed before him, his heart racing. If the shepherd's body was the dark work horse, sturdy and strong, David's was the pale thoroughbred race horse, lean and graceful. His pale skin was accentuated by soft, blond hair that grew over his chest to a thin cleft down his stomach. In the presence of such regal virility, he forgot his earlier modesty and sat back with his long legs splayed, his hand stroking his cock. It was blustery red and, although not as thick as Raul's, was a match in length.

Raul took a step toward David so his cock bobbed before his face. "Go ahead, feel it," he said. David first stroked Raul's hairy belly with one hand and cupped his balls with the other, marveling at their size and weight. Then with both hands he began to stroke Raul's cock, fascinated by its bulk and length. Copying Raul's gesture, he slowly pulled the foreskin back to expose the entire mushroom of the head. His eyes were transfixed as his own cock jerked and throbbed.

"Go ahead, suck it."

His fantasy was coming true, down to the last detail! But — but — now it was time.

David stuck out his tongue and tasted the oozing pre-cum. It had a sweet, clear taste. He wanted more, and hesitantly his tongue snaked out to cover the bulging velvet knob on all sides. He could sense the contained excitement in response, and, without further hesitation, he went further down the pre-ordained pathway. After engulfing the head, he slowly tried sinking more down his throat, but gagged.

"That's all right," Raul said, smiling down at him, "just use your mouth on the head and your hands on the rest."

David rolled his tongue over the head and continued stroking with both hands. Raul placed his hands over David's and guided his strokes, making soft moans of approval. As the pre-cum continued spilling out over his tongue, David became almost frenzied for more of this exquisite man.

Raul abruptly pulled his cock from the his lips, making a popping sound. "Lie down, my friend," he said urgently.

David lay back on the narrow bed and Raul crawled over him, settling himself down, making sure their cocks pressed together. Holding David's head in his hands, Raul started kissing David about his face and then engulfed his mouth. He rocked his pelvis against David's, their cock juices lubricating their bellies. He began kissing David's neck, continuing down to his chest, and lingered on each pink, hard nipple.

When he reached his cock, he paused and took two licks along the shaft and then engulfed its entire length. David was jolted by a wave of pleasure as he watched the shepherd's black moustache meet his blond pubes. Raul's lips quivered and sucked up and down along his pulsating cock. Then while stroking David's cock with his hands, he began stuffing his mouth with the young man's balls. He rolled them around, singly and together, in his hot mouth.

Still he proceeded downward. Raul suddenly forced David's legs up and apart and pressed his mouth between his ass cheeks. On reflex, David struggled to push his legs down to keep the man's tongue from his asshole, but the shepherd was strong and forced them back into place. Once his mouth was at his anus, David gave in to the strange pleasure. He had never realized that such bliss could come from this spot as he pulled his knees up voluntarily, feeling Raul shake his head vigorously to root even deeper, his hot, silky tongue contrasting with his course beard grinding against and around his asshole. Finally Raul straightened up while still on his knees and still keeping David's legs up.

"I really want to fuck you. I think you'd like it, too."

David stared at the shepherd's huge dick. "Won't it hurt?"

Raul smiled and leaned forward and kissed him on the lips, first gently, then harder, pressing his tongue into his mouth.

He rose, breathing heavily. "I would never hurt you, never. Only someone who is mean or inexperienced would do that. I am neither. If there is pain, it's because you're holding back. You must give yourself to me totally. I know you would like it, I can sense that from you." David was entranced by the man's words, his will melding with the man who knelt above him. Raul began kissing his mouth again. "Please, David."

It sounded like somebody else talking as he heard himself say, "Yeah, I want you to."

Raul leaned over and opened a drawer beneath the bed and retrieved a condom and a small bottle of lubricant.

"You're prepared," David said with a chuckle.

"Oh, my little brother uses this truck on his dates back home. He's always well stocked."

Raul coated his tumescent cock with a generous amount of lube, rolled the condom down as far as it would go, and then generously lubed his sheathed dick. Pushing David's legs further back, Raul expertly applied the grease to the submissive virgin duct. "Relax now, keep breathing, I'm going to put all of the head in now," he said, as he used his hand to manipulate the cockhead in circles over the tight sphincter. Gently, he pushed through into the relaxing hole.

Immediately David let out an intense moan.

"Remember, give yourself over to me, my friend." He felt the muscles relaxing. "That's right, feel it going inside you, you like it, don't you?"

With both his legs drawn above him, David felt exposed, vulnerable, yet bold and excited. "Oh, yes, give me more, man," he said gazing deeply into the dark eyes. Raul pushed forward, sinking another inch into David's butt, taking his time before giving him more. When the cockhead hit the prostate, David tensed up.

"Don't worry, you're not going to piss, just let go and enjoy it." The sensation became more pleasurable for David as Raul pushed in again and stopped, giving the sphincter time to adjust.

When at last Raul had his whole cock sunk into David's asshole, he began slowly grinding crotch against buttocks, sending his cock in deeper. David gritted his teeth through the intense pleasure and Raul carefully picked up his pace. Before long he was pulling out and thrusting back in to the hilt. They had started to sweat and his hips made slapping noises against the runner's ass. Each thrust from the big man sent him into an animalistic ecstacy.

David heard himself talking almost like a different creature. "Fuck me, Raul! Oh, it's so good," he cried. He started working his butt as best as he could under the man's weight, taking a more active role.

"I got an idea," Raul said, and carefully pulled his thickness from David's hole. "Come on over here and stand up. Be careful of your foot," he reminded him. As David struggled to stand on one leg he looked at Raul's cock which had actually gotten bigger. "I can't believe I had that whole thing up there," he gasped.

"Well, you did and you're going to again," Raul promised.

Raul instructed him to brace himself with his hands against the wall, then took the foot stool and gently placed David's knee on it to spare the wounded ankle. "O.K., now spread your legs, bend your knees, yeah, bring your butt out to me." Raul positioned himself behind him and guided his cock to David's asshole. "Come on now, push back on my dick."

Slowly, David pushed back on his dick, feeling the swollen heat going inside him. Pleasure flowed through his tense body. Raul stood still, leaning back with his hands on his hips as David did the work this time and watched as David's lily-white ass sank down to meet his dark hairy crotch. This slow, rhythmic spectacle inflamed Raul's passion even further. His jaw jutting aggressively, he grasped David's hips in his rough hands and fucked him vigorously, his strong, sweaty ass humping like a bull's. David tried to match him with his own back strokes. The camper was set in motion, rocking back and forth from the furious fucking inside. The shepherd's loyal dog woke from his dreams beneath the camper and came out into the rain to peer through the open door into the dark camper. He caught the smell of man sex, relaxed, and returned to his dry lair.

David continued supporting himself with his hands against the wall while Raul reached around and started stroking David's slick pole, his hand strokes matching his cock strokes up David's ass. The rhythm intensified and, with his face buried in David's silky hair, he felt himself exploding in what felt like a pressure cooker. Waves of pleasure jerked through them. Raul cupped his fist over David's cock and jerked, feeling the hot semen spurt in gushes into his hand. Their groans merged and crescendoed as their juices flowed simultaneously in a continuous cascade.

When at last the orgasm subsided, Raul turned David's head and, covering David's mouth with his own, kissed and licked at his lips.

Later, when their excitement had finally ebbed, David lay in Raul's arms, his head on his chest. Outside the soft rain continued like a whisper. David felt a great sense of release and happiness, of safety and love in the shepherd's arms. And as he lay there he told him his story, of his unhappiness with his life and the decisions he had made out of guilt and a sense of duty, and of his loneliness at school. Raul lay there quietly listening, stroking his hair. When he was finished, Raul responded quietly, choosing his words carefully.

"It is good that you want to honor your father. If our parents love and protect us as babies, we should regard them respectfully when we are grown. But more important than anything else, we should respect our own hearts. Only unhappiness and bitterness will follow if we don't. It is sad for the father who will not respect his child's own heart, but it must be his sadness, not the child's."

David twisted his head to look into Raul's dark eyes, but they seemed far away as if remembering another time.

"Sometimes we must be still until we can hear our heart, but if we listen, we do what is right. The heart will always be true and lead us to our chosen destiny. Maybe your gift is to be a healer of animals, maybe not. But if it is, it's a very special gift and one that would be tragic to deny." He brought his hands down to David's chest and tapped with his fingers. "Listen to your heart, my friend, only you can hear it."

They lay in each others arms in silence then, eyes closed, listening to the rain, until they both fell asleep in contentment.

When David awoke in the early morning darkness, the rain had stopped and through the open camper door he could see light along the horizon. For some time, Raul had been awake staring silently at David, his eyes burning through the dimness. David moaned softly, happy that it had not been a dream, and then began quietly kissing him, moving down his body to his already hard cock and hairy balls. The pungent, manly aroma wafted across his face. Without a word, Raul pushed him back down, rolled him over on his stomach, and spread his legs. David could hear him tearing the foil from a condom and then felt the cool lubing jell on his asshole.

In a few moments, Raul was on him, pinning him down, pushing his staff forcefully into his asshole. David thrilled to the man's aggressiveness, his desire for what he could give. And there was another factor, an unspoken realization that their time together was almost gone, that the world would shortly claim them back to their respective lives. This time they fucked like animals, with feral rutting, no words, only noises and grunts. No longer the gentle tutor, Raul reigned over him with all his power, his hands over David's, pinning him down, his thrusts so strong as if to tear him open and meld with his flesh. He bit and sucked the flesh on the boy's neck and shoulders, causing red welts, and then grabbed a handful of his blond hair and roughly yanked his head back. Their kisses were hard and violent, Raul grunting his breath into David's mouth with each plunge. As he shot his pungent come, Raul's visage was almost cruel as he slammed his weight and muscle into David. David's erection was pressed rhythmically between his belly and the rough wool blanket with Raul's thrusts. The feel of that aggressive cock in his tender ass and the friction and pressure on his own shaft threw him into that sweet, new oblivion as he squirted hot cum onto the bedding. They both lay gasping and wordless till David fell back asleep, Raul still on top, his cock still inside.

The sun was shining when Raul woke David with a cup of coffee, made creamy and sweet. He noticed that Raul had shaved, groomed his moustache, and combed his black hair. His hands were taped in preparation for moving the barbed wire fence of the goat's feeding area to the other side of the arroyo.

"Here are some clothes for you to wear out of here," Raul said. "They won't fit you very well but they're better than nothing. I need to get my work done. My brother will be here tonight with

his livestock truck. Hopefully my goats will be finished by then.
You take your time, but I need to get started."

David finished the coffee and put on the clothes. Raul was
right, they were too short and too big around but they felt
comfortable. Still hobbling on his injured foot, David stepped
gingerly out of the camper and heard the sound of a metal stake
being driven into the ground from somewhere on the hillside.
Eventually Raul appeared from the bushes.

The moment was suddenly very awkward for both of them.
There would be no dates, no plans for dinner or future fuck
sessions. This was it. Paul placed a rough hand on David's
shoulder.

"If you follow this trail around the bend you'll reach the road
over the hill and back into Berkeley. You should be able to hitch
a ride from there. Wait a second." He disappeared into the
camper and came out with a large wooden cane. "This is my staff.
I use it for herding, for guiding the animals. I have had it for a
long time, but I want you to have it. You can use it as a crutch
to get you back."

It was beautifully hand carved with deep textures and tones
in the wood grain. The handle was dark from the oil of the hand
that had gripped it so many times, and David could feel the man's
superb energy radiating from it as he accepted it gratefully.

"This is beautiful," David said. "Thank you... thank you for—
everything. You saved my life, in more ways than one."

Suddenly, tears welled in the shepherd's eyes. He took David's
face in his hands and kissed him tenderly, then turned abruptly
and disappeared into the trees.

David found the road easily and hitched a ride into town, first
going to the doctor for his wounded ankle. As Raul said, it was
a stretched tendon that needed to be taped and iced as much as
possible. When he returned to the frat house, he showered
reluctantly, for he could still get whiffs of Raul's odor from his
own body. Then he wrote a short letter to the Dean, saying he
was dropping out of school for a while to pursue other plans.

That night he called home, but his father, the maid informed him, was in Switzerland until the end of the week.

"What about the tests he was supposed to have in the hospital?" he asked.

"What tests?" she responded.

David laughed mockingly. "Please tell Dad that I'm dropping out of school at least for the semester. I don't know what I'll be doing or where I'm going but I'll keep him posted as soon as I decide. We'll have a lot to talk about when I do see him again."

He fell asleep early that night, despite his excitement, and woke up at dawn. While packing the jeans that Raul had given him, he felt something in the back pocket. It was a letter, carefully printed in pencil:

"Dear David, You are sleeping as I write this. It was a kind fate that brought you to my camp last night and I feel that a kind fate will also bring us together again sometime in life. We may be old men by then, but it will happen. Perhaps our paths will merge and we can travel together as life allows. Until that time, please know that I remain, your devoted friend, Raul Davila."

David packed his car trunk with the suitcase and three pairs of running shoes. He placed Raul's staff on the seat beside him. As he approached the freeway and the traffic moving north and south, he felt poised on the brink of a new world. From here he could go anywhere. He pulled the car over, stopped, and closed his eyes.

Raul's staff felt warm and potent as he smoothed his fingers over the worn grooves, and he could feel Raul's spirit inside. Remaining very still, even with the world moving around him, he was able to hear the beating of his heart. . . and he listened. When he opened his eyes, he smiled, put the car in gear, and moved forward.

MIXING MEMORY AND DESIRE

Joseph W. Bean

April is the cruelest month, breeding/Lilacs out of the dead land,
mixing/Memory and desire, stirring/Dull roots with spring rain.
– T. S. Eliot, The Waste Land, 1922

Yesterday, I went to Golden Gate Park and climbed down into "my" gully behind a grove of rhododendrons. Since it's just the first of April now, and the bushes in the Rhododendron Dell don't reach full bloom before May, I was pretty much alone as I rambled around paths so old the tree roots are worn down level with the hard–packed dirt of the footpath. Getting down into the minor canyon behind the bushes is a tricky ordeal, so once I'd slipped and slid to the big rocks and fallen tree trunks at the bottom, I was completely isolated. I couldn't be seen by any off–season passers by, nor could I even tell if anyone was up there.

Somehow, I had almost forgotten the possibility of being alone in the park. These days, when I come to the park at all, it's because I have classes to teach or lectures to give at one of the museums, but it wasn't always like that. Twenty years ago, in 1967 and '68, I came to the park to meditate, or to prowl (pretty successfully) for sex. I bought and used plenty of drugs in the lush greenery too, but mostly I came alone and stayed alone back then, taking refuge in my "hideouts." That's what I called the flats above the waterfalls, the shrouded ditch near the windmill, and this damp, mossy trench among the rhododendrons.

The first time I wrestled my way down into the trench, breathing its musky odor of beautiful, natural decay so deeply and gladly, I was stoned — although everyone I knew called it "flying" at that time. (Now I'd just call it crazy. I remember almost nothing that happened in all those stoned–flying years, except this one afternoon.) I was on some fresh, clean, no–speed LSD. Until I felt the buzz coming on, I had stayed up in the sunlight, drinking in the blazing, iridescent colors of the swirling blossom clouds on these same, now all–green bushes. Then, looking around for a quiet place to cool–out while the buzz passed, I ducked between the huge, globe–shaped rhododendron bushes and found this hideout. There was already someone down here that afternoon, but I was sure he was cool. Somehow, see, when I found a place to buzz, everyone around would "naturally" look like he's got a buzz on, too.

"How's it going, bro?" I asked as I slipped into the crotch of a massive fallen tree and dropped my arms flat into the damp, decaying leaves.

"Just groovin' on it," he said.

"Yeah. It's far out," I agreed, looking up at the bright blue patch beyond the silhouettes of trees and bushes above us. "Gets to me when I'm on," I added, not quite ready to be flying solo, even with the clear sky beckoning so patiently.

"Always *do*, y'know," he said, putting a powerful emphasis on the word do, which answered any question I had about him. He was flying for sure, making sense only to himself as he answered some voice only he could hear. "Always love the wind," he added to clue me in, "love it blowing through so much nature, such a filter, y'know, cleaning all the little molecules of air for us and all...." He trailed off, and I shifted my attention from clear blue to the clear invisible wind. Wouldn't want to leave a brother tripping alone. That's how guys end up freaking.

"Far out," I whispered, hoarse with surprise. "Fuckin–A, man, the wind is like singing or something. Cool." By then I was buzzing through the first wall, feeling a slight fear, a sense that any movement I could make would be clumsy and pointless. In a few minutes, I knew, I could wander around if I wanted to, but just then I needed to coast, cruise, chill, and close down all the external stuff.

I didn't usually fall asleep, but sometimes you can't tell

ordinary vision from visionary apparitions, or dreams from what straights call the real world. Anyway, some time later I shivered and felt really cold and wet, and came out of my dream or whatever it was. It left me feeling so high, but so alone.

In my dream, a huge, vaulted, white stone temple, carved with incredibly intricate patterns and figures, was slowly turning above me. If I squinted, I could turn the patterns into gods and things, things that reminded me of the temples I had seen in India, but much more complex, with hundred of little images carved in every square foot of the marble. Suddenly, as if it were the most important thing in the world, I felt a need to memorize the patterns, but I knew I couldn't. In frustration, I came to the conclusion that memorizing some small part of the grand vault would be better than losing it all.

I squeezed my eyes half shut, and scanned. There, if I held my head just so, I could distinguish one long, narrow, vertical strip of the marble, make it look a little less brightly white, so I could study it. The main figure in the whole area was a single god. I stared into his eyes intently, drinking in the wise but somehow impish gleam I found there. Then, the impossible happened: his eyes, still marble against marble, white on white, were alive. The stone eyes, not perceptibly moving, glanced downward. I realized they had already been looking at me, then—still without physically moving—their warm–marble attention was turned down the carved god's body, and I understood what he was doing. He was encouraging me to examine him further, to memorizenot just his eyes, but all of him.

As my stoned eyes slipped downward, only very slowly letting go of the contact with his stone eyes, the marble below seemed to be shaping itself into the figure of the god just in time for me to see it. At the very edge of my field of vision, like plaster being poured into a thin glass mold, the white stone sculpted itself into perfection, urging me to examine carefully and memorize exactly what it showed me.

A chin jutted out, square and smooth, with a deep cleft, then a powerful, wide, sinewy neck took shape. The stone flared wide to form the mounds of muscular white shoulders, as the chin slipped out of view above. The rush of stone becoming the shape of a god–perfect man seemed to be a revolution in creation on a scale that might change the very fabric of the universe from beginning to end. For a moment, my eyes tried to close. I was resisting the revolution. Did I, just for the pleasure of seeing this god, have the right to cause the universe to be changed absolutely? No, I did not, but how could I not follow the orders of a god whose very existence had that power? I knew I had to follow the order–no, the *command* in those eyes.

Immobile with fear that I might be one of the casualties of the world's reorganization, I forced myself to look further down. The god's chest was massive. Mountains of the purest and most perfect white stone took the shape of two identical and impeccable plains. They were separated by a smooth, round–bottomed valley that was broader at the top, almost winking shut at the bottom from the pressure of the converging pectoral plains. I could have been happy in that valley, I knew, for all eternity. His nipples—the very models of luscious, masculine nipples—were diadems, irresistible proof of his divinity, and I was powerless to resist the urge to touch them.

The urge, unaided by my immobile muscles, drew me up until my forehead was touching one stone pectoral. It was warm and yielding; it shaped itself into a cradle that fitted my forehead perfectly. Then my head was moved by a force so palpable that, for a moment, I thought someone was pushing from behind, moving my mouth onto the nipple which I now knew would be warm as life itself. I sucked and licked the nipple. I chewed it, and sawed at it with my lower teeth. Somehow I knew my life depended on the pleasure I was taking, and I wondered if it were possible for a mere mortal to lap at the nipple of god so well that even he would be pleased.

I chewed for what seemed eternities, pressing my teeth together on the first nipple until tiny drops of the molten stone oozed out into my mouth. I was delirious. He wouldn't have been willing to bleed his very essence into me if I were not pleasing him. So, I lost no time in thanking him by diving onto the other nipple. This time I chewed fiercely, licked gently, sucked hard, and gnawed wildly. Again, he blessed me with a tiny trickle of his molten essence. As soon as the second taste of salty heat touched my tongue, I fell back to the ground to continue exploring and memorizing the body of god.

I remained transfixed, gazing at the nipples. They were no longer unblemished white. Now they glowed and throbbed, they had color, and the fluid that had seeped from them was not white at all, it was red. I had kissed and drunk the miraculous blood of an icon. No, not an icon, this was the god himself, somehow living, somehow infinitely more than all the bleeding statues in all the churches of the world. The nipples that had looked moments before like negative impressions of a kiss, the shape of the space between kissing lips, were now roses dripping attar onto the contours below.

Somehow, although I could not see his eyes, I heard his great stone lips urging me down, and I moved on. I looked. Here and there on the chiseled–perfect hills and valleys of his abdominal muscles, I saw fingertips. Without taking my eyes off the ravishing perfection of his abdomen, I knew his posture exactly. He was standing, curved into the arching temple wall, with his hands on his waist, his thumbs hooked behind, fingers spread wide. On any mortal man the posture would be nothing but arrogance, but it was entirely appropriate for him.

Suddenly I realized what lay ahead, as I continued to run my eyes down his body. Moses had seen the hind parts of god. I was about to see the carved–perfect, stone–still, legs–apart fore parts of a god. Fireworks began going off in my brain, almost blotting out the image before my eyes. To calm the bursts of color, I conjured a swirling whiteness into my consciousness, and it almost pushed the god back into the intricate stone work wall. A tiny ripple in his abdomen, a single muscle moving, called me back.

Down, I continued down. More and more slowly, I eased my eyes over his shining immaculacy. Fearful, joyful, I was almost laughing, but I was sure I had not laughed aloud. "Quiet," his voiced echoed in my head. The laughter went, and I returned to the worshipful memorizing of the divine body. Down I went till the curve of his abdomen tucked in, and suddenly there it was, the first hint of his cock. Only a few strands of hair were engraved on the lower curve of the abdomen around the base of the penis. Then I noticed I was not seeing the *base* of a penis—the curve coming into view was the head of his cock, standing out from his body, rigid and motionless.

A few millimeters lower, and I could see the slit in the head of the magnificent organ. I was actually seeing it: the penis, the source, perhaps the very font of creation. I adored it before I saw anything more than the glistening head. I desired it. I wanted to touch it more than I had wanted anything in my life. This was not just a cock. This was *the* cock, the *one* cock that all others should be compared to, the one cock that defines all others.

I had let desire propel me to suck his nipples, but I knew I would need some sign from him before I could touch his cock. How could I let him know about the lustful, passionate yearning his cock inspired in me? "Get close," his voice answered my unspoken question, "but don't touch it. Get *very close*, but don't touch it unless I say you may."

I floated up till my face was close enough along the side of his cock to feel the molten–stone heat radiating from the thick, straight, solid organ. Maybe my long hair was touching it, I thought. Maybe my whiskers are pressing against the length of the cock. Since maybe he will never let me touchit any other way, I will satisfy myself with that. I froze and breathed the warm air there, taking in the scent of the decaying leaves and the fresh, "human" musk of the god with every breath.

I was afraid to look up. Would he still be there above me, or might the stone I had already seen be resolved again into the wall? I didn't want to risk it. Besides, his command echoed in my head again just as the question formed. "Down!"

I looked down, still conscious of the radiant cock next to my head. His sculpted legs, their flaring, muscular shapes the paragons of male legs, were no longer part of a wall of intricate white patterns. Nor was I floating up to meet the wall. Instead, his great stone feet were nested in the carpet of brown and orange leaves, soiled with ground–up bits of the darker colors of leaves from earlier years.

My desire to touch and engulf his cock was instantly replaced by my *need* to clean the blemishing dirt from his feet. I didn't wait for orders or even permission.

The thought of his consummate perfection marred in even the most trivial way drove me into a frenzy. I scooped my hands under one of his feet and fell on it with my mouth, licking away the moldered leaf debris, opening my mouth wide to suck clean wide patches of his foot with each tongue–swirling pass. I pushed my tongue between his toes, tearing in and out of each crevice until I was sure the spaces were as clean and unmarred as the pristine muscles above. Then I went to work on the other foot, slurping the musky leaf mold into my mouth, rinsing every inch of the ideal foot till it too was completely clean. Then, confused, I thought of the dirt sticking to the bottoms of his feet. I'd only make the problem worse if I licked the soles of his feet and put them against the ground again wet from their cleaning.

Without a thought, I ripped my T-shirt from neck to hem in one strong tear. Then I took it off, one arm at a time like a jacket, and gathered it into a line between his feet. I slipped my hands under one foot and lifted. He let me lift it off the ground, but not nearly far enough. Clinging to the foot with my hands, I twisted around until I was lying on the ground, and slid my head under the raised foot. He lowered his foot, and I thought he might crush me then and there for the impudence of touching him without permission, for lingering as I scrubbed his feet with my tongue, for being such a completely ordinary, mortal man.

But, no. He lowered his foot till it pressed on my face, but only pressed there. He was holding back, he was *allowing* me to continue cleaning his feet with my mouth.

I licked the underside of the white foot in long strokes from just behind the toes all the way back to the heel. It was stone cold and hard. I tipped his foot back with my hands so the toes were resting against my lips, and I sucked all along the crease at the base of the toes, and licked each toe to be sure everything was returned to its original unblemished condition.

Scooting aside, I cradled the precious foot in one hand while I spread my T-shirt out with the other, then gently placed the foot on the thin white cloth. I did the same with the other foot, spreading the rest of the shirt to receive and protect it once it was clean.

I didn't know what to do when both feet were clean. I rolled around and settled in a kneeling position in front of him. My hands began to fidget, looking for the right place to be or the right thing to do, and ended up behind my back, the fingers interleaved for stability. I was still looking down, admiring the restored perfection of hisfeet when the command came again: "Down."

I shuffled back away from him and fell forward onto the ground, my head a few inches from the edge of the altar cloth I had made of my T-shirt. I didn't know if it was what he wanted but it felt appropriate, and it was as far down as I could go. A few drops of rain fell on my back. I wondered if they could be rain, or if they might be splashing over from sprinklers above. But the drops felt warm.

When I realized the droplets were warm, I knew what was happening. I had so offended the god that he was crying. I sprang back up onto my knees and slowly began tipping my head up in his direction. The scattered drops had become a gushing stream by then, and I expanded my chest as wide and as far as I could to catch it. Then I saw the huge balls dangling between his sculpted thighs, the underside of his cock came into view, and suddenly I was blinded as the stream crossed my eyes and dropped down to splatter into my mouth. Not tears, the water was coming like a river of yellow diamonds and molten gold out of his colossal cock. Like piss streaming out, the divine fluid kept coming, and I stretched my mouth open to catch it, leaning forward to encompass the pattern of stray diamonds around the hot, salty gold.

I thought the stream would go on forever, and it felt like I might be unable to take it all as my stomach strained to bear the volume and weight of the outpouring. Then it stopped, started again for a moment, and stopped altogether. I kept my tongue flattened out and extended in case there might be a few more drops, even one more drop, but nothing more came.

"Up," the voice in my head commanded. I started to look up, but the god slapped my face so hard I thought my neck would snap. "Up," he repeated, and it almost seemed that I was hearing him with my ears, or becoming so accustomed to his presence that I perceived his voice that naturally. I rose to my feet in one slow motion, keeping my eyes fixed on his cock, grateful that as I stood it became possible to adore his cock and his feet in the same glance.

"Turn," he said, and I began turning slowly, aching again to touch his feet and cock as they slipped out of view. There was a sound behind me, like a lightening bolt in slow motion, I thought. Then the bolt hit me solidly in the back. I stumbled forward, but regained my place, setting my feet further apart this time in case another bolt may be coming. No sooner had I adjusted my stance than it hit. Crack! The pain, oddly, did not feel electric at first. Instead, it was more like a heavy belt crashing into my back, first one side and then the other, until eventually, I did feel the electricity in the bolts. Soon I was also sensitive enough to see the flashes of light that came shortly after each bolt struck. The light was eerie, seeming to originate inside myself, seeming more reassuring than threatening.

Very gradually, I realized that I was being tested in some way. What the living stone god might have in mind, I couldn't guess, but I was determined to prove myself worthy of whatever it might be. I spread my back, inviting the heavy blows, bracing against their force, and looking forward each time to the soothing burst of light from within.

My back was battered for so long I lost all sense of time or number, although I had at first thought to count the blows, expecting some sacred number to be the limit but unable to recall, for example, how many blows were given in the scourging of Christ or whether 21 or 100 was the holier figure. Crash, crash, crash, the rhythm of the blows closed up so tightly that it felt as though they were becoming one continuous wave of pressure vibrating as it slammed into my back. Tears were streaming down my face, collecting in salty droplets in my moustache, but I was still trying to keep my back stretched wide and available for the torture it was taking.

The beating went on, sometimes painful but never unbearable, not when the pleasure of a god was at stake, nor if it was a test of my stamina devised by the god–man behind me. Then the pain was everything, like a heavy drape of darkness it fell over me all at once. For several moments, as the pounding of my back slowed down to a rhythm of thudding blows again, I felt pain from my throbbing head to my freezing feet, fiery pain in my back and hot waves of pain coursing down my arms and legs. Then, like stars appearing against the black backdrop of the pain, there were points of light, points of painlessness, tiny, distant flickers of space and air that did not hurt. I began to strain toward those far away sparks, and felt myself tear free of the pain completely in one slow, wrenching move that happened entirely within my heart and mind. I knew my body had not moved. By thinking of it, I could still sense that it was sustaining brutal blows on the raw and sensitive surface of its back. But my body was *it,* not me.

As I drifted in this peace, I raised my arms involuntarily and thought I might fly away, all of me. Perhaps he thought so too, because he stopped the no–longer painful bolts on my back, and whispered, "Fall back." I didn't want to be turned back to earth, away from flight, but if "back" meant toward him....

I fell, and he caught me in his arms, my wet back feeling sticky and blast–furnace hot as it pressed against his cool, hard chest.

He stretched me out on the ground face–down again, and sat down on the backs of my knees. A moment later he had pulled my jeans down over my butt, and his enormous cock was sliding up inside my ass as his hands pushed and pulled, rubbed and massaged the muscles of my back. I knew that I had passed his test, the fucking I was getting was a reward, even if I had never before enjoyed being fucked.

Despite the coolness of his body against mine, his rock–hard cock blazed in my ass. It was molten stone again, burning its way into me, filling my gut completely. Then he began pumping in and out, so slowly at first I ached for the absent rod between strokes. I could "see" him arching triumphantly over me, thrusting his perfect organ into my human ass, breathing a silent cry upward, calling the sun itself to witness the magnificence of the scene as he ground my body into the leafy earth.

After several minutes—or an eternity—he began to thrust in and out of my hole so fast I felt he was sawing right through me, fucking the earth beneath, using my ass, my whole body as nothing more than a guide. Suddenly, searing splashes of the god's semen filled my ass as his body—now hot and wet like my own—crashed down against my lacerated back.

When I woke up some time later, wet and shivering, I was alone. The marble god had left no trace except that his feet pressing into my T-shirt had caused just the footprints to become wet and stained from the leaf mold beneath. When I came up out of my hide out, it was sunset, probably 6:00 or 6:30, and I was wearing my ripped T-shirt like the jacket it had become, proud that the footprints of a god were permanently dyed into the back of it.

*   *   *   *   *

That was then, I thought, looking around at the litter and debris that seemed to give my gully its contemporary purpose. Where once an acid–inspired god had pissed diamonds and gold, people now threw the inconvenient leavings of their picnics. For no real reason, just to honor the memory I had enjoyed here today, I decided to clear out the trash. I wouldn't get sentimental about it, make the cleaning of this trench the pastime of my middle age trips to the park. No, but this once, I'd leave the bottom of the gully clean enough that if any gods did come down looking for a place to stand, they might just choose to stand here.

I probably spent three hours gathering every gum wrapper and beer can top I could, stacking everything in one place, the now–crumpled crotch of the gigantic fallen tree where I had begun my adventure in the Summer of Love. When it was all gathered together, I realized it didn't amount to that much, so I stripped off my T-shirt and tied it at the bottom, making a bag to haul away the debris.

As I climbed the bank and my eyes came over the ridge, I could see the flat ground of the planted level of the park; two booted feet appeared inches from my face. When I looked up, a man a few years older than myself was offering me a hand up. I took his hand. Rather than just steadying me, he lifted me in one powerful pull until my feet came up to the solid ground, and he was able to get his arms around me.

His embrace pinned my arms at my side, and I dropped the T-shirt bag of trash. I heard it bounce away, back down into the trench, but I made no move to stop it. He was kissing me, long and deep, making me dizzy with the intensity of the feelings he inspired in me. After kissing and crushing me for several minutes, which I didn't resist at all, he let go, planted his hands on my shoulders, and backed away to arm's length. "You don't recognize me, do you?" He was grinning like a little kid.

"No," I stammered, "I don't recognize you, but I'd love to get to know you." Then I stopped. This wasn't a line, he really hoped I would recognize him, and I *almost* did.... Didn't I?

"I can't exactly say we ever met, you and I," he continued, "but we *knew* each other... uhm... in the Biblical sense."

His use of the word "Biblical" did it. This was the god of my drug–induced delirium, the subject of the very memory I had been reliving just moments before. "I do remember you," I said, "but didn't you (I stalled, lost for words) used to have wings or something?"

"No, never, but you sure made me feel like an angel at least when we got together down there. When was it?" Then he answered his own question, "Sixty-seven, had to be April or May."

"That's right, but how do you happen to remember?" I asked, still trying to reach a point where I could cope with all of it. My god was not only human, but happened to be here to pull me up out of the gully twenty years later; he not only remembered our encounter, but remembered when it happened.

"Well, I guess you're kind of wondering about how I would still be here 20 years later," he said. He still had that magical ability to know what I was thinking by the time I did. "I'm a gardener here, started in '67, just a few days before I ran into you down there. You know, you really blew me away. I didn't know then what I know now."

"What's that?" I asked, more than a little afraid of the possible answer.

"That I'm into leathersex, that I'm a Top, that I get off on body worship...." It sounded like he could go on for a long time, and I wanted to hear every word of it, but not here in the cold wind, bare–chested and damp from sitting on the ground down in the gully.

"When do you get off work, and do you want to come up the hill three blocks to my apartment and tell me all about it?" I asked trying to cover the bases.

"Now and yes," he answered, grabbing a fistful of my right tit, dragging me into a nearby rhododendron bush. "First, I need to get a load off my bladder before I try an' take a load off my chest."

"Yes, Sir!" I snapped, diving for his crotch.

*   *   *   *   *

Before the night was over we had re-enacted our first encounter—no drugs required or wanted—and he was shocked to see how perfectly I remembered exactly what had happened. I was shocked to see how completely we had misunderstood each other that day.

Someday—maybe—I'll tell him the truth, that I've been re-enacting that scene with any man half–willing to stand over me for twenty years, but *until today* no other piss was ever diamonds and gold, no other body was marble perfection, and no matter how much I praised many of them, no one else was a god.

THE PLUMBERS AND THEIR HELPERS

Lee Williams

It happened a few years ago on the job site. The after–work beer–break with Stan had become almost a daily occurrence. I guess I started it, but he seemed to look forward to it, too. I was hoping for even more.

Before we started working on that research building together, Stan and I had never exchanged more than a nod at plumbers' union meetings and the like. He stood out from the crowd mostly made up of grizzled, overweight craftsmen left over from the old days, but he was quiet, only the twinkling blue eyes under thick brows indicating that he wasn't impressed by all this mob hoopla. When I found myself assigned with him to this job, I decided to find out more about him and maybe get something started.

The new ten-story University research building, for a while a political football since it was being built within the City of San Francisco, was a big job for plumbers, as you can imagine, with all the faucets and drains for every laboratory, and for the other trades as well. The electricians were almost as plentiful around the site as plumbers, and frequently we had to work together to coordinate the construction. But after work, when everyone else had roared off in their trucks, an eerie silence fell over the empty, half-constructed building, and Stan and I would break out a cooler of beer and shoot the shit for an hour or so before wending our separate ways home.

That day Stan and I were sitting cross-legged on the floor, hard hats tipped back, in what would be a large laboratory, complete with central floor drain and bare pipes standing tall through the concrete floor like a dozen erections waiting for the word. Stan, by himself, was enough to give me a stand, but we never talked about sex, directly, that is. Everything except sex, it seemed. From our conversations and cautious probings, I gathered that he was a virgin where guys were concerned and

probably would remain that way. He wasn't hostile, just dis-
interested, or so it seemed.

Still I enjoyed those times of quiet even if there was nothing
more to be gained. His husky frame, his hairy chest always
seeming to be on the verge of bursting the buttons on his work
shirt, and his rather broad, handsome face always seeming to need
a shave, was enough to get me started, if only he would make
some sign.

That day was especially difficult for me because Stan had
ripped the crotch of his Levi's crawling over something that day,
leaving a two inch gap through which one hairy ball was visible
as we relaxed on the floor. We had joked about it, but he seemed
unaware of my glances that kept returning to that enticing view,
or the troublesome twitching in my own crotch as he sat opposite
me, so close and yet so far.

We had gone through several beers each and started on
another twelve-pack when we were startled by voices.

"Plumbers working overtime? Will wonders never cease?"

We turned to the door as two electricians, draped with all their
tools and paraphernalia, sauntered in. One was tall and quite
thin, the other shorter but square and muscular. I didn't know
them but had seen them around. I had particularly noticed the
tall one before because of a cock bulge that seemed to extend
endlessly down his leg.

"Just a beer break before tackling the freeway," Stan grinned.
"Want one?"

"Sure," grinned the square one, popping a can. "My name's
Frank, by the way." We shook hands all around without getting
up. I moved closer to Stan and Frank sat down across from us,
taking a long swig.

The tall one said his name was Rod. I glanced at that cock
bulge and thought that his name was pretty appropriate.

Rod hesitated before taking a beer. "I'd like one, but I need
to piss first. We were looking for a john that's been plumbed in.
You guys got anything finished yet?"

Stan and I shook our heads. "These central drains are the only systems hooked up," I said, pointing to the shiny drain near our feet.

"If I can use that — " "Sure, be our guests," I answered with a grin as if it belonged to Stan and me.

Rod stood over the drain and opened his fly. He started fishing down his leg and I watched breathlessly as he finally reeled out that whacker I had been wondering about. Soft it was a good nine inches with a broad head partially covered with a loose foreskin, and when he let go his stream was thick and powerful.

"Ahhh," he sighed deeply as the pressure was released. His cock hung unattended, gushing its yellow, pungent stream, as he stood with one hand on his hip and the other raising a beer to his lips. His electrical tools hung in organized disarray from his belt.

Every eye was on that huge, pendulous prick gushing its amber stream at our feet. I tried to look away — at Stan, and then at Frank — but they were clearly fascinated, too. Frank took another swig on his beer, but his eyes never left his buddy's cock and the abundant amber flow it produced.

Even after his stream had stopped, Rod didn't seem in any hurry to put it away. Instead he flopped it back and forth to get the last drops, and it seemed to me that it grew a little in his hand. When it finally disappeared again in his Levi's, we breathed easier, each man busy with his own thoughts, I guess. Rod joined us sitting in a circle on the floor, around the central drain.

Rod and Frank finished their first beers quickly and we all cracked new ones while just joking around. Both Stan and I were getting a little ripped by this time, but neither of us made any move to go.

We were all sitting cross-legged, and Rod's basket was enormous in that position. He made a wisecrack about the tear in Stan's Levi's where those hairy nuts lurked, but Stan made no effort to hide it.

Then it was Frank's turn to take a piss, and we all watched him take out his thick circumcised dick and stroke it down a few times before letting go with a gush of hot, yellow piss that smelled almost like cum. As he pissed he swung a little from side to side, and some of the stream landed on Stan's bent knee. Stan stared at the wet streak but didn't move away. Nobody said anything. My cock was growing down my leg.

Then I noticed the end of Stan's cock beginning to show at the rip in his crotch. Evidently Frank saw it, too, and this time he intentionally swung in Stan's direction, soaking his knee and moving up toward his crotch with his stream. Stan stared at his warm, piss-soaked leg, and his prick pushed out of his torn pants in a rush. But Frank was empty and his cock was growing rapidly in his fist. He shook it once and struggled to get it back in his pants. Still nobody said anything, but Stan's dick was protruding stiffly and I could hardly stand the pressure in my crotch. Frank squatted down again, and I passed beers around again.

Rod, who had been the quietest one, now spoke up. "That's quite a boner you got going, Stan," he rumbled deep in his chest. Stan blushed and looked down at the thickening protrusion. He pulled his knees together to try to conceal it but that only pushed more of it out through the hole.

"Gotta piss, but can't do it until it goes down," he mumbled.

"Yeah, I got the same problem," I joined in.

"Sometimes it's interestin' to try," Rod smiled and stood up, tugging his tool belt upward and then pushing down his Levi's to his knees. That huge prick had grown an additional three or four inches, and throbbed rigidly in his fist. Stan and I sat stunned by its enormity and even more as he moved closer to us, straining a little, and then let go with another hot stream of piss, directed first at Stan's crotch and then at mine, soaking us with hot, pungent brew. Quickly I was soaked to the skin, my cock and balls swimming in hot man–piss, and Stan's dick looked like it was about to explode as it drooled Rod's piss in a yellow stream.

Suddenly Stan stood up and ripped down his Levi's, his

beautiful eight–incher stabbing the air. He grabbed it in his fist
and pointed it directly at Rod, pushing hard to start the stream.
After a short, hesitant burst he started a strong stream directed
straight at Rod's rod, and it was Rod's turn to beam with pleasure
at the hot bath.

But Frank and I were not to be ignored. Quickly we both rose
and jerked our Levi's down, whipped out our pricks and joined
the piss pigs flooding the newly installed floor drain. Swinging
left and then right, back and forth, we sprayed each other until
our bladders were empty and we were all soaked in hot piss
shared freely by all. When a hot stream would strike my dick it
would surge violently, only to spurt freely again at the sight of
another dripping cock and pair of balls. We all wore big, happy
grins.

And then only Stan remained, his stream cutting down but
still weakly dribbling, and I instinctively fell to my knees at his
feet, my mouth open avidly, seeking contact with his internal
juices so freely flowing. That startled him and his stream shut
down abruptly. I couldn't expect a virgin to understand what the
sight of that intimate, yellow stream straight from the guts of a
beautiful man could do to a guy like me. At this point I didn't
care what the two electricians thought. I only knew that Stan
was what I wanted, and it was "go for broke" time.

I looked up with pleading in my eyes, my mouth gaping open.
"Can I have it?" I asked breathlessly. I knelt at his feet, my wet
Levi's pulling awkwardly around my knees, my stiff dick in my
fist.

He hesitated so long that I thought I had fucked it up, pushed
him too fast. But then he strained a little and pissed directly in
my face, realizing that I needed it, relished it. The heat and odor
of his virility overwhelmed me, and the piss from that stiff prick
and those dripping balls was life-sustaining fluid for my parched
soul. Frank and Rod watched me closely, realizing that there was
a new element in the picture now, one that did not include them
for that moment, and they stood quietly, stroking their rigid but

drying dicks as I paid homage to the man most important to me.

As I grew closer, Stan's flow diminished to a trickle and then stopped. Although there was only a drop left on his cock, I took it in my mouth, thrilling to the strong, acrid taste that was so singularly Stan's. I held only the throbbing head between my lips, hoping for more, but it was not to be. Stan stared long and hard at me, but there was no need for words. He knew I wanted him, and now I was pretty sure he wanted me.

Slowly I worked my way down the clammy column, dripping with the piss of all of us but hot with his own private juices. I took it into my throat and he lurched into me, burying his prick in my clasping channel. Avidly I grasped his wet, hairy balls swinging freely between his soaked legs and mashed them against my wet chin. I could feel them churning, demanding release, primed to disgorge. And I wanted that too, in me, all over me.

I looked up into his eyes, my mouth full of him. His eyes were filled with lust, but then as I watched, his base instincts were tempered with something gentler, something I had longed for but had thought it was hopeless. There was some confusion there in his eyes, but I thought I saw the dawning of an understanding that might not be fully realized for a long time. I had to make it clear and irrevocable that I was his to do with as he pleased.

Slowly I withdrew from his cock and lay back, stretching out on the floor over the floor drain. My hard hat clattered to the floor and rolled away but I didn't care. I raised my T-shirt above my pecs, leaving me bare from tits to knees and making it clear what I wanted. My prick reared rigidly in my hand, and my balls rested on the piss-covered concrete floor.

I looked up at the three men towering over me, their cocks tightly clutched in their fists, their eyes fixed on mine. Their hard hats were askew but their chests were heaving with excitement. Their pants were soaked and down around their knees, revealing the thick muscles of their hairy thighs tense and ridged.

Rod's incredible cock was clasped in both hands and the head looked ready to explode as he stroked it slowly. His horse-sized balls, dripping from our combined piss, swung heavily as he rocked back and forth on his heels.

Frank, his hairy chest bare and dripping, moved his booted feet near my chest. His thick cock strained in his fist, and I knew he was already close.

And Stan, my Stan, was beginning to understand the depths of my love. He came to stand over me, his wet boots framing my face, his cock pointing directly at me. Involuntarily I licked my lips, and he knew what I wanted, needed. Slowly he began to stroke his prick over my face and I matched him, stroke for stroke. Momentarily he looked at my cock so primed and ready and then back to my face, and his mouth hung slack with the awakening of internal desires that must have startled him.

I picked up my pace, unable to restrain myself as the focus of the trio. They all followed suit, their strokes growing bolder and stronger, their pricks preparing for that ultimate surge that makes men men. But my eyes held Stan's until I heard a sharp gasp.

Frank stiffened and arched his back, groaned loudly, and shot his hot cum over my belly. He aimed his second spurt at my prick, drenching my dripping dong and lubricating my flailing fist.

Rod was not far behind, emptying huge reservoirs of white hot juice on me, from my chin to my knees, mixing with the cooling piss that puddled between my legs. He directed the stream like a fire hose, but only added to the conflagration within me.

My own balls were clenching ready to shoot, but I held off somehow, gazing upward at Stan and what I hoped would be mine. Stan grimaced, seeming reluctant to commit himself, instinctively knowing that, when he gave me his cream, he would be changing his life forever.

"Please," I whispered. Perhaps that was what he needed. A smile suddenly appeared and he shot his cum into my face in great gobs. With each spurt he dropped closer to me until finally he was kneeling over my face, spurting his luscious lava directly into my gaping mouth. And I shot my own load high into the air, to fall down on my chest and belly and thighs to mix with the other loads already deposited there.

For a moment he rested his dripping cock on my face, its heat penetrating into my brain as the stiffness left. Then he rose, knowing what he must do to conclude the bond between us. He held his cock loosely, staring into my eyes, and then released a new stream of piss into my face and over my chest. He was immediately joined by Rod and Frank, their streams hot and almost scalding, yellow gushers of man juice that mixed with their cum, drawing swirls of white into their cascades. And I joined them, pissing straight upward and over my belly and chest, the streams joining and mixing symbolically.

That piss was like a second cum, the hot recycled beer gushing through our tortured, sensitive pricks, joining us all together in a brotherhood that would never be forgotten.

As our streams tapered off I looked again at Stan, my heart open and full. He moved to my side, looking down tenderly, and then spread himself out over me, chest to chest, cock to cock, relishing the sharing of the piss and cum that covered me. I wrapped my piss–soaked arms around him, hoping he meant what he seemed to mean. We were immersed in a sea of manjuice, strong and pungent and potent. We stared at each other for a long moment and then he kissed my cum-streaked lips.

It must have been five or ten minutes later when next we surfaced. Rod and Frank were nowhere to be seen, but they had helped to break down the first of many barriers that Stan and I have swept away since that fateful day. We still enjoy plumbing, especially our own.

HOW TO SUCCEED IN BUSINESS

Reid Dennis

I had just graduated from San Francisco State University with a bachelor's degree in business. My aspirations were toward becoming a junior executive, eventually a senior exec, and, sure... aim for the stars: president of the company. Well, at least be a member of the Board of Directors. But my dreams were slightly inconsistent with reality. I had sent my resume to every Bay Area ad agency and public relations firm in town, with the same response: "We're looking for someone with a little experience under his belt." Hell, I had *plenty* under my belt, but that wasn't what they were looking for. If I had known that I could have used my heavy endowment in the dick department to make up for my shortcomings in business experience, I'd have done it for sure. But they don't teach those things in business seminars. Can you imagine the course title? "How to Suck Seed in Business Without Really Trying"!

Anyway, after months of frustrating job searches, I finally happened upon a large advertising agency in the prestigious Transamerica Building right in the heart of San Francisco's financial district. The agency had a very understanding president, extremely personable, who insisted on doing the interviewing himself. He told me his own son had started out at the bottom with his firm, and he felt I deserved a break, even though I was pretty wet behind the ears. If the truth be told, I was also a little wet behind my pants, checking out this really good-looking, older gentleman with salt-and-pepper hair and a sexy silver handlebar mustache. The thought came to me— "How To Suck Seed in Business..." — but I quickly ignored such nasty musings and thanked him for giving me a break and hiring me. I wasn't offered a very fancy title — Administrative Assistant to the Creative Director — but at least it was a chance to get my foot in the door of an ad agency.

I set my alarm early to get a head start on my first day of employment, but upon awakening I discovered that wasn't the only thing that had a head start—my cock was rock hard inside my underwear and wouldn't take "no" for an answer. Besides, I was so uptight about this new job, I figured I might as well unwind a bit and have a morning jerk-off session. So I pictured the handsome, distinguished company president giving me my interview while I was on my knees under the desk giving him head. I was showing him my skills at dick-tation. In my fantasy I was fishing out his thick, uncut cock from his fly with my lips, hungrily taking his meat into my mouth and sucking all of it down my throat—all the while he was reviewing my resume and going over my job history, deciding that I probably could work under him quite nicely. He agreed that I would fill the position, while he filled my mouth with his spurting semen. At the tantalizing thought of the president of the company unloading his load during my interview, I shot my morning wad all over the sheets just in time to hear my snooze alarm bring me out of my raunchy reverie and back to reality. I showered, jacked off once more under the hot stream of water, shaved, and dressed for work.

When I arrived, the president greeted me and welcomed me heartily. I felt a bit sheepish when I recalled my nasty jack-off fantasy of him, and had difficulty looking him in the eyes. It was my first day on the job and I was awfully nervous. When it came time for lunch break, I just couldn't work up an appetite. My stomach was a little upset, so I went to the men's room and just sat on the throne for a long time.

After a while I heard the rest room door open and saw, through the space between the stall wall and the door, an unbelievably beautiful man entering the john and approaching the stalls. He had a classic face. A typical Frisco Financial District Clone; yet he could have been moonlighting as a male model. He was this incredibly handsome brunette, with longish chestnut brown hair and brown mustache. I'd say only a few years older than I. I realized I was rather boldly staring at him through the cracks, and feeling like some kind of voyeur, sat back abruptly. Then I heard the stall door next to me slam shut. Feeling a bit queasy, I put my head between my knees. To my amazement, the guy next to me was bent over staring at me under the partition!

At first I sat up and pretended not to notice him, but that was impossible. He was just too good looking to ignore. His hair was brushed to the side as he peered under the partition. Thick, shining, brown hair cascading from his chiseled face and a wiry dark mustache under his aquiline nose. I was clean shaven with my businessman's short-cropped haircut, but I had everything but a business-like attitude. I mean, here was this beautiful man looking up at me with absolute lust in his piercing green eyes, and I was immediately cured of my queasiness. I was no longer sick, unless you count love-sickness!

I could see his penny-loafer shoe begin to move ever so slowly under the stall wall until it touched the edge of my wing-tips. I purposely did not move my foot away, signalling mutual interest. A jolt of electricity sparked from his shoe to mine and travelled up my leg, each hair standing up and sending chills right up my spine. But if my spine was chilly, my crotch was utterly on fire! The instant I felt his foot contact mine, my cock flooded with hot, throbbing sensation and stood bolt upright—a condition he noticed immediately.

"Want that rod of yours sucked dry?" he whispered in this incredibly sultry voice, poking his head even further under the partition and gazing at the hard-on sprouting from between my legs.

I lost all sense of propriety. Here I was on the first day of my employment in San Francisco, in the company men's room, and I didn't care about anything but the sexy stud behind that bathroom wall. Like they say—a stiff dick has no conscience, and for sure it has utterly no business sense. All I knew was that I had to feel my stiff dick slide under his mustache and between those full, moist lips. So I wasted no time lowering my slacks to my ankles and easing down to the cool marble floor, thrusting my eager dick under the partition in this prayerful position. (Yeah, I was praying all right. Praying we didn't get caught. Praying he would suck me like he promised. To hell with peace, I was praying for sex!)

I immediately felt a hot, wet mouth encircling my cockhead. I thought I was going to fuckin' explode! His lips expertly massaged my mushroom head, his bushy mustache pleasantly tickling my dick, and I could feel every vein in my pecker throbbing with exquisite pleasure. I felt transcended in the Transamerica!

But my ecstacy was rather rudely interrupted at the sound of the men's room door squeaking open. Both of us jumped to our feet and resumed normal bathroom etiquette, anxiously awaiting the intruder's exit. The minutes dragged on, and finally he left. Again I slid to the floor and into his mouth. And again I felt his skillful tongue caressing the burgeoning head of my grateful prick, about to travel past the coronal ridge and lick my deliciously sensitive frenum. And again the damned door burst open and brought an abrupt halt to our little scene with the arrival of yet another person who had the utter audacity to use the facilities as a rest room instead of a play room. I hopped back onto the toilet seat in great disappointment and frustration.

A glance at my watch quickly brought me back to reality. My "lunch" break was now definitely over and I had to get back to work, reluctantly leaving that tempting, hot hunk behind. Some lunch break that was: I hadn't eaten and I hadn't gotten eaten either. So I quickly zipped up, washed my hands, and departed with lingering thoughts of the great time I might have had. The one that got away. Alas.

In the crowded elevator on my way back to the penthouse floor and my little office cubicle, my mind was racing with images of that hunky man's gorgeous face, his extremely sexy voice imploring me to let him suck me dry, and that wild tongue of his wrapping around my dick head, just about to descend my shaft and take my full load. I felt my cock stir in my shorts and start to harden from these delicious day-dream wet dreams, when I was jolted out of my reverie and into a real-life fantasy-come-true. There in that extremely crowded elevator I felt a rock-hard, throbbing cock press against the seat of my trousers and nestle in the material covering my asscheeks.

"Don't turn around," whispered that familiar, sexually-charged voice I had heard moments ago in the men's room downstairs. "I want to take up where we left off. I still want to suck you dry," he quietly spoke in my ear so that only I could hear.

My prick was now flying at full mast inside my pants, and I was dying to turn around and acknowledge him. Nevertheless I obeyed his secret, almost silent request, keeping my eyes straight ahead, but I backed up just a little in order to feel the full effect of his mammoth pulsating rod shoved up against my hungry butt. My god, I could have almost taken him right then and there in that elevator car, and the other passengers be damned! His soft, low voice brought me out of my dream state.

"I'll contact you after work. You won't be sorry." And he thrust his hugehard-on even more snugly against my ass. "That's just a preview of what's to come," the stranger whispered in my ear and then, as if to seal the deal, he licked my lobe. I then felt him back off into the rear of the car.

I was a wreck. Someone tried to make polite elevator conversation with me and I just stood there like a zombie—a zombie in heat! The elevator door opened and I walked out in a complete daze. The mystery man must have remained behind, because when the elevator closed, there was no one but me on the floor, standing there and staring at the closed door, half expecting it to open and reveal this Adonis to me. But no such luck. I returned to my work cubicle attempting to get back to "business as usual." Nice try; but no way.

Sitting at my desk I could not get rid of my stiff dick. As I typed up this mundane report, the phrase kept haunting me —

taunting me: "Suck you dry... I want to suck you dry." That deep, sensuous voice of his was lodged in my ears. And the feel of his firm tool pressing against my ass was indelibly impressed on my mind. Not to mention the wonderful sensation of his incredibly expert mouth—music that had played on my organ under the men's room stall. All these images mercilessly toyed with my libido and I simply could not concentrate on my work.

I figured I'd get my mind off sex by checking the view out my cubicle window. Gazing out the window of the biggest phallic symbol in San Francisco, the Transamerica Pyramid, and looking around at all the surrounding skyscrapers, all I could see in my mind's eye were dicks, and all I could think about was dick. Dick dick dick. Long, tall dicks. Big, thick dicks. Especially that stranger's big, long, throbbing dick pressed against the seat of my pants.

Hours passed and still the bulge in my trousers remained as I reminisced over the interrupted sexcapade in the men's washroom and anticipated its repeat in the fun to come once the workday was over. As I sat at the office Wang computer, all I could concentrate on was the feel of his mouth on *my* wang.

When I went to the photocopy room to do some copy work, I had to carry a folder in front of me to cover up the big boner I was sporting. As I stood in front of the fax machine I kept envisioning and anticipating when the handsome stranger would come and fax me! Standing at the water cooler did not manage to cool me off either, and I was sure there must have been a big stain at my crotch from the constant dripping flow of pre-cum inside my shorts. The late afternoon coffee break arrived but did not give me a break from my sexual fantasizing. Back at my computer terminal I felt like I had a terminal hard-on.

At last the clock was approaching 4:30 p.m. and some of the early-shift employees began packing up, getting ready to go home. I, on the other hand, was getting ready to explode. My balls were bursting. I was just plain fucking nuts. When the hell would this day be over and the nighttime fun begin for me? Five o'clock came and went, and so did most of the remaining employees. At last the brilliant orange of the setting sun was beginning to reflect on the Bay Bridge, but the bridge in my britches was only spanning all the longer, thinking about that man in the men's room.

Finally it was quitting time for me. Then half an hour passed, and still the mystery man had not shown up. By this time it was pitch dark outside, and all the buildings took on a silvery glow beneath the full moon. I sat at my desk staring at the twinkling lights of the beautiful Golden Gate Bridge spanning the Bay. I must say I had a gorgeous view out my window. But I'd much rather view that gorgeous hunk going down on me.

Forty more minutes went by; the office was now empty of employees, all except me and my acute case of the raging hornies. I had gone around all the office windows trying to pass the time by checking out every possible view of The City by the Bay, and still he had not arrived. I sat back down at my desk with this aching hard-on, resigned to the fact that the sexy stranger was not coming but I might as well be.

I was so horny I had to jerk off right then and there. I unzipped my pants and began to ease my frustration with a few loving strokes of my hand. It felt so good to finally touch my pulsating pecker and know that release was just a few more poundings away. All that tension would be melting in my hand, not in his mouth. I was about to speed up my stroking, when suddenly the door burst open.

"What's going on — starting without me?"

It was that sexy voice I had been hearing in my mind all day long. He stood there with a big smirk on his face, in his white business shirt and three-piece suit, with his big dick hanging out of his pants. It was at least seven inches soft, cut, with big blue veins traversing the shaft. He tore off his suit jacket, got down on his knees, and without another word, swallowed my meat. His full lips pressed into the opened fly of my pants.

Suddenly I knew I had to feel my dick down his throat without any intrusions. I gently took his head in my hands and lifted it from my crotch, loosening the button of my pants and pushing them past my knees. He resumed the blow-job, gobbling my cock right down to my pubic hairs. I could feel his furry mustache right up against my groin, sensually rubbing my bush. I pulled his head as close to me as possible and held him there, my prick pulsating at the very back of his throat. Then he slowly eased back up my shaft, his tongue constantly swirling and creating a wonderful suction sensation. He pulled away about a half inch from the tip of my cock, which by now was throbbing and dripping with juice. His tongue darted out and lapped at my piss slit, diligently catching every droplet of pre-cum as if it were precious nectar.

"God, you've got me so hot and wet, I can't stand it," I gasped.

"I promised to suck you dry, and I don't go back on a promise," he said. "But first I want to sample your nuts."

His tongue lightly flicked at the hairs on my balls, sending shivers all over my body. Then he began lapping at my furry ballsack, using a slightly heavier touch. Finally he sucked first one, then both nuts, into his hot, wet mouth, very gently biting at my nut sack, sliding the sensitive skin between his teeth, careful not to hurt, just arouse almost to the point of climax, and then ease up, so I felt as if I came, but I didn't actually shoot.

"I can't stand it. You've got me so worked up... I'm about to... cream your face," I panted in short breaths.

"That's the whole idea. I told you I'd suck you dry. I'm just churning up that cream for you."

As his lips climbed all the way up my shaft, I couldn't help snicker a bit as I happened to look out the office window and notice Coit Tower lit up in all its glory high on Telegraph Hill; it never looked so much like a towering hard cock than at that particular moment.

"What's so amusing?" he asked, taking his mouth off my own personal tower.

"I'll tell you later. Don't stop, man, don't stop for a moment!"

He went back to sucking on my pole, working his way up and down, around and around the shaft, increasing the suction until I was just about to blast, then letting up until the urge to orgasm subsided. This went on for what seemed like an eternity of prolonged ecstacy. I was begging him to let me come. My nuts were bursting with jism. But still he kept up this wonderful torture until I was ready to scream. His warm hands slowly, sensually travelled up my belly to my chest and softly massaged my nipples until they were just about as stiff and erect as my dick.

"Damn you, fucker. You're driving me crazy. I... I can't... hold out... another minute."

I felt my whole body begin to quiver. I started frantically fucking his face. I couldn't control my rhythm as I thrust my throbbing rod faster and faster in and out his burning hot mouth. I was shaking uncontrollably as I felt the first blast of white-hot cream jet out from my nuts and into his hungry mouth. Again I shot. And again. And again. I didn't think I'd ever stop coming. And he swallowed down every blast of cream with big, greedy gulps, not letting one drop of my steaming semen escape his gullet.

I collapsed into my chair, weak in the knees, satisfied beyond my greatest expectations, completely sucked dry as promised. He had kept his bargain all right.

"Oh, we're not done yet," he said, pulling out his fat, hard, donkey dick and massaging it with long, slow strokes, so the damned thing extended even longer and grew still fatter. I stood there in utter amazement staring at this one-eyed monster demandingly rearing its head at me. He barked out a command: "I want you to bend over the desk. Remember I gave you a preview of coming attractions in the elevator?"

I had thought I was completely satiated, but when he reminded me of his big, thick, tantalizing hard-on pressed against me in that elevator, I couldn't leap onto the desk and spread my cheeks fast enough. In the financial district jargon, this was the bottom line. He spat a couple of times into his palm and lubed up that beer-can cock of his, slowly pushing just the tip into my twitching butt-hole. It hurt a little, then it hurt a lot, then it hurt real, real nice. I just couldn't seem to get enough of his stallion dick. I thrust my anxious ass toward him and pulled him all the way into me, crammed to the hilt. His giant ramrod was stretching the walls of my asshole so I could almost swear I felt the head of his cock poking against my navel. I was so full of cock I could burst.

Then he started to pull out, very, very slowly, almost all the way out. Then back in, easing up my ass, making the walls vibrate. He was slow-fucking me, and my dick, drained from the previous and very thorough suck job, again began to stand up in excitement. Every time his enormous prick massaged my prostate, my cock just grew bigger and harder. I went insane. I suddenly became a total pig.

"Fuck me faster! Deeper! Harder! I can't get enough of you and that big ol' plunger of yours!"

So he did just that, fucking me faster. And deeper. And harder.

"Yes, yes. That's it. Oh, God, that's it. Don't.. ever... stop... fucking... me," I groaned with each thrust, as his body bumped against my body, and my monosyllables were pushed out with every bump. "Just... keep... fucking... me−e−e−e..."

His cock turned into a veritable piston, pumping me faster and faster. I could feel my balls filling up again, welling up with a fresh supply of jizz, and I felt I was about to empty them any second now. His breathing was so quick and shallow, I knew he was right there with me, at the point of no return, on the brink of shooting his pent-up load of man cream and bathing my insides with that warm flood of love.

"I'm gonna come, baby!"

"Yes. Me too!"

"I'm gonna shoot!"

"Yes, yes!"

I felt his shaft throb inside me and gush out jet after jet of steaming hot cream. My cock followed and shot out a big wad all the way across the desk and against the filing cabinet. I pulled him deeper into me as he kept on creaming my ass with thick load after thick load of his wonderful cum.

Eventually we stretched out on the carpet and lay in each other's arms in the warm afterglow of our wild and finally uninterrupted session of lovemaking. It seemed like there was sweat and cum all over the office. After a few moments of hugging in quiet, I interrupted the silence.

"I don't ever want you to leave, but—" I hesitated.

"I don't intend to leave."

"But this isn't what I had planned."

"What do you mean?"

"I don't have time for a relationship now."

"I don't understand."

"Damn it! I'm just starting to work on my career here at the ad agency. I've got plans to climb the corporate ladder."

"Well, hey, that's certainly no problem. Climb away!"

"You mean sleep my way to the top?"

"Yep, if I have anything to say about it. Right now I'd say you're executive material. For chrissake, I'm the President's son! Care to try for Chairman of the Board?"

MANIPULATION

Chisolm Rivers

I was pissed by the time Harry drove up in his polished black Jetta. I had arrived at his house a half hour earlier, at the time we had agreed upon for our rendezvous. I told him I had a house guest where I lived in Diamond Heights and said that the week-end wouldn't be a good time for us to get together, but he made it sound as if he couldn't meet me during the week, so I agreed to drive down to his house in Pacifica. I arrived to find a note on his door that he had gone to the market. I walked up and down the badly paved street of the hill he lived on, admiring the occasional glimpse of the Pacific from between the houses but getting angrier with each passing minute. I put a premium on punctuality myself and don't subscribe to the notion of "faggot time."

When Harry stepped out of his car, however, I immediately forgot my wrath. He was much handsomer than I expected. An older man with straight brown hair just beginning to thin, he stood 5 foot 10, only two inches shorter than me, and had obviously kept himself in good condition. His features were boyish in spite of the lines of experience radiating from his eyes, and his grin told me that he was pleased with my appearance as well. As he walked toward me, I noted with further pleasure the spring in his step. He was wearing jeans and an artsy tee-shirt of people sitting in a cafe captioned JAVA JIVE. I could see he had no ass and that his chest was concave, but he was tight and I liked the long muscles in his arms.

After we introduced ourselves, he took a grocery bag out of the back seat and I followed him into the house. The first thing that struck me was the view from the front room, a magnificent panorama of the ocean and coastline. It was a cloudy day, and so the Pacific blue was mottled with grays and greens. In the distance I could see the foam of the ocean striking against the rocks and headlands of the jagged coastline. The town of Pacifica itself was hidden by a yellow, rocky point. In the foreground, a wide crescent of sandy beach hosted a scattering of people walking their dogs; a couple of wet-suited surfers lay on their boards waiting for a wave to catch.

"I brought us something to eat," Harry said, going behind the counter that separated the kitchen space from the living room. The house was snug, well-suited for Harry's bachelor existence.

"I don't want anything," I said. "I told you I have a house guest, and he's cooking dinner for me tonight."

"Oh, I'll bet a big man like you could easily eat again later."

I didn't appreciate the reference to my size. Of course, that was how I advertised myself in *The Advocate*, in the Big Men section. Like any other visible distinguishing feature—like muscles, black skin, Asian eyes, a big dick—my weight was a turn-on to certain men, but I wanted to be loved for everything about me, not just for my size and belly.

"Look," he continued. "I'm hungry. If you don't mind, I'll make something for myself, and perhaps you'll change your mind later on."

"I don't mind."

And with that, he flipped over a package of frozen pot stickers. "These look good," he said. "And listen," he continued, reading the label, "there are only 120 calories per serving, five grams of fat, and ten grams of carbohydrates. Furthermore, they're steamed, not fried, which is better for you."

This nutritional talk frosted me further. People always think that fat people are the way we are because we're pigs, that we have no self control and eat junk food. I won't deny that I have a healthy appetite, but any attempts I might make to conform to the mesomorphic ideal of male beauty would be sabotaged by my metabolism. I made peace with myself about my physical appearance long ago, but I get tired of having to educate others.

"You're still standing," Harry said. "I'm sorry. Please, have a seat. Take off your clothes." He laughed. "I mean, take off your coat." I shrugged my way out of my leather jacket, and he hung it up in the closet near the front door.

"Can I get you some wine? I have a wonderful Riesling I found in a Napa winery last summer."

I sank down on the leather couch facing the picture window but kept my head turned to Harry, working in the kitchen behind me. "Do you go up to the wine country often?" I asked.

"Not as often as I'd like. I try to get up to the Russian River once or twice every summer, and then I go through Napa or Sonoma. There's a marvelous restaurant, incidentally, near Healdsburg, the Scuppernong. They serve an amazing coquille St.-Jacques. It's a huge oyster shell brimming with scallops, prawns and leeks bathed in a sauce made up of raclettecheese and créme fraîche, browned and seasoned with freshly cracked peppercorns, bits of dill and tarragon. Each bite is its own mouthgasm, and you eat it slowly, with your eyes closed and your lips slightly puckered." He demonstrated the facial gestures, looking both impish and charming. I had to laugh.

"Is that what you do instead of sex?" I asked.

"That *is* sex, my fine furry friend."

It was inevitable, I suppose, that twenty minutes later I should have found myself seated at a glass-topped table overlooking the ocean view with a glass of white Burgundy and a plate of pot-stickers before me. The food and the conversation were equally tasty, all spiced with the mutual attraction.

"You know," he said, leaning over the table and touching my forearm, "I'd seen your ad in *The Advocate* for some time. Now that I've met you, I'm sorry I didn't answer before."

I was flattered. "You haven't lost anything for the wait," I replied.

"Are you seeing anyone?"

"Well, people answer the ad, so I have what I'd guess you'd call a steady supply, although it can be erratic. I'm in a bit of a dry period now."

"What about your house guest?"

"Oh, he's just a friend."

"Well," Harry smiled beautifully and reached over to take my hand. "I'm glad."

His touch turned me on, but his conversation was even more exciting. It was a genuine interchange. I've found when I'm meeting someone for the first time that people either want to talk about themselves or they want you to talk about yourself, but it's rare to find somebody who will risk an interaction with a stranger. Harry was bold about presenting himself, and he was genuinely interested in me. When he rose to get another bottle of wine, instead of returning to his seat after refilling my glass and placing it on the table, he stood behind me and started massaging my shoulders.

I closed my eyes in involuntary pleasure. "That feels good," I said, as his thumbs dug into my trapezoids.

"You're tight," he responded.

I opened my eyes again and looked out over the ocean. The heave of the water against the shoreline seemed an echo of my own desires. I had told Harry, when I agreed to meet him, that we were just going to talk and get to know one another, but I could feel from the tingling in my body that I was entertaining the possibility of more. After massaging my shoulders and back for about five minutes, he leaned down and nuzzled my beard.

"I'd like to kiss you, fuzzy bear," he said.

"That could be arranged." And with that, I stood up and he came against me. I liked the feel of his body. He made sure I knew he had an erection, and then we kissed. As I had hoped, Harry was a great kisser. Kissing him was like unwrapping a gift. He moved his lips against mine in a sensual give-and-take. Soon his tongue followed the rhythm of his lips; then he drew it back in an implicit invitation for me to reciprocate more deeply. I found this intensely exciting. When we kissed, he was kissing *me*. I could feel that. He wasn't focussed on getting a nut; he wasn't looking for sexual validation. I excited him; he wanted me. That, of course, was the greatest turn-on. Pretty soon our cocks were rubbing against each other through our pants. Harry pulled my shirt up and found my nipple. This sent another sensation of pleasure through me. I felt flattered because he was seducing me.

"Why don't we go lay on the bed?" he suggested. "We don't have to take our clothes off."

I assented, knowing what would follow. He took my hand and led me into a small room dominated by a king-sized bed with a green comforter. The bedroom also had plate glass windows overlooking the ocean, but these were shaded by green mini-blinds. He pulled me down on top of him and grunted in both pleasure and surprise at my weight. I tried to roll off, but he tightened his arms around my back. "No," he said. "I like it."

"I'm afraid I'll crush you."

"I'd like that too." And with that, he kissed me deeply, his hands running along my back. Soon he hiked my shirt up again, and his mouth was on my nipple. This too he was good at, expertly negotiating the border between pain and sensation. As I sank into the sensuality of getting serviced, I lost my sense of time. I don't know how long we engaged in this nipple play before he asked, "Can we take our shirts off?" In response, I pulled my polo shirt over my head, and he did the same with JAVA JIVE. The pants and underwear soon followed. Then, when we were naked, he rolled off me, withdrawing his body as his kisses became more gentle. He was deliberately turning down the heat, and I was enjoying it. I loved not having to be in control all the time. He lay beside me, hand on my hard cock, and once again nuzzled my beard.

"Is there anything you've ever regretted sexually?" he asked.

Now I was totally hooked. I had tricked enough to know when my partner was following a formula in his love-making. I've had men whimper with excitement while rubbing their cocks on my belly, and it's left me totally cold. What turns me on is talk, interchange, communication. If I'm real for my partner as a person, then we become intimate. Harry had seduced me through conversation earlier; now he was capping that strategy by calling a halt to the love-making.

"Is there anything you've ever sexually regretted?"

I lay back on the pillow and cradled his head in the hollow of my shoulder. As we talked, he stroked my chest and belly.

"I broke up with my last boyfriend about three years ago. We had been together almost five years before that, and the break-up was pretty devastating to me."

"Were you living together?"

"Not at first, but as soon as we bought our condo together, the relationship started going downhill. I finally asked him to leave and had to buy him out. It was messy, like all divorces. Anyway, about six months after he moved out, I placed my ad in *The Advocate*. I was lonely and hadn't been with anybody for almost a year. This one guy from Utah started corresponding with me, and eventually we exchanged photos. He asked if he could come spend a week-end with me, and I said yes. The minute he stepped into the airline terminal, I could tell there would be no chemistry between us. I don't know why. I thought he was attractive enough from his picture, but he just didn't come alive for me. We spent the day sightseeing together, and I kept trying to psyche myself up into being intimate with him. I must have seemed kind of remote, but he didn't pick up on it.I found him bland. Well, when we went to bed that evening, he was on me as soon as the lights were out, and it had been so long since I'd been intimate with anyone that I went ahead and had sex with him. I wasn't feeling very good about myself, and perhaps that's why I let him fuck me. To this day I don't know why I did it. Since he didn't turn me on, I didn't particularly enjoy it."

"Did he fuck you without a condom?"

"Yes."

Silence at this.

"I don't understand it myself. I felt in some weird way as if I was getting back at Steve. That was the name of my lover. Anyway, after our first night together, I couldn't *wait* for this guy to get out of my life. He finally got the message because the next night, although we slept in the same bed, he didn't touch me.

"After he'd gone back to Utah, I was in a *panic*. I couldn't believe I'd let this happen. I obsessed about AIDS for about a week and then I joined a support group. That helped me tremendously. I had other issues to work on as well."

"Like what?" Harry asked.

I was silent for a moment. "That can wait 'til we know one another better."

"You said in your ad you were HIV negative."

"I am, but I could have reversed everything in one monumental act of self-destruction. I wasn't even turned on to the guy, so I didn't have that as an excuse." We were silent for a moment. "And now, what about you?"

"My sexual regret?"

"Yes."

Harry smiled. "As you know, I like big men. I like playing pool at Badlands because sometimes bear–types come in there. But you know the Castro. If you're not hung, young, or dumb, it can be intimidating. One night I was at Badlands and this big bear of a man walked in, young and kind of goofy looking. He took stock of the place and was about to leave when I went up to him and invited him for a drink. I thought he was gorgeous, but he was very shy and couldn't believe I was interested in him. Turned out he'd just moved to San Francisco a few weeks before, so he was new to the scene. He came home with me that night, and the sex was fantastic. We began dating, but after the third or fourth time, he didn't want to have sex any more. He said he didn't want to be rushed into anything. This inflamed me all the more, but I tried to keep myself under control. I decided to let him call me.

"Up 'til then, I was the one who had taken the lead in the relationship. A week passed, and then he called one evening to ask me to help him buy stereo equipment. I was delighted to agree, and we spent the following Saturday going from one store

to another looking for the best bargains.   He was totally
dependent on my expertise—such as it was—which excited me
even more. When we got back to his place, I set his components
up, and he came to sit on the floor beside me as I explained the
hook-ups. I couldn't keep my hands off him. At first he was
playful in resisting me, but I only took encouragement in that,
and pretty soon we were wrestling around on the floor. I was
thoroughly aroused, but Jimmy got angry. Of course I was no
match for him. He pinned me under him, and started shouting
at me to leave his apartment. He never wanted to see me again.
I tried to apologize, but the damage had been done. I called and
wrote for the following couple of weeks, but I couldn't get through
to him. And that was that. I really liked the guy, too."

The sadness in Harry's voice touched me. After he had
finished, I pulled him to me, kissing him deeply. He maneuvered
me on top of him, and we both groaned as our bodies joined in
waves of motion. This too I liked, this demonstrativeness. After
many minutes of this, ebbing and flowing on his green comforter,
I found myself on my back, massaging the nape of his neck while
his lips fluttered kisses around my naval. Occasionally he would
lick it, and the sensation was just shy of intolerable. When he
finally went down on me, I sighed deeply. He was able to take
me all the way in.

We had spent so much time in foreplay that I quickly felt
myself coming to climax. "Back off," I said, "or I'll come."

His response was to tighten his lips and take me in deeper
strokes. "God!" I groaned, "I'm going to come." I arched back
to pull out of his mouth, but he grabbed my buttocks and sped
up his motion. I had tried to warn him so that he could jack me
off. When I realized he wanted me to come in his mouth, I had
irreversibly crested. "I'm coming!" I cried. "Goddamn it!" He
grunted in encouragement of my own pleasure.

As soon as my penis stopped flailing in his mouth, he jumped
off the bed and ran into the bathroom. I could hear him spitting
into the sink. Shortly afterwards came the sound of water. I now

felt like a condom washed up by the tide. I liked to cuddle after coming and was unpleasantly surprised at Harry's instant abandonment of me. As I waited for him, I focussed on the digital clock on his headboard, which handed me another shock. We had been making love for almost an hour. I would soon have to get dressed in order to make it back in time for dinner. The sun was about 30 degrees above the ocean, and its rays, weakened by the late afternoon slant, directly pierced the narrow blinds of Harry's windows.

When Harry returned to the bedroom, he was no longer erect.

"I don't feel very comfortable with what we just did," I said.

"Why not?"

"We didn't discuss my coming in your mouth."

"If I didn't mind it, why should you?"

"That's not the point, Harry. If we're going to be intimate we have to discuss beforehand what kind of risks we're taking."

He got back on the bed and began stroking my belly. "I'm sorry," he said. "I got carried away."

"Yeah," I replied. "That's what they can put on the tombstones of half the gay men in this state."

"Don't be mad," he said reasonably. "The next time we'll lay out all the rules beforehand. Neither of us planned for this to happen."

I didn't believe him but held silent a moment. "Do you want to come?" I asked.

"No," he said. "I'm tired."

I was glad. I had neither the energy nor the will to continue. "Well, look. I told you I could only stay 'til five, and it's almost that now."

"O.K. You want to take a shower before you go?"

"No. I don't have the time. Anyway you were so efficient there isn't much to clean up."

Harry smiled mischievously. "They don't call me 'blowfish' for nothin'." And with that he dove onto my belly for a final time.

During my drive back to San Francisco, I found that the anger

I had felt while waiting for Harry had returned, and I was sorry I hadn't called him on his being late. The faster I drove along the freeway mounting the low hills separating the coastline from the main part of the city, the angrier I became. As I thought about the events of the past few hours, I decided that I had been thoroughly manipulated. I hadn't wanted to eat, and he fed me. I hadn't wanted to have sex, and he seduced me. I hadn't wanted to come in his mouth, and he blew me. All of the negative feelings I'd associated with bad tricking scenes rushed in upon me. I had been used, objectified, reduced. It had all been done so artfully that I hadn't recognized the pattern. All I was to him was a belly; all he wanted from me was sex. "I like to feed big men," he'd said. "I like to suck them off." That he hadn't said, but he might as well have. It didn't matter whether or not he announced his agenda beforehand. He was expert at getting what he wanted.

When I arrived home, I found that the table had already been laid. Greg was making a salad when I walked into the kitchen.

"How was work, sweetheart?" he asked.

"Fine," I replied. "How close is dinner to being ready?"

"It's ready whenever you are. Shark steaks with fettucini. The shark'll only take ten minutes in the broiler."

"Can you hold off serving for about twenty minutes?" I asked. "I've got to take care of something before I can sit down and enjoy myself."

Greg gave me a look of suppressed frustration I knew so well. He stood in the kitchen doorway with a wooden pasta spoon. wish you'd leave the office at the office," he said.

"I try, honey, but sometimes things come to me in the car on the way home. I just want to jot down a few notes, and then... I'm all yours."

Greg smiled at this. I went over to hug him, and he swatted me playfully on the buttocks with his spoon.

"That's meat, baby, not pasta."

"I don't care what it is as long as I get to eat it tonight."

I squeezed him again and went into my study, closing the door behind me. I took from the drawer a piece of personalized stationary and began writing.

Dear Harry,
First of all, I want you to know that I'm not angry with you; I'm angry with myself. You are clearly the kind of person it is most dangerous for me to be around. I feel like an anemone that has responded all too predictably to the probing of a fat finger . . . .

WAIF

Frederic Trainor

"How many times do I have to tell you, Kurt, not to—Jesus! Now look what you've done!"

"Ohhh, take a chill pill, will ya?" he groaned, rolling his indolent blue eyes ceilingward. "Isn't anything to be having a *baby* over." One overturned ashtray and the fucking queen was ready to short-circuit. The petulant outbursts and bitchiness were getting worse, day by day, steadily mounting toward some catastrophic finale, some ugly confrontation that he had successfully skirted and dodged with the agility of a ferret up to this point.

Slowly Kurt leaned over in the overstuffed armchair, the sweeping mess of his oak-brown hair falling forward around his face as he began scooping up Camel and Salem Light butts from the dingy, multi-colored rug, then negligently rubbing his hand around to smear in ash residue. He ignored, or pretended to, the tongue–clucking and impatient sighing noises, the irregular shifting of feet, the brisk swish of cloth. Dramatics. Miss Jonathan had a flair for them.

He looked up, casually spreading his long legs. His jeans were faded and ripped, a host of haphazard patches sewn here and there. A yellow "Shit Happens" patch rested over his worn-down crotch, lumped and conspicuous. He scratched there now lazily, flashing one of his innocent boy-meant-no-harm smiles. Through the partially-opened living room window drifted the faint melody of the late San Francisco morning, underemphasized yet sinuous, a vague dynamic in the distance.

Jonathan, forty, frustrated, his patience stretched taut and needle-thin, nervously paced the short distance between living room and dinette, a streamlined menthol cigarette dangling down over his pouty bottom lip. It was unlit: a pacifier of sorts employed when he was extremely agitated. His blinky, squinty eyes appraised the youth in the living room in an instant, top to bottom, his emotions a disorderly mass of conflict. Too old, he mused. Too fucking old for this in my life. Finally unable to withhold it any longer, he blurted out what was really gnawing at him.

"Where were you last night? *All* night?"

"A friend's," came the too casual response.

"You couldn't call? Couldn't let me know you were still alive? Still—"

"What's the beef? I'm here now, ain't I?" And that's what bothered Jonathan the most: the arrogant disregard.

He turned to face the boy and sighed. "Is there anything in this world that solicits real concern, real involvement from you, Kurt? Anyone or anything you really *care* about?"

The youth's smile slipped a notch on his dull cast, handsome face, the bearing of his drug-dreamy eyes assuming a look of ingenuous puzzlement. He burped, inclined his dark, bushy head slightly to the left.

"Come again?"

"Con*cerrrn*," Jonathan stressed, his high-strung, nasal voice dragging significantly, his round balding head craning forward with almost comical emphasis. "What do you *care* about? Elementary English, sweetlips. Five word sentence structure."

Kurt stared at him like a vegetable for a second, slowly blinking his eyes. Then, in a saccharine-sweet tone, he said, "Well, so's this, love*errr*: Suck... my... big... white... dick. How's that? Five word sentence." A wheezy snigger followed.

Jonathan blanched at first and then his pale, acne-blotched cheeks colored crimson. "I want you out of here by Friday, Kurt! You're a worthless user. I pulled you up from the Polk Street *gutter*, fed you, shared my bed with you, put clothes on your pimply back—"

The boy belched loudly his unconcern, gazing indifferently at the Sony Trinitron broadcasting mutely in the corner, then at the ever-gurgling eighty-gallon fish aquarium along the wall by the hardwood bookcase.

"Your pimply *back*," Jonathan continued, his pitch rising perilously. "Let you bring your drug-addict hustler friends over here and fed *them*, too—"

"And took it out in trade," snickered Kurt, perversely enjoying his middle-aged benefactor's increasing frustration. Chunky framed, diminutive in stature, hungry and furtive of eye, pampered, soft-white-underbelly face with a bleeding martyr air—typical. At eighteen, Kurt Huntsinger had known many Jonathan Housers, consummate tricks, compulsive chicken hawks. Complain and whine though they may about young predators with ruthless intentions, heartless takers with street-toughened chips on their shoulders, they nonetheless invested considerable money, countless hours of valuable time and energy pursuing them—and being pursued by them. Vicious circle. Self-fulfilling misery.

"You think you're *sooo* smart, don't you?" Jonathan sneered like some peevish Buddha, a stew of convoluted emotion brewing in his expression.

"Jonathan, why can't you just kick back and let it flow, man?" Kurt cooed languidly, stretching one of his stork-like legs straight in front of him. "You're never satisfied. You tell me to go down and get food stamps, I get food stamps; to apply for general assistance, I do that. *All day long* I spend down at that fucking zoo, spun-out freaks and weirdos gawking at me, trying to hustle me..."

Jonathan made a disgusted, agitated noise in his throat. With a series of quick little ungraceful steps he traversed the distance separating them and stood looming over Kurt, to the side of the armchair, face pinched and livid with petulant anger. The purple monogrammed bathrobe he wore fell just short of his knees, exposing his hairless, pulpy legs. His baby-pink chest, also hairless, peeked out unglamorously through the wide part in his robe.

"You're a pitiful specimen, a loser," he snarled, thrusting a shaky finger down at the infuriatingly indifferent boy. "You don't appreciate anything I do for you. I know boys who would—"

"Sell their souls to be in my place," Kurt finished for him, his tone annoyed, bored. The trace of a smile passed over his face. "Oh, chill, Jonathan. Your nose is twitching like Bugs Bunny again."

Enough was enough. "No. No, you get out, Mister," the older man retorted, his anger boiling over. "Right now. Today! Take your damn *skateboard* and your — your barbaric metal tapes and *hit* it!"

The youth looked up at him, gauging countenance with voice tone. Oh, oh. Miss Thing was serious this time. Diffuse. Pacify. With practiced smoothness, Kurt switched to alluring charmer, twisting his athletic frame just so in the chair, his narcoleptic gaze now yielding and attentive.

"Come *onnn*, man, what're you so pissed about? Work late last night? Huh?" He reached for Jonathan's hand.

The older man stiffened and gave a quick, emphatic little side-to-side shake of his head. "Don't try it, Kurt," he said, steeling himself, refusing to weaken. "You're a user and I'm... I'm sick of it. I want you out. *Today*."

"Come on, Jonathan..."

"Uh, uh. No." The boy took hold of his wrist, a soft, pleading look in his drowsy blue eyes.

"But where will I go?" the youth queried softly, running his fingers over the man's plump forearm with light, wispy strokes. "It's Tuesday. I won't get my GA check until Friday. You want me out on the street with nowhere to sleep? Huh?"

Jonathan tried to pull away from his touch, that wretchingly magical touch. The fingers entwined around his wrist, gently tugging. He started to speak, then halted at the sight of Kurt's pants crotch, the way his slouched position showcased the indecent bulge there. Shit happens. The boy grinned, quick to notice the familiar double-take, the reluctant, lingering glance. He lifted his butt slightly, splayed his legs without a hint of shame.

His grin turned sultry.

"You know you'll miss ol' peter here if I go."

"You're not the only hot cock in town," Jonathan protested, somewhat feebly now, doing little to resist the effort being made to pull his hand downward. "I want you gone today, Kurt."

" 'Kay."

"You hear me? Gone and out of my life."

"Uh huh."

"I... I can do so much better than this. I don't—"

"Just feel it, Jonathan," the hustler whispered silkily, seduction incarnate, placing his mentor's hand square on the patch where shit had a tendency to happen. "Feel it go hard in my pants, man. Ol' Pete." He kept a firm grip on Jonathan's wrist while studying his face.

The battle was raging inside the man. Second by precious second his shameful weakness for this lewd street boy was chipping away at what little resolve he had left.

Kurt slumped lower in the chair and lifted his hips, urging Jonathan to get a good, broad feel. A triumphant little smile spread over the youth's face as he watched raw glaze of lust replace uncertain reluctance in the beady eyes. He had him where he wanted him. Confident now, he released the man's wrist and spread his legs further. His obedient cock hoisted and thumped hot against the palm of Jonathan's hand. The older man shuddered and leaned weakly over the chair. His breathing grew more shallow. Color had risen to his cheeks. Seeking final confirmation, Kurt reached inside Jonathan's bathrobe, between his legs. The man gasped and stiffened slightly as the boy made contact. The thick little cock was hard as marble, a taut rage inside his skimpy silk briefs. As Kurt deftly pawed him, Jonathan uttered a sudden strangled growl and lunged, pressing his mouth against the youth's in a torrid lip-lock. His fingers tightened around Kurt's tangled crotch package, pulling and squeezing with such roughness that the boy wondered if he wasn't trying to rip his plumbing loose.

To calm him a bit, the youth gave a sharp yank on Jonathan's testicles and bit down on his tongue. The older man made a yelp in his throat and collapsed on the floor on his knees, dazed and breathless. At that moment he reminded Kurt of some middle-aged survivor of a hurricane or shipwreck; thinning light hair askew, nostrils flared, eyes bewildered and gleaming. Drool dripped from his lush lower lip. His robe was undone and hanging crookedly.

"Wanna lick ol' Pete, Jonathan?" the young hustler teased, tracing the ridged outline of his erection through his jeans. "Huh? You ol' cocksucker, you. Wanna licky?"

Impulsively Jonathan attempted to scramble forward. Kurt stopped him cold with a Reebok planted on his chest. "Wait, man. Let me get up."

The boy stood up and popped the buttons on his jeans, one at a time. As he ceremoniously parted the flaps, a phallic, flesh-toned missile lunged from the recesses, sinfully stiff and formidable. He was a tall, lithe youth, rock musician-lean with long stalks for legs. He towered over the older man like a conquering warrior, tossed mop of amber tresses rippling in waves down around his shoulders, hands on his slender swivel-hips, waiting.

Though uneducated and not exceptionally bright, the street had taught Kurt at an early age that his ultimate leverage was found below the belt—in the bludgeon-thick penis he'd been distinctly endowed with. His cock was his Easy Street ticket, his vulgar magic wand. He gazed with disinterest at the mute television, some game show inanity, then down at the inelegant bald spot on Jonathan's gyrating head. A sloppy, ravenous cocksucker. Desperate hands clutched Kurt's buttocks through his thin pants. Obligatorily he yielded, bucking his hips with just the right amount of passion, casually glancing about the expensively furnished living room with a detached, lazy air.

The crass gulps and slushy sucking sounds both repulsed and excited him simultaneously, and he envisioned Skinhead Skip,

Dusty Riverton, and Gangster Charlie, delinquent boys he'd known at the foster home back in Michigan, boys who had gone that extra obscene mile to show him what queer love was all about. Hungry fingers burrowed up the crack of his Levi's, rough, intrusive. His hips thrust harder. The choked sputtering started then, music to his ears. There was an insistent, furious tapping against his right shin. He glanced down, watching his muscled stalk piston back and forth between Jonathan's voracious, slip-shod lips, the man's fist a bumping blur against Kurt's leg as he masturbated.

A grunt, a retching cough, an indelicate fart, and a ropey glob of semen was splashing the hustler's pants leg. The youth grimaced and then brutally rammed his cock forward, doing his godawful best to shove the thing through the back of Jonathan's head. His buttocks clenched in spastic little jerks as orgasm came, more relief than pleasurable satisfaction.

A Golden Gate breeze, cool and embracing, swept through the room, nipping lightly at his legs. He'd done his duty, met the requirements. There would be no more mention of eviction... for a while. The golden goose had been appeased.

"I had a trying, frustrating night last night, Kurt. I didn't mean..."

"I know, Jonathan, I know."

A pause, rearrangement of clothing. Then, "Can I give good head?" his tone diffident and child-like.

"You're the awesomest, Jonathan."

Pot was on his mind as he strolled up Van Ness, his mood light and undisturbed by concerns over his capricious lifestyle. Things had a way of taking care of themselves. It threw him off balance to think too deeply, too extensively about the future and its myriad possibilities. He wasn't designed that way. Kurt Hunt-singer had learned to operate successfully within a very basic framework of ambition, namely, the less the ambition, the greater the chance of achieving it. A place to stay. A daily minimum of one hot meal. A sugar daddy with a careless wallet. He smiled, a lazy, so-what smile, giving a casual shake to his billowy, heavy-metal mane. Jonathan was incredibly easy, almost embarrassingly so. But Kurt felt no pity. Why should he? Hell, no one had ever felt pity for him. Sure. Of course. I'd be happy to, Kurt. I just want you to do a little something for me, okay? Whore training.

Those secret, lurid trysts with trusted staff counsellors at the boys' home back in Michigan—perverted family men with sons and daughters Kurt's own age. 'Come into my office, Mr. Huntsinger. Lock it, please. What transpires here remains here. Is that understood? Good. Now... step closer, Kurt. Touch it. It's big, isn't it? Don't be scared. I'm your friend. Friends help each other.' The price. Everything has a price. Whore training...

He walked past the cubic sprawl of city-county office buildings, a foreign/domestic auto lot, a sterile-looking McDonald's with its sleekly tinted windows splashing harsh, reflected sunlight. He ignored the intermittent roar of noon traffic beside him, scanning from habit the edge of the sidewalk and gutter for anything of interest or value. So absorbed was he in his thoughts that he failed to notice the bouncing shadow entering his path.

"Quit tweakin' so hard, Kurt," a familiar voice admonished.

Kurt looked up, blinking his eyes. A handsome, smiling black youth in a blue Troop windbreaker and gleaming tight spandex shorts stopped in front of him. His hair was close-cropped, crinkly, the sides shaved in decorative designs. Three gold earrings dangled from his right ear lobe. His face had a lustrous cuteness, its features gentle yet strong and certain in their symmetry. A lighted cigarette rested daintily between two fingers.

"In your *own* little *world*," he teased, making his luscious brown eyes widen and then laughing richly.

Kurt smiled. "What's up, Maurice?"

"Not much," the boy said, his gaze mechanically sweeping up and down the boulevard as he talked. "Just left a trick's house down by the Marina. You should have *seen* all the antiques and shit he's got. Monet and Dali prints on the walls; Louis the

Fourteenth and Sixteenth loveseats and chairs. He's an import-export dude or something."

Monet and Dali meant zip to Kurt.   "Probably a dope smuggler," he said with a cynical grin.

"Probably," Maurice giggled, taking a quick drag from his cigarette. "But, no, he's pretty straight-laced. Pays well, though. Hey, nice leather."

"Thanks," Kurt glanced down with pride at his charcoal Diesel varsity jacket. "Miss Jonathan," he added before Maurice could ask. The black boy's smile was knowing.

"How goes that?"

Kurt tossed hair from his eyes and then blew sputtery air through his lips in a disdainful gesture. Cocking one hand on his hip with the other bent at the wrist, he batted his drowsy eyelids and pranced about on the sidewalk in mimicry of Jonathan, shrilling crying, "You're a *loser*, Kurt, a *user*! You don't appreciate me!"

Several people passed them, pointedly staring. The boys were too busy laughing to care.

"He told me to vacate," Kurt said and they walked together up Van Ness. Someone screamed something from a passing car. A horn blared.

Maurice frowned with concern. "Really? You're on the street?"

"Naw, he blew me 'til I juiced his tonsils. Now everything's cool again. Dizzy queen." Then, glancing sideways at the black youth, Kurt asked, "Where can I score some pot, Maurice?"

"Chris and blond Mike are holdin', I heard."

"You smoked any of it?"

"I just heard." The black boy leered amorously at a pair of handsome Arab youths exiting a corner deli. "Let's cut down Golden Gate," he suggested. "I've seen 'em round the park lately."

"Some crazed fucking wino types chased me through there the other night," Kurt said, his tone vaguely sluggish, surfer-lethargic. Maurice giggled, earrings tinkling musically. He glanced up.

"You're a stone trip, Kurt," he said, studying the tall white boy with mild amusement. Kurt blinked at him quizzically, mouth slack.

"What's to trip on, dude?"

"Your Valley-boy drawl," answered Maurice. "Like you've been doing 'ludes for weeks at a time. You don't wanna check out the park?"

"Not especially." Kurt took out his Walkman, positioning the headphones snugly on his head. "But, hey. If Chris is down there, like, that's cool 'cause he owes me anyway. Gimme a smoke."

They walked on, speaking minimally, Kurt rhythmically bobbing his rocked-out mane, semi-absorbed in his music while Maurice, his eyes keen and promiscuous, idly assessed various male faces, torsos, and crotches on both sides of the street. They were a striking pair, a conspicuous and contrasting pair, as much from their different demeanors as from their racial differences. They had known each other for several months, in the curious way that Polk Street denizens knew one another—familiarity compounded by the routine of casual association. When you see the same face in the same place for a consistent duration of time, it grows on you.

Kurt had always liked Maurice. The black boy had a whimsical quality, an upbeat poise that was reassuring somehow. Life never seemed to push him to the ropes.

A gale of crisp Bay breeze assailed them suddenly as they crossed Golden Gate and Polk Streets, kicking up pockets of miniature tornados of leaves and litter by the steps of City Hall. As they walked through the park and passed a group of lounging addicts, a sandpiper voice crudely called out, "Say, boy! I bet your mama's right proud of that set of buns you got!" Drunken hoots and whistles followed. The statement was directed at Maurice who chose to ignore it, rolling his eyes at Kurt with a nasally snicker.

"What?" said the lanky headbanger, turning down his Walkman

and glancing back.

"Nothing," answered Maurice. "Some wino admiring my caboose."

"Yeah?" With a slack-lipped toss of his hair, Kurt spun around and dramatically flipped the bums off with both hands. Then he grabbed his crotch and violently gyrated it at them. A wine bottle came sailing in their direction, bouncing wildly across the lawn.

Kurt ran and caught up with his friend, smiling. Maurice frowned. "Why'd you do that?"

"Fuck those assholes. Probably the same dicks who chased me the other night. Besides, you like a buncha stinkin' winos talkin' about your ass?"

Maurice shrugged. "Like it matters or something, Kurt? And the drunk fool's right. My mama loves my boodie. It's bigger than hers." He laughed pleasantly and exaggerated the sway of his prominent rear, tossing his head from side to side like a cocky queen.

Kurt chuckled in spite of himself, his eyes settling on Maurice's behind. The black hustler's ass was definitely an enticing distraction. It jutted outward into a blossomed bubble, clenching and jiggling with a lush sort of rebellion inside the snug, gleaming spandex.

Kurt felt a vague tingling in his belly which gradually grew warmer, spreading down to his groin. An erection threatened. He shoved his hands in his pockets, looked away, and spat. Shit, he wasn't queer, so what's the deal? Still it was a far better ass than many he'd plugged for a few bucks or a warm bed. "So where are they?" he said, his annoyance showing through; he stopped and pointedly looked around the park.

"Don't see 'em."

"Screw this. Let's jet up to—"

"No, wait." Maurice spotted a familiar face in a group across the way. One ring-adorned hand reached for Kurt. "Cash. Sleazy Sherry's got pot. It's that real stinky, horny shit, too."

The white youth dug into his pocket, then hesitated, casting an uncertain, wary look at Maurice. The black boy rolled his eyes, snapped his fingers.

"Come on, come on. Don't insult me, man. I ain't hurtin' for ends. Miss Art Collector was very generous. What's with you?"

"Man, it's my last twenty and..." Slowly, reluctantly, he handed over the bill.

"And what?" countered Maurice., matching stares with him. "I'm not into burning people, Kurt. And hell, I'm just going over *there*." He chuckled incredulously. "Paranoid *Pauline*. Where you think I'm gonna go?"

"Okay, okay," said Kurt, fidgeting, suddenly embarrassed. "I'll be right here. I just... um, like, don't take a lifetime," he finished lamely.

Maurice left him, pivoting on his heels and striding across the grass without a backward glance. Kurt watched him immerse himself in the colorful, ragged group of mohawked punk rockers and cupid-faced longhairs clotted around a row of benches, saw him engage a thin, dark-haired girl with a thousand bracelets on her wrists in furtive conversation. In less than five minutes the transaction was completed and Maurice returned; the two walked silently together out of the park and up Larkin Street.

The black youth slipped a small plastic envelope to Kurt who, feeling slightly foolish over his unwarranted mistrust of a few moments earlier, declined to inspect it.

"I thought we were better than that, man," Maurice mumbled, glancing up at the white youth in mild disappointment. Kurt wouldn't look at him; he found two Korean women struggling with a wailing child more interesting; a stringy-haired musician strumming a beat-up guitar in a doorway; a passing MUNI bus.

"I'm tripping, Maurice, just tripping. Jonathan's being a cunt. All my stuff's still over at Robert's—"

"So you think I'm gonna burn you for twenty fucking bucks?"

"Been burned for less," Kurt blurted feebly, then, immediately recognizing his mistake, added, "But, hey, man. We go back a ways, Maurice, and I know you wouldn't—"

"Fuck you, man," the black stud muttered, suddenly angry. He stopped and glared at Kurt. "Stick your prick up your skinny ass and fuck yourself." The righteous indignation in his voice slapped at Kurt, leaving him tongue-tied and momentarily bewildered. You really are an asshole, Kurt Huntsinger. A true dick. Annoyed with himself but unable to voice his regret, the tall youth cursed to himself and did a comical half-spin in the sidewalk, tossing his hair back with a fierce gesture. Maurice started walking away. Kurt's fumbling voice halted him.

"Well..., um. Damn, man. You wanna smoke with me or what, Maurice?"

The black youth turned and appraised him. Kurt appeared disheartened and vulnerable just then, little-boy lost and contrite. Maurice was helpless—he yielded. Resuming their walk in an uneasy silence, they turned down a glass- and garbage-littered alley, inadvertently reaffirmed their bond through the mutual cursing of a tattered, wheedling pair of tramps, and laughingly tried to outdo one another with the most creatively–scathing epithets they could think of to hurl.

Sobering, Kurt suggested, "There's an old abandoned van down toward the end of the alley. We can kick back in it for a while."

Maurice nodded. " 'S cool."

The alley was half filled with various vehicles, a sort of surplus parking area for city commuters unable to secure parking on the street or in lots. It stretched along the back entrances of Asian-owned laundry and textile businesses, corrugated doors rusted closed, swirling puffs of processed steam escaping from metal-slatted fans. The old Ford Econoline had been there for weeks—three flat tires, one side window broken, a multitude of parking tickets gracing its filthy windshield. The boys climbed in through the passenger side door and over the rear seat into the back.

"I crashed in here one night when Robert's drunk landlord caught me sneakin' up the fire escape to his place," Kurt revealed softly, settling back against the hard wheel well, his long legs stretching across the van's width. "It was weird 'cause I was stoned and cars kept cruisin' down the alley, honking and doing strange things."

Maurice scooted next to him, hugging his knees against his chest, scanning the van's stark, stripped interior indifferently. Their jackets grazed lightly. Outside, the grating crunch of gravel and broken glass as a car cruised down the alley slowly.

"Robert got a big wang?" The question made Kurt giggle. He pulled out the baggie of pot and some papers and began rolling.

"Depends on what you call big," he said evasively, smiling.

The black boy absently tapped his foot on the floor. "Big means does it make you feel all weak inside when he slides it up your tushie."

"Robert never did that to me."

Maurice lifted an eyebrow. "He never fucked you?"

"Nope. Never. I ain't queer, ya know." The headbanger's lazy eyes turned lusty sly. "My boodie's as virgin as Mother Mary's, man."

Maurice snickered. "Get real, Miss Snow White. They never packed that pooper at that boys' home you were in? How long were you there?"

"Too long," Kurt responded. "Here." He passed the lit joint to Maurice. The black youth raised it to his full, delicate lips and inhaled noisily, allowing his right leg to stretch out over Kurt's left. He didn't follow up on Kurt's claim that he wasn't queer.

The rocker's gaze dropped without thinking to the peach-sized mound between his friend's dark spandexed legs. It bulged healthily, indecently, like a tumorous growth lodged at the top of the inner thigh. There were slurred voices and a muted laugh in the distance, and the forlorn wail of an ambulance.

Maurice coughed and passed the joint back. "Tastes like Humboldt," he wheezed around a dusky visage hazed in smoke. Kurt took a hefty toke, suddenly remembering Skip Barrett, an emotionally-disturbed skinhead boy who had killed his brother

Michigan foster home. Those lust-filled times during the staff-sponsored movies in the pitch-dark dayroom, excitable, adolescent heads silhouetted in uniformed rows, inclining toward one another, craning around slyly. Kurt and Skinhead Skip sitting together toward the back, the punk rocker sporting trousers ravaged up the crotch, no underwear, his big chicken-egg balls and deep buttsplit indelicately exposed. He invariably sat with knees raised so everything spilled out gracelessly, softly mumbling disjointed, nihilistic jibberish in Kurt's ear while the tall head-banger took furtive liberties between his thighs, groping, massaging, burrowing. Spun out puppy, yes, but *damn*. Biggest *schlong* Kurt had ever seen. And that inevitable night, lots of vaseline and teeth-gritting, the two of them bucking and grunting as if their very lives depended on the outcome, the crampe , stuffy broomcloset a hothouse choked with pungent sweat, Pine Sol and damp, moldy neglect. Hot. Quick. Filthy. He had been the only boy at the Home bestowed the rare privilege of that huge meat up his ass.

"Hey." He nudged Maurice's arm.

"Huh."

"How do you spell *troll*?"

The black boy glanced sideways at Kurt. The van's muted gloom gave the metal-head's eyes a leaden look, partially obscured by ragged tresses of rustic hair, his face lightly flushed, lips decidedly moist and generous. Maurice shrugged his ignorance.

Kurt offered a stoned half-smile. "J-O-N-A-T-H-A-N," he recited slowly. A low, fleeting chuckle escaped from the black mouth. A delicately ringed, white hand absently traced circles on one mocha thigh, then up to his groin, tentatively hovering.

"What happens when he boots you, though, man? Back to Polk or what?"

"Whatever's clever," Kurt replied, not particularly enthused about thinking ahead that far. The marijuana was doing its work and edges were blurring nicely. A hazy complacency.

"Shit gets old."

"So does life but you still live it." Kurt reached for his lighter, the gesture definitive, his way of stating unwillingness to pursue the subject further.

Maurice shifted his dark legs, fished in his windbreaker for a mint, and popped it into his mouth. Idly he watched the white youth toss back his wild mane, light the remainder of the joint. He toyed with the earrings in his lobe, cleared his throat.

"Just stuff I think about sometimes. You know."

Kurt glanced at him, exhaling smoke. "What's that?"

The black boy shrugged. "Things. Having my own spot. Money around when I want it." He paused, vacantly fondling the bulk between his legs, shifting it. "And, you know, only *doing* it when you feel like it and with who you feel like. I think about school..."

Kurt looked at him sharply, smirking. "School?"

Maurice met his gaze, held it. "Yeah. School."

The headbanger snorted with disdain. "Fuck school. Head-trips, phonies. All dressed up, no one to blow. No thanks."

"That's *high* school," stressed Maurice. "I'm talkin', you know, college. Enrolling, gettin' a grant or something. Taking dance and music classes, some writing stuff. You read?"

"Not much."

"Finish high school?"

"Nay." Kurt burped, passed what was left of the joint. He gazed at the black boy under heavy eyelids and hair, studying his clear, dark countenance, his almost effeminate features. The eyes had a mercurial, knowing quality; the nose well-shaped and slightly flared; the mouth pouty, pooched a little; tapered yet sturdy jaw; hieroglyphic hairstyle; talismanesque earrings. Zulu princeling. Exotic excitement. Suddenly the van seemed charged with a shadowy, slow-burning tension, a vague impression of gentle decay mingled with illicit opportunity and desire.

Kurt felt himself stir; that tingly, insinuating heat that precedes a hard-on. He touched himself gently, glanced down at the conspicuous lump between Maurice's thighs.

"Soooo," he ventured, seeking distraction. "What sorta writing stuff?"

The black boy, preoccupied now with a stubborn lighter, replied without looking up, "Different stuff. I think I wanna write fiction or something. Action stories. I dunno."

"Yeah?" A lost attempt. Kurt's mind had regressed back to his penis. He was absently pinching it, gently, steadily, through the denim, making it throb, harden, his gaze insistently drawn to Maurice's groin.

"Action stories, huh? Like... what? Big-dicked boys meeting rich guys on the beach? That sorta schtuff?"

Maurice giggled, shaking his head. "Mind in the gar*bahhj*. Is that all you—" He looked up and stopped, noticing the crotch of Kurt's ragged jeans, the familiar protrusion, the persistent, diddling fingers. Smiling knowingly at the gangly rocker, he reached over and boldly touched it. "Oooo," he cooed admiringly. "Got a big one, don'tcha, for a straight dude?"

Kurt grinned and moved his hand out of Maurice's way. "Just goes and bones up when I least expect it. Must be the pot." He parted his long legs to encourage better access, still grinning, watching the black youth's slender fingers explore him in lazy, lingering sweeps, causing the entire area to expand, to breathe, rising and falling with ardent plumpness.

Glass exploded in the alley, followed by strident female voices. Running sounds. Wild, malicious laughter. In the van there was dull, clumsy–sounding metallic bumping. The hollow scraping of bodies shifting. A lengthy groan. Crotches, at once hard and tender, squashing together in seething cadence.

Maurice, on top of Kurt now, their lips locked together in sloppy-tongued greed, wanton surrender, unrepentant, mingling saliva, soulful moans. Kurt's hands, expertly roaming over the jutting hills of his black friend's ass, up and down, in circles, as if to steady, to steer its unruly gyrations. Stiff erections dueling, roughly colliding through the prison of fabric.

Dick bump. Bump thump. The sharp screech of Reeboks and

Adidas. A clash of radios filtering in a brief overlap of distant, familiar music, then drifting back out along the perimeters of background traffic sounds. A sudden wet smack of release, of liberation. Gaspy breathing.

"Slow... slow down, man. I'll jizz off in my jeans." Kurt's hair, sweeping spaghetti mess across the dirty van floor, his face suffused with blush, waif lovely, lips bruised and glistening sybaritic. Maurice's lips were buried in the crook of the white neck, his breath hot and agitated. Pelves continued to churn to a clumsy rhythm, Maurice's bulging, distended buttocks lifting and dropping in a lewd roll, hypnotic motion pushing inside snug, taut elastics.

"You can do me," Kurt whispered hoarsely, "but I want some, too."

"Some what?"

Kurt gave the black rump a solid slap and clutched a cheek, squeezing it firmly. "Some of this, man. Some of this. I've wanted to pork this big, juicy fucker ever since we first met," he admitted.

Maurice uttered a soft, dirty chuckle, and then Kurt's hand was easing down the back of his taut spandex, creeping between the twin knolls of smooth muscle, seeking. The black boy sighed, wiggled his buttocks.

"Mmmm. Like that." He pushed his legs out over Kurt's in a wide sprawl, knees rubbing the cold metal floor, ass thrusting upward, perilously straining fabric. They kissed. Sluggishly. Lusciously. Kurt's hand sank deeper. A small ripping sound. A grunt.

He was in Maurice now, in his ass. Suck spit. Bump dick. Bit butt black boy. Like Charlie. Gangster Charlie at the Home. Peppermint sticks, Public Enemy cassettes and a drawer full of girlie magazines. Perpetual grin. Copious mouth forever sucking on barber pole swirls. Never talked about why he was at the Home. Kurt never asked. They took a shower together once and Kurt got his chance to really assess Gangster Charlie firsthand.

A deep umber-colored boy with a broad chest, crude 'Diana' tattoo over the left nipple, tight, flat belly, piano-stump legs. Added to the lineup was a thick anaconda cock and big, bulging spheres for buttocks. Even trapped in baggy trousers the black youth's robust behind tossed and tumbled prominently, protruding outward in a gorgeous swell. Watching him had Kurt shuddering with ill-concealed lust. But Gangster Charlie hadn't been disposed to befriending white boys. Kurt had to struggle hard to disguise his longings. It wasn't easy.

Maurice made a choked sound, opened his mouth wider, moaned, then resumed. The van rocked gently. Kurt squirmed beneath him. His pants were down around his calves, slim, knobby hips slowly thrusting upward. They faced away from each other, mouths embedding warm, bulky genitals. Feeding. Maurice's tool overwhelmed Kurt at times, stretching his lips and jaw muscles uncomfortably. They writhed in a tight yin-yang undulation on the floor, the black boy's dark, nappy head dipping and circling in blissful earnest, earrings softly jingling, lips noisily slurping. His hands were clasped below Kurt's buttocks, eagerly pushing the white youth's bushy crotch into his face, heavy balls bouncing gently against his chin.

He paused briefly, mouth lewdly distended with thick, fleshy prick, hunching the cheeks of his corpulent behind with unrestrained vigor until Kurt retched sharply and squeezed his leg. Maurice eased up. Groaning pleasurably, he gobbled downward, filling his throat with Kurt's savory rigidness, then shoved a wet finger up the headbanger's tight ass.

Kurt grunted, rolling his hips in agitation, relaxing his sphincter. Maurice worked his finger in deeper, round and round, out, than back in, teasing, loosening resistance, then lifted his own buttocks slightly, heard the vulgar pop of release, and lowered his ass to Kurt's upturned face. Rubber soles squeaked and slid, rattling old discarded newspaper, fast food containers. Pale fingers spread over lush brown haunches, pressing with urgency, spreading them fully. His tongue went searching immediately, nose and lips and eyes immersed in musty darkness. Hot black butt. Like Gangster Charlie's. Yeah. Like his. Murky and gaudy and irresistible. Sweet chocolate cushions, pressing snugly at his face, sublimely smothering him.

Like the night Charlie cornered him in the upper dorm bathroom, just the two of them, and asked him sneeringly if he was a fag. Point blank. You a fag, white boy? Huh? You a fruiter? And he wanted to speak, to deny it, to act indignant, but couldn't, *dammit*, and Gangster Charlie took his silence for acquiescence and slapped him, hard, like a bitch, blocking his escape with that stout, pit-bull frame, and Kurt, terrified and oddly thrilled, his arms raised to shield his face, felt the bathroom spin out of focus, his knees buckle weakly, his pulse thunder, then a blunt blow to his unprotected belly, his body fold on impact, collapsing in slow motion, his knees hitting the cold, pissy tiles, hands groping desperately for support, dragging at his assailant's flannel leggings without intending to, feeling them give, slide, then Gangster Charlie pushing them down the rest of the way, spinning around and ordering Kurt to lick his big black ass, to shove his faggot face deep up the hot, funky crack and rim it *gooood*, pulling and squeezing that long, greasy fire hose of his, elongating it, pushing his mountainous buns backward, back into Kurt's face. And Kurt obeying him, wallowing like a drunkard between his smelly, bloated buttocks, tasting his foul aroma, extended tongue surging upwards, up into the warm, murky rectum, dragging his whole face tortuously up and down the entire length of the bully's cavernous ass crack, feeling Charlie buck back fiercely, hatefully, slamming Kurt's head against the bathroom wall, over and over, breaking hot wind in his face, in his mouth, humiliating him, degrading him, never suspecting the perverse truth, the undeniable truth that Kurt loved every raunchy second of it, his cock so frightfully stiff in his pajamas that he was certain they'd burst before he could manage to...

"Family *styyyyle*," Maurice moaned, breathless, hips churning slowly, pacing. Lust impure, beautiful, drenched his handsome brown face.   His minstrelish mouth was cock-swollen and dripping. Kurt chuckled a husky concurrence, slipping his hands under the other's shirt and windbreaker, caressing smooth, scorching skin. Spandex and jeans lay discarded at their feet.

Kurt's knees were back to his ears, his long legs hooked over Maurice's shoulders, stylish white Reeboks carelessly untied and swaying in mid-air. The soft squish-splutter of his asshole being impaled by a thick, black turgid log reverberated crudely in the hollow spaces of the van.   He gripped Maurice's rounded buttcheeks, richly stroking them, urging him to push harder, deeper. Weighty testicles slapped his behind — almost lulling, the sound.

His mouth fell slack, luscious, his tongue wagging in wanton invitation. The black youth's hovering face descended, eager to oblige. Maurice kissed him as though trying to inhale intestines, lungs, and *soul* through Kurt's throat, forcing the rocker's jaws wide apart, fearlessly swishing spit, breath, tongues entwining frenziedly.

The thrust of hips grew less tentative, more careless, impassioned. Every inch of Maurice's cock penetrated now, pistoning in, then out, searing the headbanger's clenching, suctioning rectum with a steady, grinding onslaught. Throaty, husky grunts escaped Kurt's lips with each of Maurice's forward thrusts, their lower bodies seemingly at war with each other, bumping and colliding in brutal unison on the hard van floor, the crescendo swelling wildly until Kurt screamed, "Fuckin' shootin', man! I'm going, ohh..."

He gripped Maurice's buns in a death clutch and pulled him forward, forcing every last inch of the black sex up into his bowels.   His back arched severely, eyes tightly shut, body shimmying as a torrent of juice spewed from his cock, squishing wetly between them. With an urgent whimper, Maurice pulled himself from Kurt's hot, slippery ass and squashed dicks with him in a rough, fevered hump, biting the rocker's lips, licking him, tonguing his cheeks, his chin, locking mouths and growling deeply as the paralyzing spasms seized him, erupting from within, a slimy, pleasurable coat of wetness blending on their shirts and bellies as their hips continued to gyrate, to grind, genitals sleek and sliding lushly.

Kurt's feet slapped the floor. His chest heaved erratically. The smell of Right Guard and hair grease, boy sweat and cum teased his nostrils. Cheek to cheek. Maurice's and his own. He started to speak but then heard soles shuffling over gravel outside. Gruff, mumbly voices. The clicking sound of someone trying the driver's side door. Maurice rolled away in an instant, peering expectantly in that direction. Kurt quickly pulled himself up into a sitting position and gave a brisk shake of his dense, tangled mane. He glanced at Maurice, then toward the door.

"Occupied, *dude*," he called out, loudly enough to be heard. No response at first, and then a slurred, sarcastic, "All right, *dude*," accompanied by a resounding kick to the side of the van. Disgruntled mumbling. Shuffling feet moving away. Relative quiet.

The boys looked at each other and snickered. "You owe me, fucker," Kurt said softly, smiling.

Maurice laughed a quiet, fond laugh. "So I do. Next time, honey buns." He retrieved his tights, wiggled into them. "Let's book up outta here before some cop comes."

Kurt got dressed and they left the van, walking together up to Polk and Geary, zipping up their jackets against a sudden stab of mid-afternoon breeze. At the corner, Kurt stopped and assumed a negligent pose, a hustler's pose; pelvis pushed forward, one leg thrust in front of the other, fishing around in his pockets for Walkman and headphones, the intersection a clamor of constant, streaming traffic.

Maurice had stepped over to speak to some skate punks he knew, a group of them hovering by the public telephone a few feet away. When they left, Kurt walked over and called Jonathan, making funny faces at the nearby Maurice, idly watching cars as they passed, winded scatter of Valhallic tresses whipping his face.

The phone rang for a long time. He scratched his crotch. A gaunt-faced teenager with a bulky boom-box and an arrogant swish strode by, muttering, "Doses? Water?", and continuing down Geary, his furtive, cryptic salespitch summarily ignored.

"Maybe he's gone," offered Maurice, observing Kurt's growing frustration. The tall boy made an anxious gesture with his free hand, indicating his need for a cigarette. The black youth lit one and gave it to him, then eased Kurt's headphones from around his neck and his Walkman from his jacket, and walked to the corner. When he turned back a moment later, Kurt was speaking into the phone and gesturing animatedly with his head and upper body, long legs shifting restively, his face an ever-changing array of unpleasant expressions.

As Maurice watched, Kurt's movements became increasingly stiff and agitated, switching the receiver from ear to ear with sharp, sudden jerks of his head, wild chops at the air with his hand to emphasize whatever point he was making. Finally he cursed into the receiver and slammed it into its cradle, stomping his foot in petulant outrage. He flipped off several motorists who ogled him rudely.

Just as quickly as the anger developed, it dissipated, leaving in its wake a dazed yet oddly collected and resolute Kurt. His hands were stuffed deep in his thick Diesel, lazy bedroom eyes calm and beckoning Maurice.

"Jonathan?" asked the black boy, handing his friend's radio and phones back to him.

Kurt nodded, staring up the street. "Dizzy queen threw me out. All my shit's sitting in his hallway, packed."

Maurice was silent a moment, then, for something to say, asked, "How much stuff?"

"I dunno, I... fuck." The day suddenly seemed oppressive, mocking. The stench of car exhaust, burnt rubber, and fresh tar emerged sharply, pervasively.

As did the imminent stench of destitution.

"So, what you gonna do, man?" Maurice asked. "You know

you're welcome to stay in my room at the Lindsay. I'm paid up 'til next week."

Kurt brightened a bit. "Desk man cool about visitors?"

"Lonnie is. The rest are dicks but I can sneak you up." He shrugged, cringing a little against the wind's chill. "Better'n crashing in some squat like Sunshine and Bones and them."

"Yeah." Kurt's pale, chilled face grew momentarily dark. "Fuckin' troll."

Maurice smirked and shook his head. "Don't trip, man. You knew it was coming. He'll be cruising around out here tonight, scouting fresh dick, talking that, '*My*, you're a *lovvely* boy' shit." Kurt laughed.

Pleased, Maurice stepped up and kissed him, adding, "Gotta go, sweets. It was fun. You need anything? Couple bucks?"

"No, I'm cool," Kurt lied, slightly embarrassed.

Maurice lingered. "So, what's up with you?" The headbanger tossed back his hair and gazed thoughtfully up Geary Street.

"I dunno. I think I'll check out the bookstore for a while. Can't hurt." Their eyes met knowingly in brief, silent conspiracy.

"Got enough for tokens?"

"Four or five bucks."

"That'll do ya." Maurice, grinning playfully, reached to pinch Kurt's behind. The rocker pushed his hand away.

"Don't act like a fag. I hate fags." Kurt looked away.

"Four seventeen," Maurice said. "The Lindsay. Meet me out in front at midnight. Later."

Kurt watched him go, then shifted his gaze to the adult bookstore across the street, considering. Yeah. Why not? Although the day was sunny it was steadily growing colder. At least it would be warm inside, especially in the dark back room with the twenty-five cent booths. And, who knows? Perhaps he'd strike gold and find a wallet stuffed with money and plastic like he did a couple weeks ago, or even land a quick date with some horny tourist. The two of them might stuff themselves into a cramped booth for a lewd and spirited romp.

One moment to the next. Keep it simple. One to the next. "Fuck it," he said loudly, and then crossed Polk with a tentative, increasingly purposeful stride that said the future be damned, today is the day...

A SHADOW ACROSS TIME

Joseph W. Bean

Shipman W. Reid III had everything. He was young and handsome, intelligent and sensitive. His family had a bit of money—old, Barbary Coast supply money, he was told—so he didn't have to earn a living. But, to live with his father, he had to have a job. So, he became a museum docent at the California Academy in Golden Gate Park. He led guided tours of the early American art collection mostly. What he wanted to do was art work, not paintings or sculpture, but papercuttings. He had a collection of papercuttings from all over the world, everywhere he had travelled with his parents.

Collecting papercuttings and making them had always been just about the only things that gave Shipman any happiness. But, as his father had said so many times, collecting 'paper dolls' is not a career. Neither, in Mr. Reid's view, was the making of cut paper art anything more than a pastime. He was satisfied, but only barely satisfied, when Shipman began volunteering his time at the art museum.

Shipman, though, was not satisfied. In fact, he often felt that he was a mistake. When he was working out at the health club, he thought his muscles—already impressive after less than a year of weight training—should have been developed doing productive labor. In fact, he often wondered if he belonged in some other world, some place or time where artists were appreciated more, and where he would be allowed to spend his time the way he wanted: alone, doing for himself whatever needed to be done and, of course, designing and cutting pictures in silhouette.

One day, while Shipman was examining for the millionth time the only papercutting in the museum's art collection, he was approached by a museum patron. He hated wearing the camel-colored blazer that identified him as a museum staff member. It didn't hang on his newly muscular frame all that well, but it did, as he often thought, "attract idiots." People were constantly asking him where the Picassos were kept ("There are none here, Madame. Unfortunately, Picasso was a Spanish–born painter in Paris, not an American."), or where the little boys' rooms or the powder rooms were ("The comfort stations are located next to the elevators on every floor. You'll know them by the big blue and gold signs over the doors.")

As he turned to the gentleman who was trying to get his attention, Shipman thought, "I am going to say 'I don't know' no matter what the question is." He put on his official smile. "May I help you, sir?" But then, looking into the man's rugged face, he felt a tug. It was more than duty, not just a matter of doing his job. This man, whatever he wanted, was not one of Shipman's usual idiots.

"Sure can. I think that painting is mighty nice, but I can't help wondering why it's all just black and white."

He couldn't mean the papercutting, Shipman thought, no one notices that, but me. There was an uncomfortable pause during which the man's deep brown eyes seemed to flash, throwing strangely comforting little pains into the pit of Shipman's belly. Shaking himself free of the unusual feeling, he asked, "This?" He felt as if the way he pointed at the papercutting suggested that he thought little of it.

The gentleman nodded. Shipman noticed then that the man was dressed in what seemed to be real, rather than "drug–store" variety cowboy clothes. Neat and clean as he was, he seemed a little out of place in an art museum. His brown leather chaps were shiny with wear, his vest darkened down the sides where sweat had been rubbed in by the man's heavy arms. The huge tan felt hat in his hands had a smooth, dark patch around his fingers, showing that it had been taken off many times with dirty hands, although the hands – and the man – were well–scrubbed at the moment.

"This," Shipman said as he stepped back to let the cowboy move in closer, "is not a painting. You're looking at a single sheet of black silhouette paper, cut into this expressive and intricate pattern by an unknown artist. Using tiny, pointed scissors and sometimes a knife, paper has been carved into pictures like this for more than 1,500 years."

"I'll be," was all the cowboy could say.

"This particular cutting was apparently done from life, or, at least, sketched from life, possibly cut later. But, probably, it was actually cut on the spot, in Promontory, Utah, on May 10, 1869. The artist was obviously south of the railway tracks when he observed the driving of the famous Golden Spike that completed the transcontinental railroad line."

"South," the cowboy whispered, turning his face from the papercutting. They were standing so close that Shipman could feel the man's hot breath on his face. He wanted to step back, but something from deep inside himself wouldn't let him move. "How'd you know that?" the cowboy asked.

"Because he's put Central Pacific Railroad's engine on the left. It was coming east from Sacramento, and the Union Pacific engine, which was coming west from Omaha, is on the right."

"Makes sense 'nough, I guess," the cowboy said. "But you are a sharpie to notice that!"

"I enjoy this cutting," Shipman said, trying to shrug off the dizzy feeling that was sloshing around in his head. "I like most of our Western Americana collection, especially the cowboy stuff, the big–sky paintings with nothing taller than a *suguaro* cactus breaking the horizon line..." Shipman trailed off. He was certainly not in the habit of speaking about his own preferences, or saying anything that might be called revealing, to the museum's patrons.

"Don't say?" The cowboy seemed amused, and his free hand reached toward Shipman's forearm. The attention was embarrassing, but Shipman liked the nervous warmth it caused. "Y'know," the man went on, lightly touching Shipman's arm as he spoke, "that's where I *live*." He put a very strange accent on the last word.

"Promontory, Utah?"

"No, under the sky, out away from all this... buildings and cars... and, no offense intended, but away from people, too."

Shipman was really feeling uncomfortable having this personal conversation in the middle of the museum floor, but he was hooked. He felt deserted when the cowboy withdrew the hand that had been resting on his arm. He wanted very much to hear about life out under the big sky, as he let himself call it for the first time (except in the official phrase "big–sky paintings"). "Too bad you don't like being around people," he said, "I was just about to ask if you wanted to go out onto the concourse for a cup of coffee." Then a little more emphatically than he intended, he added, "To talk."

"First things first," the cowboy said. "I don't mind people all that much, I just enjoy the solitude, the peace that soaks into a body deeper and deeper as he gets out farther into the desert. Then, I suppose, we'd ought to meet before we go making appointments. I'm Richard Skinner," he said, offering his hand, "but 'cause of my summer job – leading tourist mule trains – most of my friends call me Muleskinner, or just Mule."

"I'm glad to meet you, Mr. Skinner," Shipman started.

"Mule, please. It's summer now."

Shipman checked an impulse to remind the man in front of him of the date: May second, still spring, not summer. "Glad to meet you, uh, Mule. My name is Shipman Reid."

As they shook hands, Mule asked, "Folks call you Ship, maybe Chip, do they?"

"No, I'm afraid I'm not the sort of person who gets nicknamed," Shipman answered, adding hurriedly, "but, sure, you can call me Chip. I'd like that. Now, what about that cup of coffee?"

"I'd like to, Chip. I would, but I got to get myself on into Mr. Boseman's office now."

"Boseman? The museum director?"

"Yep." As he spoke, Mule broke out in a broad smile. When he spoke again, it was in a lighter voice, without the appealing cowboy twang. "I'm working for the museum this summer, leading six different groups on pack–train vacations around the Northern California Gold Country."

Shipman laughed. "What do you do the other three seasons, teach school?"

"You guessed it. I teach speech and drama to gifted students at Horace Mann Middle School, but I never teach summer classes."

Chip and Mule arranged to get together for lunch after Mule's meeting with Mr. Boseman. At lunch, Chip said next to nothing. He spoke, mostly in questions, only to keep Mule rambling on about the joys of the wild, wide open spaces of the Utah desert. And all the while, Chip was fascinated with the man sitting across from him. Even though the bodies he worked out with at the health club wore less and often had more massive muscles, he had never felt much like looking at them. Now, every gesture Mule made sent ripples across the muscles of Chip's chest and tightened the knots in Chip's gut. If he breathed deeply, Chip could smell the rich, warm scent of Mule's leather. If he watched closely he could see, along the edge of Mule's vest, one pec thicken as he lifted his coffee.

Of course, the California Academy of Art in Golden Gate Park, San Francisco, didn't send its valued members to the Great Salt Lake Desert. Mule's pack trains on the museum program would start and end at Plymouth, California, on the Cosumnes River. But, after the third excursion, he'd be taking a nine–day break. Of those nine days, he planned to spend seven riding from Wendover, Utah, through the base of the Silver Island Mountains, then northeast around the Great Salt Lake. He even said that at the place where his trip turned around, he wouldn't be more than an hour's ride from Promontory Point.

Mule's eyes were closed and his head had dropped to one side. Chip was entranced. He'd never wanted anything as much as he wanted, just then, to pack up and go east into the wilds with Mule. He wanted to feel the desert "rush up and sit on ye and not move for an hour," the way Mule said it did. He wanted to hear the Indians singing, and to know just how it felt to have that peace "soakin' deeper 'n' deeper" in him as he went farther into the desert.

The rudest thing the world could possibly do to Chip and Mule when they woke from their daydreams was just to still be there. And, it was. Reality came knocking in the form of the waitress sloshing coffee into their cups and dropping the bill right into a coffee puddle.

Before Chip went back to work, he had to ask, "Is there any chance I could go with you when you go out to Utah?"

"Heck, Chip," Mule said in full Western character, "I swear ye'd never like it a bit. I know I make it sound sweeter'n a blonde whore on a Saturday night, but it wouldn't be, not for you." Chip thought of his own blond hair, and he wished he could be there on Mule's mythical Saturday night.

As they walked back to the museum's visitor parking area where Mule's modern, teacherly Toyota was parked, Chip felt he had to somehow get through to Mule. He absolutely *had* to be allowed to go along on the desert ride. "I know how to ride a horse," he said, recognizing the sound of a little boy begging Dad for a favor in his voice. "I took lessons for two summers when I was 10 and 11. And...." He was stumped to come up with any other arguments against his being left out, but he wasn't going to give up easily.

Mule suddenly seemed far away. Chip thought he might have blown it, whining wasn't going to get him invited along. Just outside the employees–only side entrance to the Academy, a yard or two behind Mule's car, the two men stopped and turned to look at one another. Suddenly, like a loose fence post blown by the wind, Chip felt something in himself lean toward Mule. It was all he could do to stop his body from following through as this inner weight strained toward the other man.

After a long, tense moment during which Chip was sure he felt something also straining toward himself, something from inside Mule, the silence between them was broken. Mule sighed deeply, gave a taut grin, then looked down at the ground as he spoke, still sticking to his cowboy voice. "A few fancy, city–boy lessons in arena riding are not the same thing. Won't do, you know. Out on the trail, it's all different. Ye need ropin' an' knot–tyin', the right kind o' habits about food 'n' water. Ye need to be able to saddle up, take care of your own horse an' a pack horse. Ye need to know how to pack a horse and pace a horse, an' how t'pace y'self, too."

Chip wasn't sure what he was hearing. Was he being told to learn all of this in the next several weeks, or was this really an argument to prove he couldn't possibly go? "I could learn," he said very tentatively. "I could enroll in a survival course. No, a riding school—whatever it takes. Believe me, Mule, I can be ready. I learn fast."

Mule looked into Chip's eyes and screwed his face into a look of complete disb lief which slowly faded into a rather condescending smile. Then, taking a deep breath, he spoke in a very serious tone, completely free of the simple, cowboy twang. "Maybe you can learn it all, the basics at least, but you won't find it in any survival school or riding classes," he said. "I have a friend who used to ride with me when I did the bigger vacation groups. He knows everything." Mule had put an odd twist on the word "everything" as he said it, then he repeated it two more times. "Every *thing*," he said, "everything?"

Chip was relieved and frightened. That "everything" made it all sound impossible. Then Mule stepped closer. He reached out and patted Chip on the chest, sort of cupping one pec in his hand and giving it a bit of a squeeze. "Be home tonight at six," he said in a sharp, commanding tone, "and I'll have my friend—Dick's his name—give you a call. You're listed?" he asked, to which Chip only nodded, shocked by the tone Mule was taking. "If he'll take the time to work with you, and you'll pay him whatever it is he's asking for... well, maybe things'll work out after all." Mule's voice had slowly switched into the cowboy register again, and he had put that strange spin on the word "whatever."

Whatever Dick asked, though, Chip would pay.

Three times over the next seven weeks, Chip and Mule met for lunch. Each time Mule grilled the younger man about what he had learned. Each time Chip was sure that he would impress Mule, but each time Mule seemed disturbed about something in Chip's description of his progress. At their last meeting, Mule seemed on the verge of finally saying that Chip could not go on the ride. This brought Chip's reserve plan into play: "Let me come with you," he said, "and let me show you how ready I am. You'll never know any other way, really you won't. And..." Chip swallowed hard as he prepared to say the last bit of his speech. "And, if I can't keep up or can't do all my own chores–in fact, if I'm anything less than a *help* to you–just say so, and I'll turn back on my own." After a couple of long deep breaths he added, "I'll turn back with no hard feelings."

For a moment Mule's face looked hard, and Chip knew that his own face must be showing the fear he was feeling. He closed his eyes and tried to brace himself for what Mule was going to say. He heard nothing, but he felt both of Mule's hands close around his own hand which had been lying on the table between them. This, being touched, not pulling away had even become a part of Chip's training. Suddenly he knew that, and he realized he now felt none of the discomfort he had felt when Mule had touched his chest on the day they met or when Dick touched him, time after time, in the training sessions. Trembling, unable to be sure whether the trembling showed, he waited.

Eventually, in a calm, low voice, Mule said, "I know y'been doing real good with Dick. There's a thing or two, though, he doesn't think yer ready to learn. Do you have any idea what I'm talkin' about, Chip?"

Looking at his own freshly–calloused hand wrapped in Mule's weathered grip, Chip nodded. Then, very tentatively, he cupped his other hand over the three on the table. "I think I know," he said without looking up. "I think it's something Dick wanted to teach me, but I'd rather have it from you... Sir."

Mule whispered, "That's Mule, Chip, always will be. Has to be."

On June 21, the day Mule and Chip flew out of San Francisco to Salt Lake City, Chip felt he had as good a cowboy act as Mule did, and he knew he had learned everything Mule said he needed to know to make the trip easy. The one big lesson, the one he wouldn't let Dick teach him, was haunting him, though. He wondered if he had really understood what it was. Mule was a little less sure of Chip's new–found trail skills, but he knew they'd be all right.

In Salt Lake, a friend of Mule's met them and flew them to a ranch near Wendover. Chip found it "darned funny" to hear Mule's friend calling him Ricky.

By sunset Chip and Mule were ready to go, and they took advantage of the full moon to ride almost 20 miles in the night before they made camp. There were no books, cameras, radios, or tape players in their packs, but Chip had brought along a heavy roll of silhouette paper and two pairs of tiny surgical scissors.

As soon as camp was set up, while Mule put supper on the fire, Chip started to sketch. After supper he cut out the first picture he'd made in months. It had the two saddle horses and two pack horses standing together to one side, and Mule squatted down next to the fire in the center. The other end of the paper-cutting was open space with just a couple of short, twisted trees breaking the line of the desert horizon.

After he mounted the black silhouette on a white background, Chip handed it to Mule. When Mule didn't say anything, Chip began to apologize for his work. "Of course, I know it's nothing like the cutting of the meeting at the Golden Spike. I mean, I'm no good at this yet, and I do a lot better job with a tabletop to work on, but..."

Mule looked up, his eyes were wet, and he was smiling a tough but radiant smile. "Dammit, Chip, shut up! This is the most beautiful piece of paper in the world, and I won't have you talkin' against it."

Chip was shocked. Without thinking for a moment of what he was doing, he stood up and just about fell in Mule's lap. Mule whipped the cutting out of the way, dropping it safely on the ground to his right, and caught Chip in his powerful arms.

Chip's legs ended up stretched out on the ground behind him, his arms were pinned to his sides in Mule's embrace. "Mule," he said.

"Shut up," was all Chip heard as Mule rolled to the left. The stars spun and shimmered as Chip, feeling almost paralyzed, just lay there gazing up. Mule pulled his arms out from under Chip and gripped both Chip's biceps in his hands. He leaned forward, putting all his weight into his hands and lowered himself onto Chip's body.

A moment later the stars were blotted out by Mule's face hovering over Chip's. Mule pushed Chip's vest back off his shoulders. Although he could have shrugged the stiff, new leather back into place, Chip let the folded cowhide prevent him from moving his arms. He felt the cool night air rush through the light brush of hair on his chest as Mule peeled back his shirt. And he felt a searing heat as Mule's mouth clamped over his right nipple.

Chip began bucking wildly. He didn't know, he didn't think, he didn't care what was happening. He just wanted to press every inch of his body against Mule. Suddenly Mule pulled away and stood up. "Simmer down, boy," he said, "just simmer down."

Chip sat up, and the stiff edge of his too–new chaps seemed practically to cut through his hard cock. Mule reached over, grabbed the neck of Chip's vest, and lifted him to his feet, twisting him around as he did. Chip felt he must have done something wrong as he straightened up, trying to get his balance. He stood for a second facing away from Mule, feeling lost and lonely. Mule took Chip's vest and shirt off him with one easy motion.

Chip heard Mule step away from him, but he still didn't move. Then, a moment later, Mule was back. He wrapped a rope loosely around both of Chip's wrists eight or ten times, looping the end of the rope back up between the wrists. Then he tied all the bands of rope around Chip's wrists together, tightening the cowboy handcuffs.

"March," was all Mule said, and Chip started walking. He was confused, but he was not resisting. As the toes of his boots bumped into a saddle on the ground, Chip stopped. Mule moved around him, picked up a pack saddle and stacked it atop the riding saddle at Chip's feet. "Sit there," Mule said in a deep, threatening voice, "and get out of your clothes."

Chip turned, sat, and wondered how, with his hands tied behind his back, he could do what Mule said. He found that he could slide his bound hands down over his ass and legs, and get them in front of himself. A minute later he had stripped off his boots, socks, chaps, jeans, and underwear. He stood still for a moment, knowing Mule's eyes were examining his body. For the first time in his life, he felt proud of himself. He knew every muscle was well defined and beautifully developed, that the symmetry of his bodybuilding had been perfectly supervised. Even his cock, stretching nine inches out into the night air, was looking fine. He knew it was.

"Pretty soggy bunch of muscles," Mule said, "with nary a trace of honest work in any of 'em." Then he moved toward Chip, picking up a six-foot length of rope from the sand. He folded the rope in half and stepped nearer still, off to one side. Slam. The rope bit into Chip's chest. Crack. The second stinging blow was harder, but somehow it was easier to take. Again and again the rope snapped against Chip's chest and across his thighs until he knew he was going to start screaming with the next blow. No, the next... the next, but then it stopped. Chip felt free, light, relieved, then lonely, aching again for Mule's intense attention. Nothing happened for a long, long minute, and Chip couldn't see where Mule had moved to.

"Get your hands behind you," Mule ordered, "and kneel by those saddles." Chip found that the boiling pain on his chest and legs turned to an unbearable, raging fire as he bent to step over his wrists, but he did as he was told. Mule pushed Chip's face down against the pack saddle. The mixed smells of the pine frame, the thick leather, and the horse sweat rushed into Chip's lungs. He breathed deeply, eagerly stretching his senses in the direction of The West.

Again the rope began to tear at Chip's body. Up and down his back, across his ass, even on his bent legs, the rope was raising welts. He could feel each stripe rise, heat up, and then disappear in the wake of new welts.

Chip was lost in the pain, thrilling to a pleasure he didn't even try to understand when he saw Mule's stark, moon–made shadow shoot across the sand and bend up the stack of saddles beneath his face. It seemed the shadow itself added a musky odor to the hot smells he was already breathing. He turned his face up to find Mule—his Levi's unbuttoned, his cock and balls sticking out, huge, just inches away.

"They say if y'piss in a dog's water, y'make him loyal t'the death," Mule snarled. "You my dog now? Are y'boy?" Chip nodded and felt something new pressing at him from inside his head. Fear. That was it. His eyes were stretched open with fear, and just then Mule's piss began splashing against his face. Slowly, his mouth drooped open, and Mule directed the foaming stream against his teeth before he stepped up and stuck his still–pissing cock into the waiting mouth.

The piss stopped. Chip needed more, he *needed* to please and serve Mule, so he started sucking. Mule stiffened, grabbed Chip roughly by the hair and ears and shot his load down Chip's throat. Then, without a word, he reached down Chip's back and gave the rope around his wrists a sharp tug before he walked away.

Chip soon realized that he could just shake off the rope from his wrists. He picked up the rope and rolled it into a neat, tied–in coil the way Dick had taught him. Then he looked around. His clothes were already stacked next to his pack. Mule was stripping down for the night. He had spread both bedrolls out into one. Then, without looking Chip's direction, he walked away from the bedrolls, further away from Chip. He looked magnificent in the moonlight. His broad, square shoulders stayed level as a table until he sat down on a rounded boulder at the edge of the flat–topped rise they were camped on.

Chip was suddenly quite shocked. It wasn't what had just happened with the ropes, and saddles, and Mule's cock. Even though he had never before touched a man's cock, that all seemed perfectly natural. The thing was, he remembered what Mule had said earlier. Mule felt about his cutting the way he himself felt. It was perfect, completely different than anything he'd ever done before. He wanted to give the cutting to Mule, but, on the other hand, he didn't want to break the silence that stretched across the open space and connected the two of them. A little later, just after Chip slipped in among the blankets to wait for Mule, he saw the powerfully beautiful silhouette of the man he wanted to be with as it moved still further away from the camp. At the very brink of the mesa, Mule stood and sang a couple of bittersweet cowboy songs to the moon.

Each of the next two nights Chip made another new sketch before supper, and cut it afterwards. He knew they were even better than the one he made the first night out. He also noticed that Mule sang better and better each night as the desert got into him. And the interludes between Chip's art work and Mule's songs got hotter and hotter, too.

Every night Mule tied Chip's hands. Every night the lashings with the rope were longer, harder, and sweeter. Every night Chip got a faceful of salty, smelly piss, a belly–full of hot, delicious piss, and a mouthful of Mule's sharp, thick cum. Through the days, he felt his clothes riding against the rope marks, and twice in one day he came. Just riding along, feeling the weight of his leather and denim against the red creases in his skin, his cock pushed down into the tight space between his chaps and his leg. It lay there being squeezed with every step his horse took. Then, slow and easy, his aching nuts drained into his jeans.

On the fourth evening, shortly before sunset, the short–term cowboys came around the north end of the Great Salt Lake.

Almost immediately after they had turned south again, they came to a railroad line. The tracks were gravel–banked, about eight feet up from ground level. To make the crossing easier on the horses, the men decided to ride east to a road where, fortunately, there were no cars.

"Down there a piece," Mule said, "is the Promontory Point you were talkin' 'bout... guess 'at's where the east meets the west... was once, anyways." Chip looked down the track. It was a remarkable sight, barley fields showing bright green on either side of the railroad's right-of-way. Promontory Point, Mule guessed, was about six miles out, northeast.

"Let's ride over to the Golden Spike National Monument, Mule. I'd love to see it." Chip was excited enough to forget his cowboy voice.

Mule's answer was sharp. "You're fergettin' y'SELF now, boy!" He went on, more calmly. "They'd be crowds and cars and all such stuff as belongs to a time yet-to-be over there t'the monument. 'Member, we're here... out in the west, on our own. Got that, boy?"

Chip understood and, after a moment's embarrassment, accepted what Mule said completely. This close brush with the 20th Century chastened him. He found himself actually disgusted by the thought of what he might have seen just over the next rise, at the monument and in the park. Symbols of everything he was escaping on this trip would be there. Families, reminding him of his discomfort with his own family, would be poking around the site of the Golden Spike. He didn't want to be reminded of families. He loved his parents well enough, and he got along with them most of the time. Still, the simple life he wanted and the *successful* world they wanted him to live in just weren't a match. Nothing clicked. And, it wasn't just his parents. Schools, museums, hurrying, frozen food, noise, and even people he didn't know... it all just fit together in a pattern that was inescapable back in Chip's real life. The pattern—whatever it might mean to anyone else—was a dreary round of necessities and requirements, nothing in it made sense to him.

The men rode on in silence, easing eastward with the terrain. They must have ridden about four miles beyond the railroad tracks by the time they stopped for the night. As he built the fire, Chip heard a car horn. He looked up and caught Mule's eye. "Kiowa, I'd say. What d'ye think?" Mule didn't wait for an answer. "I do wonder what brought 'em this far north. Kiowas usually stay down about the Oklahoma Territory."

Mule was not making a joke. He was dead serious. Chip had to help him patch the atmosphere and erase the car horn, or they'd have to pitch in and move before they even had supper. "Well," Chip said after a moment, "dunno, Mule, but they been tryin' to round up 'n' trap six bands of the Kiowa an' put 'em together on one reservation down there."

"So I hear. Like as not, one band is up here, just hidin' away from the Cavalry."

"Yep," Chip said, "like as not."

They made it through supper all right, but with the extra effort to keep their minds back in the middle of the Nineteenth Century, Mule didn't feel like singing, and Chip couldn't work up any sketch to cut out that night. So, silently aware that it was mostly to be sure they were out of reach of the next noise from the highway, they turned in early.

On the three previous nights Chip had stayed pretty much on his side of the sleeping spread, always being sure an arm or leg was out far enough to touch Mule, but just touch him. Tonight, with no lashing or cocksucking, he felt almost as though he had been sent to bed without his dinner. He hesitated. He couldn't reach over to touch Mule, no matter how much he wanted to. So he lay there, holding his own cock in one hand and keeping the other floating a bare inch away from Mule's tight stomach muscles.

Mule was awake too. "Dammit, boy, get down there and suck my cock," he said in a easy, even–toned drawl. Chip started crawling under the blankets, feeling that his arms and legs had somehow gotten tangled and were slowing him down. Then Mule kicked the covers off and, in one powerful move, rose to his feet, bringing Chip half–way up at the same time.

As Mule's thick, hard cock began plunging into Chip's throat, he fell onto all fours, stretching his neck and mouth to reach and accommodate the welcome assault. It seemed to go on for hours. Mule would plug away at Chip's mouth for a while, then stop. He'd fuck the upturned face again, and stop. Mule's cock stayed rock hard, but Chip knew something was wrong.

"Spread out there, boy," Mule growled. Chip wanted to do as he was told, but he didn't know what Mule wanted. After a moment's confusion, he flattened out, face down on the blankets, spreading his arms and legs out, making a taut X of his body.

"Good form," Mule said, almost chuckling, "but get over in the sand, we don't need to fuck up our blankets." The sand felt rough on the still–red stripes all over the front of Chip's body, but it was also cool. Chip could almost feel himself melting into the sand, but as he relaxed that way, the soothing cool was replaced by a grating pain.

Chip heard some rustling noises, then nothing—a long, deep, silent nothing. "Just about tore it all down today, didn't y'boy?" Mule's voice was harder than Chip had ever heard it. "Didn't y'boy?" Mule punctuated the repeated question by slapping Chip's ass hard with his broad, heavy, tooled–leather belt. After the third hard stroke, Chip heard Mule muttering to himself, "Teach him to go thinking about the future." He deserved his punishment, and he took it. When Mule finally stopped belting his ass, Chip lay still. He didn't expect to get to suck Mule's cock again. He didn't expect anything more. Then the piss started flowing, playing over the hot, aching bands of swollen skin where the belt had been tearing at his ass.

Then Mule walked around and stood by Chip's head. He knelt and lifted Chip's face up in one hand. With the other hand, the belt still dangling in it, he wiped the tears off Chip's face. And he leaned down and kissed Chip. The kiss was long and hard;

it left Chip's lips feeling as bruised as his ass, but it let him know he had not ruined everything, that the punishment was over, that he was forgiven... and loved.

Some time in the early hours of the morning, Chip woke up. From over the ridge north of the camp he heard a lot of noise. It sounded like a lot of people, including a lot of children. Then he remembered: The Promontory Point, the Golden Spike Park... it must be that close.

He pulled up out of the bedding and walked to the top of the ridge to look in spite of an inner voice that kept saying "don't." He stood for several minutes at the very brink of the ridge not looking north, but breathing in the peaceful view of the campsite. Mule was still sleeping.

Atlast, Chip turned around.

What he saw below was amazing. There, on the tracks at the bottom of the slope, were the Central Pacific and Union Pacific engines and their coal cars. Between them were a dozen men. Some of the men were in suits, some were laborers with hammers. All of them and everyone else in sight were dressed in the clothing of the Nineteenth Century. There was a band standing by, and a huge crowd.

It took Chip several seconds to work out what he was looking at. It was a celebration of some sort, a re-enactment of the meeting of the rails. He would surely have understood much more quickly if he hadn't just spent three days and four nights acting out a life for himself in just about the same historic period. "Why," he whispered to himself, "is the day of May 10, 1869, being celebrated on. . ." He couldn't remember the *actual* date right away. He knew that it was the summer of nineteen-eighty something. It didn't matter.

He ran back to the camp and woke Mule. "Hey, look alive! There's a big party down in the park right now and everyone's dressed up like it's 1869 and they've got replicas of the trains there and everything."

"Whazzat? Hold yer horses." Mule sat up, rubbing his eyes,

then he squinted hard and raised one eyebrow. "I don' care if they're fightin' the Injun wars down there, or diggin' the transcontinental canal. Fer Pete's sake, I'm not goin' anywhere's near *them*."

Chip saw there was no hope of budging Mule, but he had to try one more time. Calmly, he said, "Don't you see, Mule? They're kinda doin' the same thing as we are."

"No. No, they ain't!" Mule sounded at least a little bit angry. "Having a party about Yee Oldie West is not the same thing as being there." Chip gave up on Mule, but he was going down the slope anyway. As he stood up to go, Mule slipped back down under the blankets saying, "Wake me up in 'bout 'nother 30 minutes... when the light's clear, boy."

"Sure, Mule, I'll do it," Chip said. Then he saddled a horse, picked up his canvas bag, and rode over the ridge.

When Mule woke up, the sun was high and Chip was nowhere to be found. After an hour or two of searching around the mesa where they were camped, Mule went over the ridge to the tourist information office in the park. He asked about the celebration, whether the festivities had been carried into town or over to the lake front. No one there knew anything about any party. No one had seen any young man fitting Chip's description, or, for that matter, anyone at all besides Mule on horseback.

Eventually, Mule decided Chip had taken their little disagreement too hard and gone back to San Francisco. They had agreed he'd do that if things didn't work out. Mule had insisted on that agreement being perfectly clear before he'd let Chip come along. So, he put it out of his mind—except he did realize that a missing saddle horse would be hard to explain if Chip hadn't found a way to return it.

Still, the ride back without Chip didn't have the magic of the ride out. Mule sat in the evenings staring at one after another of the three papercuttings Chip had made. There was magic enough in them, almost, to make Mule feel like Chip was there, somewhere just out of sight.

Back in San Francisco, Mule went to Chip's house right away. There was no one home. So, with the papercuttings rolled up, ready to be handed over when he found Chip, Mule went to the museum. He stopped at the desk. "Where'll I find Shipman Reid?" he asked, almost laughing at himself remembering to use Chip's whole name.

"Second floor, north gallery, Western Americana," the receptionist said, as if there were no other place Chip would ever be.

Mule looked around the gallery. There was Chip, dressed in his docent's jacket, standing in front of the papercutting of the meeting at the Golden Spike. "Chip," Mule shouted as he crossed the room. Chip turned around, but he wasn't Chip. It was some other docent, hushing Mule with a finger to his lips.

"Sorry. Do you know where Shipman Reid is?" Mule asked in a whisper.

"Right here," said the docent, pointing to the papercutting and stepping aside.

Mule looked at the cutting, back at the docent, then back to the cutting again before he noticed that, snipped out in neat letters along the bottom edge of the silhouette, were the words, "For Mule, By Chip Reid."

After a minute or two and a lot of long, slow breaths, Mule turned to the docent. "Amazing, isn't it?"

"Did you know," the docent volunteered, "that this picture is a single sheet of silhouette paper cut into this expressive and intricate pattern by Shipman 'Chip' Reid?" Mule just stared at the cutting. "Using tiny pointed scissors and sometimes a knife," the docent went on, "paper has been carved into pictures like this for more that 1,500 years."

Mule smiled. "I'll be," was all he could say.

AND THEN THERE WERE THREE

Bill Lee

The lift rack crashed to the floor and Brian looked up startled at the forklift operator. He knew immediately that he had met his Master. The green eyes flecked with brown stared straight through him, set off by the red-blond hair and freckled skin of the type the British called "ginger."

Gordon, Brian's new boss, had characteristically, audibly reacted to the noisy greeting, giving a little squeal. Gordon was showing Brian around on his first day on the job as assistant director in the graphic arts department, and they had ended the tour in the warehouse. Brian wasn't sure why, since he would have little if any contact with the shipping department. He guessed it was just fate that he met Steve in just that way at that particular time. Steve's rugged face, his thick muscles, his broad chest sweating through the black T-shirt — all seemed designed to capture Brian's fantasy and weaken his resolve to approach the new job without distractions.

Steve hadn't wasted any time. The next afternoon Brian received a curt phone call from the warehouse. Without any preliminaries, the gruff voice had said merely, "Meet me at the parking-lot entrance at 5:30," and Brian immediately knew who it was. When the truck pulled up in front of him, Steve gestured for him to get into the cab and Brian complied with little hesitation, except for the minor concern about his best suit in contact with the obviously greasy cushions and having to straddle his briefcase.

Steve had taken him to his house in his pick-up, ignoring Brian's car in the parking lot and his attempts at conversation during the ride. They entered the back door of an older house on the seamier side of Oakland, and Steve pushed him down the back stairs into his dark dungeon with a growled command to undress. A few minutes later Brian was naked, pale, and trembling in the chilliness of the basement and with trepidations about his fate as he watched his new Master strip off his sweat-soaked clothes.

"Come here," Steve ordered, picking up a cat-o'-nine tails and smacking the handle against his other paw. Brian's legs wobbled as he started to obey, but Steve's "Crawl, dammit!" solved the problem of walking. The concrete floor with a thin covering of black rubberized mat was cold as he scuttled across the floor and looked up at the forbidding figure above. Steve was massively muscular although not actually tall; his broad chest had a nest of red hair around each nipple and a streak of red strands coursed down the midline of his belly to end in a flaming bush surrounding a thick, uncut cock. It was growing large as he stared down at his new slave.

"After a long, hard day I need a bath, and you're going to give it to me."

Brian fell to with enthusiasm. His Master's raunchy feet, spread staunchly on the mat, reeked strongly as Brian's nose drew near; he encountered rolls of grime between the toes when his tongue snaked out to relish those workman foundations for the red-decked, muscular pillars. The dried sweat coated his taste buds as he lapped greedily, the blunt toes with their coarse, red hairs curling with his efforts.

"Between them, slave," Steve growled. The whip slashed down unexpectedly over his naked back and trembling butt, and Brian groaned as the pain heightened his ardor. Quickly his tongue intruded between the stubby first and second digits, but when he moved on before Steve was ready, the whip slashed down again. When both feet were finally cleaned and polished to his Master's satisfaction, Brian's back and ass cheeks were streaked with welts and his cock was lurching rigidly against his belly.

"Work your way up," Steve commanded, and the coarse red hairs on his thick legs were soon plastered wetly against the muscular columns. When each hair had been lovingly cleansed and smoothed, Brian concentrated on the grooves between the tense calf and thigh muscles, outlining the massive strength and superiority of his new Master.   When he neared the groin, the thick and heavy rigidity nudged his forehead and tangled in his dark, curly hair as he worked, but he did not dare to touch it despite his nearly unconquerable desire to worship it as it deserved.

"My armpits need cleaning, slave," Steve snarled, and he raised his arms for Brian's face, the damp, musky odor permeating his senses. He rose to nuzzle and lap the sweaty pits, the red hair long and luxurious, and when Steve clamped down on his face, the bulging muscles trapping him in those aromatic valleys brought his tortured balls close to explosion.

His cock probed stiffly against his Master's hairy thighs, and Steve encircled it along with the threatening balls in a work-roughened fist. He bore down hard, nearly suffocating his victim in his armpit as he compressed the throbbing genitals, and Brian's control was lost. He gave a strangled cry and jetted thick streams of juice over his Master's thigh. His knees gave way, his only support the vice-like grip on his balls and prick gushing white and viscous.

"Fuckin' pig," Steve grunted disgustedly, as the white cream ran downhis leg in thick rivulets. He swore repeatedly but did not release the pressure until the streams began to taper off. "Lick it up!" And even as Brian continued to dribble, he knelt to lap up his own cum as it coursed down his Master's hairy leg. His cock lost none of its rigidity as he worked, the ingestion of his own spending seeming to preserve his potency.

"Clean up my asshole, pig!" was the next command. Quickly Brian scurried around the spread pillars, and his Master's hard, round globes beckoned invitingly. Between them the red hairs grew sparsely, but as his Master bent forward he could see an abundant thatch surrounding the pink pucker. Brian pressed his face deep into that valley, his tongue searching and probing, and he tasted and smelled the heavy musk and sweat of working-man's asshole. His cock lurched strongly again, the red hairs curling on his tongue even as it lapped up the deposits left there. He could feel the muscle ring dilate as he probed and the butt cheeks tense around his face as he licked it clean.

"Eat it out – clean it up – eat ass, pig!" Steve grated through clenched teeth. "Lap up my shit!" Brian grasped the rock-hard mounds, separating them for his avid service, trying to reach further and further into the hot, murky channel. Steve grunted and panted, shoving back hard against the gobbling face. Brian's dark, bristly mustache seemed to bring special enjoyment to the sensitive tissues.

After only a few moments of this bliss, Steve straightened and swung around, his heavy prick slapping his slave's face like a bludgeon. "Suck it down, pig!" he ordered, and Brian, long deprived of this most precious gift, slurped as much as he could into his gasping throat. He was filled with pulsing prong, his lips spread widely to accommodate as much as he could, the bulbous head pushing everything else aside as it plundered his mouth and gullet. Tortuous veins ridged the massive shaft, and Brian could taste the oozing precum on his tongue as his Master set up rapid fucking movements. Brian clasped the hairy thighs for stability in the storm.

"Ugh, shit," Steve growled, his knees beginning to tremble. "Get up in that fuckin' sling," he snarled. "Got to fuck you now!"

Brian rose quickly but not quickly enough for his Master. Steve picked him up and literally threw him into the swaying sling. Not bothering to wait until the ankles were supported by the stirrups, he smeared some lube on his thick prick and shoved it into his slave's asshole in one continuous movement. Brian screamed from the massive and painful invasion, the hot poker sending searing swords of savagery through his shaking frame. But then the encompassing, throbbing fullness overtook him and turned his terror into aching desire and acceptance of his new Master with the monster prick.

Steve held the stiffly–thrusting legs wide and high and began a furious raping of his new slave. In and out the thick club moved, penetrating deeply and withdrawing fully, and with each movement the slave's cock gave a fresh lurch, dribbling precum over his spasming belly. Brian moaned and shuddered, ravaged relentlessly but exhilarated to the peak of his passion. He clutched the chains holding him with fervent hopes that he could withstand the vicious onslaught. The fire-red crotch beat against his asshole with each thrust, the heavy balls aching to unload, and then there was no turning back.

Steve emitted a bestial bellow and crested, his massive prick jerking and throbbing deep in the cavern and spurting his man-juice deeply into the quivering receptacle. Over and over he plunged, each time jetting hotly and heavily, filling the clutching tunnel with his virility. Brian met each stroke with avid greed, begging for more, seeking no solace.

Even after Steve's fury had subsided, his cock softening and relenting, Brian continued to twitch and jerk spasmodically in his Master's fists. His cock slithered helplessly in the pool of juice collecting on his belly, and as the softening cock slipped out, Steve bent to take his slave's aching tool into his mouth. Immediately he received the dammed-up flood rushing to overflow its constraints, the rich brew spurting thickly down the Master's parched throat.

That was Brian's introduction to his slavery to Steve. Soon it became a routine — each night after work he would join Steve in his truck and, with little conversation, they would return to the ramshackle house for a heavy beating or lashing until Steve's balls demanded release, and then Brian would receive the hot load that had built up in the sweaty crotch of his Master during the day. Frequently there would be a second session later before going to sleep, but at those times Steve seemed tired and the tempo was more leisurely. He was not quite as vicious with the paddle and whip.

As time passed, Brian became more proficient in his job, and his talent inevitably revealed his supervisor, Gordon, as relatively incompetent. The older man's queenish peculiarities had become more and more grating with everyone at the office, and one day

Brian was informed that Gordon had been terminated and he was now in charge. This meant that he had a staff of ten or twelve people to supervise and his administrative abilities were called into play. Although unusually young for that amount of responsibility, Brian found he liked being in charge, especially in an atmosphere requiring a combination of artistry and executive skills, and blossomed professionally under the challenge.

That meant nothing to Steve, of course; to Steve he remained a thing to ravage, a hole to fuck, a servant to carry out the household chores. Their conversations were usually stilted, since Steve had no sensitivity for artistic subjects and Brian cared nothing for batting averages; he could not force himself to become engrossed in watching baseball games on TV, Steve's favorite pastime.

They rarely left the house at night, but if they did visit a bar or any place other men congregated, Steve always ogled the young, preppy boys. To Brian's relief, however, few of them responded, probably because Steve was nearing forty years old and they were usually interested in others their own age. Sometimes they went across the Bay to The Eagle where many master/slave couples made themselves apparent, but Steve never seemed to want to talk to any of them. Steve and Brian always returned home by themselves.

Brian took to working out in the gym and jogging when he could, much to Steve's ridicule, although his muscles thickened and his body improved with each passing day.

One day Steve showed up unexpectedly at the gym as Brian was finishing his workout, growling that he wanted an early dinner so he could attend a night A's baseball game. Brian hurried to shower but noticed Steve hanging back, his eyes devouring a doe-eyed kid barely out of his teens struggling with the weights. When Brian returned from his shower, Steve was in conversation with the young blond, and when they left for home the boy Roger was wedged between them on the seat of the truck.

Steve forgot all about the game. When they arrived at the house, he led the way to the basement and locked the door behind them. "All right, you great fuckin' body-builders," he sneered, "I want to see you get it on together — two slaves showin' their artificial muscles while waitin' for a real man to take you both on. Strip down — let me see how you kin amuse me."

Roger blanched and started for the door, but Steve had the only key. The blond looked to Brian for help, but Brian was already undressing, responding to his Master without hesitation but his mind in a whirl, not sure what was expected of him.

As he looked more closely at their captive, Brian realized that there was more to Roger than he had originally thought. He was young, that was sure, but he had broad shoulders and a maturing body that invited admiration, and the expression in his eyes was hardly naive fear that Steve apparently wished for.

"Come on, kid, take 'em off — I liked what I saw of that fuzzy, blond ass," Steve snarled, and Roger hesitantly complied. In a moment, a nude Brian, several inches taller and twenty pounds heavier than the trim blond, seemed to tower over the naked, muscular boy, although the long, slim cock was hardening in its silvery nest. Steve had also stripped and was fingering his thickening cock in a hairy fist, his eyes fixed on that extra-long cock with a loose foreskin. Two perfectly-matched balls swung cleanly in their lightly-haired sack. Roger's eyes flicked from Brian to Steve and back. Brian took charge as ordered.

He strode purposefully to Roger and gently tweaked his nipples. Roger looked at him questioningly but with awakening desire as his its peaked in the convincing fingers. Gradually Brian became more forceful, eventually gripping them tightly and twisting between his fingers. Roger cringed a little, but his cock was jerking rigidly. He looked up into Brian's piercing eyes, but could see only a dark blankness. Abruptly Brian pulled him close and, bending him over his knees with one arm, began to spank him soundly. "Hey!" Roger gulped, but the stinging hand brought further starch to his cock while bringing a flush to his face. By the time his ripe melons were glowing pink, he was gulping and groaning but no longer resisting.

Brian pushed him into the sling face down, his reddened butt protruding lewdly. Quickly the new Master shackled his wrists to the chains at the head end of the sling, and Roger was swaying helpless on his toes, his cock trapped pointing downward at the ass-end of the sling. The legs were unexpectedly muscular, the thighs swelling massively to end in trim, rounded buns. His back was broad for a young man, showing evidence of the heavy weights he was lifting. Brian picked up the cat as Roger watched apprehensively, his eyes wide and intent. Brian raised the cat high over his head and —

The knotted thongs struck briskly but gently, not even leaving stripes on the youthful shoulders. The Master drew the thongs back slowly over the curving back and into the ass crease, and Roger sighed and shook from the liquid contact. He had gripped the chains tightly in fear at first, but then almost fondly as his bondage began to embrace him. With each succeeding blow of the whip, the surge became stronger and the thongs cut deeper; each time the kiss of the leather drawn down over his ass became more intimate, more demanding. Soon red welts began to appear with each stroke, and Roger was gasping in awe of the power of his Master. His cock continued to jerk and thrust alone, aimed at the floor.

Steve stroked his thick prick as he watched the action, but he was ignored by the pair whom he had put into action.

Brian dropped the whip to the floor and picked up a broad leather paddle with a large wooden handle. Roger's eyes followed it fearfully until his Master returned to the boy's ass, smiling at the red welts that criss-crossed his muscled back. Roger began to protest, realizing the damage that thick paddle could do and knowing he was powerless to resist. Brian raised the paddle and — gently stroked down the backbone of his victim with the raw edge. Roger jumped with the first contact, but when there was no pain, no massive infliction of injury, he seemed almost disappointed and arched his back, trying to increase contact with the rough leather, but Brian refused to cooperate. Over and over he caressed the twitching back, first with the edge and then with the flat of the paddle, watching the torment within the tethered body, the boy obviously wanting and yet horrified of the tempting taste of leather.

Brian's touch was subtle but persuasive, giving the boy opportunity to use his imagination while the leather played its own tune on his trembling frame. Steve shifted restlessly, his prick swelling stiffly in his hairy fist and his eyes consuming the twisting young body. Perhaps he was impatient with Brian's "master" technique, so different from his own brutal approach.

Brian unshackled the boy's wrists; he knew he wasn't going anywhere. When he returned to the pink ass he had left, he said, "Spread your ass, boy. Let's see that little pink asshole of yours."

Obediently Roger, one hand on each cheek, spread them wider, and the hairless hole winked nakedly. Repeatedly Brian traced the backbone down with the edge of the paddle, continuing into the ass crack and over the puckered portal. Roger moaned each time, his ass twisting and circling, needing more as time went on. Again he gripped the chains, his knuckles white.

"Please, please," Roger began to plead, and Brian knew what he needed. The next swing of the paddle brought a resounding "Smack" from the bulging buns, and pink became red, blooming brightly. "Ahhh!" Roger moaned, but swung back toward the paddle, needing another taste of its ruthless magic, and again and again Brian brought the paddle to bear. Each time as he raised his arm, the ass crept toward him until Roger was nearly out of the sling, finally using it only for support of his shoulders.

The obvious frustrated desire of the boy brought Brian close to his crest, knowing exactly how the boy felt, and he ached to enter the hairless valley between those young ass cheeks. Roger's feet were firmly planted, spread wide, his muscular legs quivering and his cock lurching rigidly. He gripped the chains at the ass-end of the sling tightly, his biceps swelling as he swung from them.

The long hooded cock of the slave dripped clear fluid in long strings, and Steve moistened his lips as he watched.

Brian was ignoring Steve now, reacting only to his own need and those of his slave, and after one more blow, more emphatic than the others, he dropped the paddle. Quickly he spread some lube on his rampant rod and thrust hard into that tiny asshole winking deliciously. "Oh, God!" Roger cried, swinging forward on the chains, but Brian followed him, his prick shoving hard and straight to the boy's core. The next thrust buried him to the hilt, his black curly hair rasping against the hairless asshole, the hot channel sucking him in to his balls.

With an agonized groan, Steve abandoned his voyeuristic stance and scrambled to his knees in front of Roger. He gobbled the boy's long cock into his throat while Brian set up an agonized fucking rhythm. Each time Brian thrust, he pushed the young cock deep into Steve's throat, and each of them moaned loudly as the depths were plumbed. The black, the blond, and the ginger in a continuous series.

Roger continued to move backward, begging for more and more of that stiff prick that filled his ass so completely. Steve followed on his knees, refusing to give up that long, silver dick that was coating his tongue with sweet juice and promised even more. Roger steadied himself by gripping Steve's bulging shoulders, but Brian continued to hammer those pink buns, his balls tight with impending explosion.

"Yeah, suck — fuck — give it to me..." Roger grunted incoherently, his ass hot and clutching, his prick stiff and threatening. "Fuck my ass — suck that prick, cocksucker — "

Brian gave a hoarse cry and shot deeply and thickly, his legs rigid and trembling, each spurt bringing shudders to his struggling frame. It was his first time to fuck in many months, and he was enjoying it to the fullest. Roger groaned with each jerk of the prick spurting hotly in his ass.

As his Master's thrusts tapered off, Roger almost whimpered with need to discharge. Steve was gobbling him furiously, but it was not enough. Roger bent to pick up the discarded cat and brought the whip down hard on Steve's back as the older man gobbled the boy's prick.

"Suck it, Daddy — suck my fuckin' prick," he gritted, and Steve lurched in shock as the whip whistled down. "Ughhh–Ughhh–" he groaned, impaling himself on the boy's thrusting prick, his pale skin immediately showing the marks of the whip clearly. His fist flew on his own cock as he knelt to service the beautiful boy. "Deeper — deeper, cocksucker!" Roger cried, the whip singing and lashing the broad back bent over its task. "Oh, yeah — take it, cocksucker!" Roger shouted, and flooded Steve's mouth with sweet cum as he continued to lash him with undiminished force.

Steve moaned, the boy-man juice filling his gulping mouth and cascading down his avid throat. Roger began to thrust in and out, facefucking savagely now that Brian had ceased his movements. Then abruptly he pulled out and clamped his still streaming cock in a tight fist to hold in the remaining cum. He began to use the whip as he snarled, "Pull that prick, Daddy! Let me see you squirt your fuckin' juice!" And Steve, his eyes bright and worshipping, the whip streaking his back with each swing of the young, muscular arms, flailed his cock wildly until he shot long streams of white heat over the floor.

The cum splashed over Roger's feet, and then the boy dropped the whip and drew near, shoving his engorged cock into Steve's mouth for his final gush, emptying his balls while Steve moaned with his own climax.

Brian watched this scene with tumult in his brain. There was no question that Steve had thoroughly enjoyed his unaccustomed role. When Roger pulled back, spent and exhausted, Steve bent to lap up his own cum covering the young feet.

But Roger turned to Brian, his lips trembling, and knelt at his feet. He clasped Brian around his knees, kissing his thighs, and rubbing against him with smooth, almost beardless cheeks. "Thank you, Master," he breathed.

Steve stared at the pair and then rose to join them, his mouth working. Roger turned to him briefly.

"On your knees over there, Daddy-slave," Roger ordered. "My Master and I will let you know when we need you again."

THE KANSAS TRAVELER

Starr Delacroix

Marshall looked up at the street clock. It said seven-thirty. He looked at his watch and it also said seven-thirty.

The appointed time had been seven pm. Ninth and Market, south-east corner. Seven pm.

Well, he thought, I'll give it another fifteen minutes and maybe that'll be it. Damn. Tyrelle hadn't seemed a fellow who'd play fast and loose with the feelings of another. No, certainly not. Well, maybe something had come up. Yes, that's probably what happened. Marshall gave that some more thought and decided he'd better wait until eight.

He looked up at the street sign one more time. Ninth and Market. Right. He was new in town but not that new. He sure ought to know Market Street. Stepping aside to avoid a mishap with a street dweller and her shopping cart, he caught his reflection in the glass of the shop window. Momentarily entrapped in self-doubt he indulged himself in a passing, reassuring study.

His eyes, he knew, were his best feature. Blue going to green, clear and unwavering, they offered serious concern and loyalty, but if need be that earnestness could be, and often was, mitigated by a wide and friendly smile dedicated to the very real matter of getting along in the world. He smiled now. Good. That ready smile, his eyes, the loose waves of blond hair and regular features gained from the determined march of battalions of WASP ancestors into history rendered him a handsome young man; he was twenty-three years old. At five foot ten, his body carried the lithe, forward stance of the track and field athlete. Smiling once more, he turned away from the window to resume the watch for Tyrelle's tall, classy figure.

Marshall had been in San Francisco barely a month and was already more than pleased with the way things were going, even if the fact weren't the fancy. He had a decent room in a decent hotel on Mission street, his money was holding up better than he'd expected, and one of several pretty good job prospects would probably open up in a few more days—a week or so at the most. Equally important, but not crucial as if it were a matter of health, he'd met Tyrelle.

Warmed by that thought, he turned back to the window and smiled: not bad for a guy who'd taken a bus out of Leavenworth, Kansas carrying two obituary notices, one suitcase, and a little over fifteen hundred dollars. Left behind were a cranky older brother, unemployment, and a reputation spattered with the mud of local ugliness and prejudice, always so handy in the great heartland of America.

His parents had died within three weeks of each other. That upset had brought on a whole new series of eruptions in the always boiling relationship with his brother, Bob. And then Myron, oddball, screwball, hysterical Myron, decided it was time to spill his guts about the weekends out at Motel Six with those two fellows from Iowa City, and to his uncle—of all people!—the most powerful Pentecostal preacher in the whole county! As the stories spread, the town, in gleeful malignancy, had been all ears and then, of course, one big wagging tongue. The fifteen hundred dollars had been his brother's buy-off: get out of town and, for God's sake, don't ever come back. That was what he'd done, and don't you worry about the other, Bob.

So, that was that and good enough. Fuck it.

Though he'd never been particularly exacting in his expectations, his listable assets, while certainly not vast, were at least genuinely his and he was happy as hell with each one. And right at the head of the list was his incredible luck in meeting Tyrelle. Perhaps there was some corn silk still stuck in his pockets, but that meeting was an event never once occurring to him as having been anything less than miraculous. In moments of pleased disbelief he was almost certain he'd found a man whom he could in daily fact share himself—and life—with honesty. In the softest of early morning light he believed that love could be built on that and, maybe, just a little bit more. In fact, he'd already made a good start at it, and he still had to grin self-consciously at its recollection.

"Well, to begin with," Tyrelle had said after that first inconclusive attempt, "you gotta relax. The key to the whole thing is relaxation, and you gotta know that."

"Okay," Marshall had replied, "I'm relaxed."

"No, you aren't, honey."

Well, he wasn't and he knew he wasn't; but he also knew that he could be and would be, soon enough.

Gleaming with confidence and capability, Tyrelle sat back on his haunches. His black body was trimly muscular—crafted through centuries of rigor overcome by daily endurance and discipline—crisply male and defined with unassuming excellence. Adorned with medallions of a sensuality synonymous with wickedness in the tree-lined Kansas streets of Marshall's recent history, Tyrelle was, oh God, Olympian abandonment wrapped in sable warmth—and less than three feet away! However true that was now, Tyrelle, even with a nature more laid back, was himself only three years into liberation from the insidious confines of southern New Mexico.

But there in his narrow room hung with awful blue wallpaper, his glow was incredibly enchanting and refreshingly direct. His erected cock stood forward in an attentive way, its head an elegantly symmetrical crown on the long, black staff.

"I've got some lotion here," he said, "which helps loads but you gotta relax."

"Okay, I got it."

Marshall was lying back on the murphy bed. His runner's legs, decked with casual golden fleece, were spread in willing invitation. Tyrelle's hand was between them, high in the buttocks where his fingers were working gently against the anus.

"You really mean to be fucked, huh?" he said.

"Yes."

"And right now?"

"Well... yes."

"I mean, I can do it, baby, and I want to. I just haven't ever run across such a good-looking white guy so intent on it in such a anxious way."

Tyrelle moved down to Marshall's side. Placing soft kisses on the lips, he moved to the nose and then the brow. He ran his hands along hard flanks to masculine hips.

"Why is that, baby?" he whispered. "You being so urgent."

"I'm getting a late start."

"Well, you can't catch up, honey. You gotta start where you're at."

"I know. I just want to get going, that's all."

"I see."

Marshall put his hand at the side of Tyrelle's face. He ran his fingers into the tight, defiantly personal curls that fell over exquisitely-formed ears.

"God," he said, "you're every one of those guys out there on the field I wanted so much to touch."

"Now, what field was that?"

"You know, the track and field sports field."

"Oh, that. Umm... that wasn't our kind." His gaze swept Marshall's body. "But, God, it sure fits on you all right. Jesus, just the look of you!" He paused. "And while you were out there you wanted to touch all those other guys, huh?"

"Every one."

"And I make you feel like that now?"

"More than you know."

"C'mon, man, you're pulling my leg."

"No I'm not."

"Well, now," Tyrelle said softly, "that's nice to hear, I'll say that."

Marshall crossed his hands at the back of Tyrelle's neck.

"Come on," he said, "no more talk, now. Let's do it."

Tyrelle smiled. "Okay. Boy, I bet when you set your mind to do something, you're a fast learner."

"The fastest."

Tyrelle knelt between Marshall's legs, his knees against the thighs. Marshall's cock, staunch in erection, lay back toward his belly, the scrotum draping above the secret alley leading to the anus. Tyrelle put his hands at the backs of Marshall's knees.

"Okay, we're gonna go up now," he said.

"Right."

"And then... say, you ever been rimmed? Had your asshole sucked?"

"No."

"Well, I bet you give it some good goosing when you jack off, don't you?"

"Yes."

"It's about like that. Lot better, though."

Tyrelle pushed Marshall's knees down to his shoulders. The crease open, the buttocks wide, the jewel hanging there in careful placement as if an emblem of royal games, he gazed on it in thoughtful lust.

"You white guys' assholes always look like they got something to hide."

"Like what?"

"I don't know. Something. But that's not to say they aren't handsome. They're all handsome."

Marshall's knees were pressed to the sides of his head. With the butt up so invitingly meaty and the sphincter brought to the glory of exposure for a blunt purpose, Tyrelle put his mouth low, near the magic juncture of thigh, scrotum and anus.

"Had me a guy once," he said, "who, when I got him pushed up like this, could suck his own dick. He did it while I sucked his bunghole." He paused. "I'm gonna throw some suck on yours now, honey. See if you can do something about the other if you want."

Tyrelle set into the sucking of Marshall's asshole with a casual greed and the ready, steady rhythm of a man devoted fully to the connecting rings of sexual enactment without the necessity of a conscious—and deadening—review of options. In life's whirl of conflicts and inconsistencies he always swam with the ever-changing current. He had that innate facility for anticipating inevitable change and accepting it without difficulty. Marshall, on the other hand, was more orderly and given to logical objectives. At the moment, trying to get his cock and mouth put together in the manner suggested was not all that orderly. Staggering along in earnest effort but soon falling into failure, he took up instead a jerking masturbation. He was, however, very much in touch with the willful scrubbings Tyrelle was delivering to the loosening twist of his asshole.

"Oh, Jesus," he moaned softly, "that's got the ticket."

"Like it?" Tyrelle murmured into the smooth flesh.

"Do geese fly?"

"They do fine, baby."

The tissues grew wet, dripping with spit; the tongue, while excellent but lacking in stamina, soon sagged in its effort. Tyrelle then called up a phalanx of fingers. He pressed a pair against the twitching pucker.

"I'm gonna go in with some fingers now."

"How many?"

"Maybe two to start."

"That a lot?"

"For some, but not for you, I think."

"Okay."

"I got the lotion for this. It don't taste good if it gets in your mouth, though."

He poured out a spot of aloe vera lotion. Pale yellow, it spread across the pinkish-brown asshole. Given a quick rub the target glistened with the invitation of a seeping, experienced whore.

Tyrelle said, "Don't this stuff feel cool?"

"It feels all right, I guess."

"Oh. Well, okay."

His finger tips doing a pattering dance on the rim, he made a few soft punches against the breathing fissure and then went in with a sly abruptness. Making tight swings left and right, he reached in and ran a lubricated palm on Marshall's cock, closing his fingers around the head.

"Oh, God!"

"That feel good?"

"Oh, God!"

Tyrelle fingerfucked and ran the jack-off for a time, his black eyes alight with the lascivious pleasure to be found in digging in the catacombs of the forbidden. Slipping into the rhythm of the fleshy exertion, Marshall's anus worked in a tight collar around the fingers, sending upward the thrills of the threatening stretch, the pulls toward the imminent penetration.

"Now," Tyrelle said, "I'm gonna put in something extra."

The thumb went in along side the fingers.

"Oh, Jesus!"

Marshall's butt swung up, joining in on the churn. His hips were hiking up the slope. He was moving rapidly toward the long shadow of the shimmering temple of fuck ready to stride manfully over its threshold into the miraculously everyday clutch of nirvana.

"That's fine, honey," Tyrelle whispered. "You're doing just great."

"God, I feel like I'm going to hell dressed in crepe paper."

"That gets it."

Putting bites, gentle, rapid, urgent bites, to the backs of Marshall's thighs, Tyrelle withdrew his fingers from the slackening sphincter and filled the void with his cock. The magnificent prod, elegantly black and girded proudly in excellent African regalia, made the entrance with calm, quiet consideration. The anus, glowing with the ripe flush of cherries hot on their twigs, accepted the inward march bowing low, sucking in the monarch, the inches heavenly markers, to its hot, moist throne.

"Oh God, baby," Tyrelle breathed, "you're the fuck named for me on heaven's golden plates."

Marshall, engulfed in billowing, nudging clouds of floating pain blown against him by Tyrelle's skillful use of their anatomies, entered the glistening cavern of anal penetrations. His bowels, his tubes, the very twists of flesh that held him together were assaulted under the wide, light tent of glorious aggression. He was celebrated; his asshole, his cock, his nuts and the skin bound up into his tits were celebrated, and he, the celebrated, celebrated the celebrator.

"God, Tyrelle," he murmured. His blue eyes, alight with delight, were turned up to those of black coal, hot in shimmering possession, burning down into his own. "God, if this could only last forever."

"It does, baby, in one way or another."

Marshall's arms, strong and supple, closed across shoulders broad, black, and capable as he gained the field of sexual effort he had truly sought. Tyrelle's lips, bringing him loose bundles of flowing kisses, were loving and in full flower, but it was the press of flesh, the ancient and venerable fitting of cock into asshole, that guided in the quest. With each thrust fattening the communion growing between the two healthy, vigorous bodies captained by two open, inquiring minds, the spew of seed was being prepared in the fiery furnaces burning in their nuts.

"Fuck me down, baby," Marshall intoned, his voice a bucket slopping with passion.

"Oh, down, honey. You bet. Down with dogs humping a post. Down with a squat on a cob."

His cock in his fist, Marshall rolled in the wonder of rut. The elusive saintliness to be sought in it, the debauchery that dripped from its creases, its curious offer of nothing of substance all, all of it, had grabbed him. At that very minute, with Tyrelle's cock pounding on his prostate and putting the tissues of his anus under a terrific strain, he was made a willing pawn in the always precarious game. Among the millions and millions of those inducted over the thousands and thousands of years, there could never have been another more comely, more desirable than Marshall in being flung upon the rack, and now straining toward the simple proposition dedicated to the dumping of a load of jizz. His hand laboring at the climbing of the invisible mountain, the first whack of the coming heave got him in the belly, spun there a moment, and then danced away. The second came faster and hit lower, grabbing his balls and going toward his asshole.

"Oh God, Tyrelle," he moaned, "I'm going to come."

"That's good, honey," Tyrelle said pulling his mouth from a kiss at Marshall's throat. "Oh, that's good. Pop us a wad, honey."

In less than seconds Tyrelle stoked the Olympian fires with swings into Marshall tagged with an increase in cadence. The thrusts thrown were to the hilt in penetration, the retreat at the maximum to mount still another loving assault.

"Oh! Oh! God!" Marshall groaned. "It's here."

The silvery sap shot out of Marshall's cock in jerking squirts. His belly rolled in the delicate torture, his legs stiffened, and his chest heaved. The turmoil seethed in a stiff strut, made the tight turns, and then began the fade into the curls of spent passion. The lacy jelly-juice lay like a frayed fan across Marshall's flat belly. Riding hard above, every fiber of his body fully energized in affinity, Tyrelle made a hero's mighty grab and plucked stars from the tilted crown of the dippy deity running the paper on the game. The wash of love in a high rush, he twisted in the marvelous affliction and, coming in gushes, bent to Marshall and swamped him in a flood of feverish kisses that soon ebbed into pools of soft, sweet pecks. Their arms folded into an embrace secure in the flight from the clamoring itch.

"Oh, man," Marshall murmured.

"Oh, baby."

"Oh, God."

Tyrelle moved back to lower Marshall's legs to the bed. His cock pulled from its wet nest with a small smack. He lay along side with an arm across Marshall's chest. He leaned his head on the other. The moment was softly strung with delicate and uncertain expectation.

"I don't think," Tyrelle said, "that you're going to have a whole lot of trouble in all this."

Marshall put his hand up to Tyrelle's bushy crown. In it he saw tiny twinkles of light thrown in constellations carelessly royal.

"No," he said, "I don't suppose so. Well, not when I'm with someone like you."

"Haven't you been with others?"

"No. I mean not here in San Francisco. There were, well, collisions in Kansas."

"I see, and, God, don't I know. Try New Mexico, baby. Throw in black and you've got the same pretty picture."

Tyrelle got up from the bed and took two short steps to the pullman kitchen. He rummaged in a drawer.

"How about some cookies? I've got chocolate chip and raisin oatmeal. Pick one."

"Um. Raisin oatmeal."

He brought both packages. Each taking a handful, they munched and chomped for a few minutes.

"Why'd you decide to come to San Francisco, Marshall?"

"Oh, God. Why? There were so many reasons back there in Leavenworth. Dozens. I don't have a single one right now. Well, except that I'm here and I'll never go back."

"That'll change. At least it did for me. And I bet it will for you, too."

"But you're different."

"Well! Now, other than the obvious, just how?"

"You're special. You look it and act it. You walk special. When I saw you in the BART station I knew right away how special you were."

"Me! Jesus, honey, where've you been! You're the special one. When I saw you I said to myself, fat chance, honey."

"Oh, come on."

"It's true, baby. I don't lie."

They sat on the bed and in the course of their conversation

devoured the two packages of Cable Car Cookies. They shared, compared, doubted, applauded and laughed. In the comfort of company they found self-awareness in each other, and in doing so planted the seeds of friendship.

It was almost midnight when Marshall stood at the door getting ready to leave. Tyrelle pasted him with a fast kiss which led to a long embrace and another and even longer kiss.

"I have to work late tomorrow night," Tyrelle had said, "but maybe we could meet the day after. We could maybe see a movie."

"Okay."

"Let's meet at Ninth and Market. South-east corner. Seven pm. That okay?"

"Great! I'll be there. You bet."

"See you."

"Good night. See you at seven o'clock."

"Right, honey," Tyrelle had said closing the door. "I'll be looking forward to it."

And now it was eight-ten.

Well, God, he thought, just because some guy hits these streets from the sticks doesn't mean he gets a prize. Dandy Jesus, use your head, fella!

Figuring a long walk would dull the edge of loneliness just renewed, he walked to the curb turning his attention toward the Embarcadero.

The traffic light was red. He waited.

That's it, he thought, a long walk, then the luxury of a piece of pie and a glass of milk and on to his room and bed. He'd make the rounds tomorrow, maybe shake loose a job. He knew he would probably run across Tyrelle again sometime. What then? Well, he'd see.

The light turned green. He started across the street.

"Marshall! Marshall, dammit! Over here!"

He looked up. There was a cab on the opposite side of the

Market wedged in between a Muni bus and a beer truck.

"Hey, Marshall!"

He saw Tyrelle waving from the window. There was a flurry of activity inside. Then Tyrelle exited the cab and hurried across the street, dodging cars and side-stepping a motorcycle.

"Oh God, Marshall, you waited. Mr. Blue brought in a whole pile of... Oh shit, the hell with Mr. Blue and his damned pants. You waited!"

"I thought maybe you'd been hurt."

"Really?"

"It's possible."

"Well, I suppose so." He smiled, looking very fetching in the last light of spring dusk. "Maybe it's too late for that movie. What do you think?"

"Yes, I suppose so. Anyway, I was thinking maybe I'd make the job rounds in the morning."

Tyrelle laughed. "I'm sort of short now, too. I had to give the cabbie a twenty. He said he couldn't make change in the middle of the goddamned street."

"Oh, Tyrelle!"

"Hell, that's nothing, honey. You waited. That's what's important."

Tyrelle put a hand on Marshall's arm and then moved an arm across his shoulders. He looked into his eyes.

"Do you want to come by my place?" he said. "I've got some more cookies. We'll stop at Ching's and I'll get some ice cream."

"Okay."

"I've got chocolate syrup, red sugar cherries and nuts."

"I said okay."

"Do you like whipped cream?"

"Sure, I like whipped cream."

"Would you settle for non-dairy topping?"

"Yes."

"Okay, I'll get some of that, too."

They made the trek up Turk Street to Ching's market, bought

the ice cream and the Kool-Whip and went around the corner to the narrow entrance of the frame building housing Tyrelle's third floor walk-up.

"Do you suppose there's a vacancy in here?" Marshall wondered as they climbed the stairs.

"Honey, there's always a vacancy here. Why? You figuring to move?"

"Sure. Well, as soon as my job comes up."

"There's a nice place one block over," Tyrelle said. "One bedroom. Outside entrance. Everything."

"Does it cost a lot?"

"Not too much. Of course it'd be better with two to share. It's a pretty big place."

Marshall stopped on the landing. Tyrelle, two steps above, turned. Marshall looked up smiling.

"Say, what would you think about maybe us moving into something like that together?"

Tyrelle shrugged his shoulders.

"We could talk about it," he said. "It's nice. Just repainted. No wallpaper. Just paint. Beige. I know you don't like the blue wallpaper I got here."

"Oh, hell, Tyrelle."

"C'mon, this ice cream's cold and I'm hot."

"So am I. Hot, I mean."

"I know."

Draped with chocolate syrup, sugar cherries, nuts and Kool-Whip, the ice cream didn't stand a chance. Tyrelle had forgotten about the cookies until he took the paper plates to the pullman kitchen.

"I forgot the cookies," he said.

"That's okay. I'm full."

"Want to stretch out with me for a while?"

"I'd love to."

In just seconds Tyrelle shed his sweater and shoved his chinos to his ankles and off. He stood in trim blue boxers with one knee on the murphy bed, looking more casually elegant than a whole catalog of models.

"Don't hurry," he said. Marshall was still fiddling with his shoes.

"Oh, sorry. I just like to look at you, that's all."

"That's all!"

"Well... I mean... Well, you know."

"Never mind, honey."

Tyrelle leaned across the bed to fluff the pillows. The thin cotton cloth of his shorts was pulled tight across the crease and, provocatively hidden, the furled brown rose was just a scant inch or so beneath. Marshall was transfixed by the possibility he might find in that hole. The erection he felt burgeoning in his underwear was more immediate in demand than any he'd ever known. He was almost faint from the desire he felt for this man who shone with the color of a gleaming nut. When he stood to drop his Levi's, the protrusion pushing at his briefs was anything but that.

"Oh, Marshall, you devil," Tyrelle said, "I'm so flattered. C'mon, to prove it I'm gonna give you a blowjob."

Stripping off their underwear they fell into the exalted sixty-nine configuration. Marshall went on the ebony staff with care and deliberation, making the plunges with his lips pressed firmly to the flesh. His tongue found its work in the nooks under the glans. He learned quickly that flat, lapping caresses there produced jerks and squirms in Tyrelle. They in their turn induced a feeling of warm power in himself which was fed fast enough into his own crotch to fuel the hot, wet exchanges being made there. Tyrelle held the nuts in the masterful grip of one hand while rolling the dickhead in his mouth. His tongue slapped impeccable insults at the slit as the fingers of his other hand danced fancy May Day steps on the asshole. Marshall was caught in the circular puzzle of dizzying actuality and reeling possibility.

To suck, to lick, to feel, push, squeeze, hold, to handle it or prick it? Smell it, taste it, tease it, grab it, twist it—gently—or spit on it. To make it go in, to make it stiff, to make it purr, jerk, spin or drip. God! And then Tyrelle eased a thumb up his ass.

He flopped back on the bed. "Oh, God!"

His belly heaved, he could have farted but he was quickly called back to the job of carrying the golden bricks.

He went above Tyrelle, forcing the man to his back. With his knees on either side of the handsome face, proudly brown from millennia of African sun, his cock thumped ruffles and flourishes, declaring the coming celebration. Then, taking ownership of that excellent, glistening torso, he yanked it to him, knees beneath his biceps, opening the cleavage to his hungry mouth for the ancient feeding. The anus, sly in a snotty smirk, greeted him in knowing complicity, brown, rude, and lovely in the way of a wedding cake mangled in devoted hunger. In his leap into the pit Marshall groaned with the grief of angels. He flung kisses of ruinous denial against the loop of desire, he raped it with the tongue of a gargoyle, he worshipped it with the purity of the unchained, the tenacity of the convinced. He spread it with spit, dressed it in the infamy of twisted gospel and inquisition and, with the condiment of liberation, ate it.

Tyrelle was thrown to the dirt of the tilting arena. His belly heaved, his cock screamed, his balls swung low in mindless joy as Marshall sailed the kites of his longing, no, his destiny, from the slick brown spot between Tyrelle's buttocks.

"Can you take a fucking, Tyrelle?"

"I could take it even if you were a Cyclops."

"I am."

"Fuck me, then. And keep your eyes wide open. Watch me do the churn, baby."

Anointing his dick with a slug of spit, Marshall put the head at the asshole turned up to him in welcoming triumph. His shoulders bedecked with a weightless fleece he bent into the special nook and took from it as it was offered, giving in return a measure equal in reach.

"Oh, baby," Tyrelle whispered, "come home to me."

The entrance gained in a fluid suck, the skid into the duct an exhilarated win, the plunges that followed were delivered without haste. The cock, hard with vigor, was gorged with elan, it glittered with style. And the anus receiving it danced with a quiver about its soft black lips as the tube, milky cream at a slosh in its cans, pushed deep into the hot milk house. Fingers, black and white, moved in skittering arpeggios across planes of skin, into creases, onto knobs, around thick things to pull, tease, urge, tempt and dare. Kisses took flight in flocks. Gropes grabbed in groups. Balls flopped in good-humored confusion, caught in a simplicity simpler than their own: destiny lay dead ahead in the eruption being forged in the guts straining at the harness of growing devotion.

"I think," Marshall murmured, "I'm about to jump off."

"Jump, honey. I'll catch you and every drop."

Tyrelle made a temple of his flanks, its construction of the smoothest, finest, most round, black marble on the market. Under a canopy of stiff corkscrew hair, the tabernacle, wet with the holiness of sodomy, prepared to receive the host.

"It's here, honey," Marshall groaned. "Oh, God!"

The spurt, the triumphal ooze, made its transfer under the shelter of an embrace most ornate in the sharing of the tremors of the explosion and the schools of darting kisses it spawned.

Tyrelle, pulled to the thinnest of his endurance, clutched at an elusive swing far above his head. Marshall pulling from the moist glut of the asshole, bent to the sweet duty and sucked at the staff, his tongue at a mean coax against the slit. Moving with nimble perception his fingers manipulated nuts and bung. Tyrelle threw his hips to the handsome face and pumped the gobs of fabulously funky slop into its lovely smooth mouth. In beads and clots, strings, and busy clusters the stuff washed about in Marshall's mouth, crossed his tongue, swamped his teeth until, the mass increasing with its affinity for spit, found the trap into the throat and made the drop downward.

Falling into an embrace of conquerors, Marshall and Tyrelle

listened to heartbeats, fingered hot body parts, and breathed the aromas of healthy exertion. Soon Tyrelle pulled a sheet to their shoulders to ward off an invading chill.

They dozed for a few minutes, Marshall going deeper into the sweet euphoria. Tyrelle slipped from the bed and tripped lightly to the bathroom.

Marshall awoke, stretched and lay back on the pillow in an expectant wait.

Tyrelle made the few strides back from the bathroom, his cock swinging at its indolent best. The color was that of the barrel of an expensive shotgun.

"Do you ever wear pajamas?" he asked.

"Yes."

"Flannel?"

"Yes. You?"

"Un huh. Sometimes I wear socks, too."

Marshall turned on his side. His butt was sleek, inviting, complete. Tyrelle put his hand near the perfect spot. Marshall rolled back and spread his legs.

"Do you like a big bed?" Tyrelle said.

"Oh, God, yes. The better to get at you."

"I think that the bedroom over there is big enough for a king-size."

"Really!"

"Un huh." He tickled Marshall around the balls. "How about it? You want to go look at the place tomorrow?"

"You bet."

"Then we could go downtown and look at some wallpaper samples."

"Fuck the wallpaper. They have wallpaper in Kansas!"

JASON, CAT

David May

Now let me in turn inform you:
I am a Cat. The name alone is enough.
— Collete

You can't tame a cat.

But you couldn't tell Bernie anything either. He thought he knew everything. He always had dogs, too, and in a way that explains why Bernie wanted Jason in the first place: Jason was a cat and couldn't be tamed.

When I first saw Jason he was lying on Bernie's floor, naked. His body was stretched out in the sunlight shining in from the window. I remember that his skin was pale, but darkly so; the body lean and neatly muscled; his black hair tousled about like a disobedient child's. He hadn't shaved for a few days and the angles of his face were accentuated by the dark stubble. His chest, stomach, legs, butt and forearms were covered with black hair/fur. His face was handsome with a straight nose and well defined chin. He was nothing less than beautiful.

He seemed asleep as I admired him, though I'd never know for certain that he wasn't watching me the whole time.

*   *   *

Bernie had been my first Master, and he felt a certain responsibility for having brought me out into the scene. He called once a week and asked how I was, who I was playing with (and if he disapproved he'd say so) and sometimes suggested that we get together. After a while he introduced me to his new slaves and taught me to top by sharing them with me. More than anything else, he was my friend.

When I'd come to see him that morning in his second floor

flat, he motioned for me not to talk and nodded towards Jason
who lay asleep (we thought) on the floor.

"I'm letting him rest," said Bernie when we'd gone into the
kitchen. "I only took the collar off an hour ago. He was so ornery
I kept him in chains. He couldn't have gotten much sleep."

"Ornery?" I asked. I couldn't imagine Bernie putting up with
any disobedience. I was always slapped silly for any sign of
resistance.

"Yeah. It sounds funny, but it feels like he only obeys me
when I'm in the room, like he's disobeying when he isn't. And
when I slap him, he glares at me."

"Just like a cat," I said without thinking.

"You and your cats, Jimmy. For a cat–boy you sure loved
being a dog."

This was true. I never really liked dogs, though I liked
Bernie's shepherd, Max. But being treated like a dog was great.
I got off on humiliation, and what could be more humiliating than
being called an animal that I didn't even like?

I accepted the coffee Bernie handed me as Jason walked in
with more grace than seemed humanly possible.

Bernie is a big man, six-three maybe, barrel–chested, with
enormous arms and big hands. He had a beautiful red beard that
he kept full but neat, and was bald on top but furry everywhere
else. (Another of his boys and I used to call him Bernie Bear, but
never to his face.)

He was a demanding Master who knew just how far to push
a slave, how to get everything out of him. He'd treat you so
mean, then hold you close and let you feel so safe in his big,
brawny arms that you knew the hell he'd put you through had
been worth it. At least that's how I always felt with him.

The point is, I really loved Bernie, and I doubted this new boy
of his appreciated him.

Jason looked at me now and nodded as if he already knew
me. He was smaller than Bernie, of course, but taller than me
though not as big, not as muscular or heavy boned.

"Jason, this is Jimmy. Jim, Jason."

He nodded again in the same way.

"Hi."

"Coffee?" asked Bernie.

"Sure."

"Feeling okay?" asked Bernie, resting one giant hand on Jason's furry little bottom.

"Yeah," he said as he stretched out his body with the same grace that he'd walked into the room. "Feel great." He gave Bernie a perfunctory kiss.

"Jim and I are going to lunch. Hungry?"

"Sounds good," he said matter-of-factly, as if the invitation were expected. He sat down opposite me and looked directly into my eyes. I looked out the window, already afraid of him. I felt devastated, almost violated, but also elated. And I knew he sensed all this without being told.

The dog, who'd been asleep in the corner of the kitchen until Jason had come in, got up and, almost cowering, backed out his pet door with a low whine to sit with deliberation on the back porch.

"What's his problem?" asked Bernie, looking after the dog through the kitchen window.

Jason looked directly into my eyes.

"Dog had a bad dream," he said with calm authority.

I looked back at him, still awed by his beauty, and grunted a garbled agreement.

"What would you know about dogs, Jimmy? Jason, Jim here is a cat fancier. Sometimes I think he prefers them to people."

Jason's eyes sparked with new interest.

"Really, Jim?"

"Usually," I laughed, trying to make light of it.

"I'm not surprised," said Jason, his voice almost hypnotic.

Bernie laughed, apparently thinking that it was all a joke. I laughed with him, but could think only of how I'd do anything for Jason, to feel the strength of our two bodies locked together.

How could Bernie want to break him? I'd rather have been Jason's slave, to be played with as cruelly as he pleased, to be his completely. But belonging is a two–way street: a Master must belong as much as a slave belongs. Jason could belong to no one, I knew, but my desire to own him, or to be owned by him, was only fueled by its futility as I watched him pad softly out of the kitchen to get dressed.

*   *   *

Jason stayed on my mind. I wondered how I could see him alone, wondered who he really was.

When I played with other men, put myself at their mercy, I was never satisfied. I felt nurtured when I wanted, even needed, to feel used. I, who had disliked dogs, became like one, ready to sacrifice myself for my Master's affection.

I waited for Bernie to call me, as I knew he would, to confide in me his doubts about Jason. I knew Bernie well enough to know that there would always be doubts.

"I can't break him, Jimmy."

"He's like a cat, Bernie, and you can't tame a cat to your will."

"You and your cats. If he doesn't want to be my slave, why is he living with me?"

"He is?"

"Didn't I tell you? He's gonna be my slave full time. It's what I want, Jimmy. I love him."

"And him?" I asked, afraid my voice would betray all.

"Who can tell? He's a mystery to me. Sometimes it's as if I'm the one being trained. It's the craziest thing..."

He *is* a cat, I whispered to myself.

"Where did you meet him, anyway?" I asked aloud, as cool as I could.

"At the Cell. I'd never seen him there before and thought he should be treated right on his first visit, so I —"

"Is he from around here?" I interrupted.

"He says from up by the River. But I don't ever remember seeing him up there, do you?"

"No," I answered. "Not that it matters."

Even if I hadn't felt the way I did about Jason, I'd have said that he was bad news for Bernie. But we were both powerless to resist him

Bernie invited me over that evening. I already had a date for later, so I arrived in my leather, feeling pretty hot. My cock was half–erect like it always is when I wear leather next to my skin.

Bernie handed me a beer in the kitchen and we went to the front room where Jason, naked except for his collar and two weeks of a soft, black beard, sat on the floor, his leash tethered to Bernie's big arm chair. I nodded to Jason as I entered the room. He stared at me with the same open curiosity as before, but revealing nothing. I sat down on the couch, stretched out my legs, and looked around the room.

"Where's Max?"

"Out," said Jason with the trace of a smile.

"No one was talking to you, Jay," said Bernie without much conviction. "He and Jason don't get along," he said turning to me. "Max is afraid of him."

I watched a brief smile creep over Jason's lips. Sibling rivalry, I thought, and poor Max is losing.

"Since you're already in your leather and ready for a workout, Jim, why not borrow Jason for a spell. You'd like that?"

I looked at Bernie, than at Jason who was looking up at me instead of at the floor as I would have done in his position, as Bernie had trained me. I knew right away that Bernie's offer was prompted by Jason. He was challenging me. I wavered for only a moment before I remembered what I'd told Bernie: you can't tame a cat.

"Can't tonight, Bernie. Gene's expecting my full attention." I grabbed my crotch. "I've been saving it for him for a few days so I'll have a lot to give him." I rubbed the leather to show my hard cock. I was ready for some action, but not this action, not the uneasiness I felt in Bernie's house.

Bernie looked relieved and disappointed at the same time. He stroked Jason's hair as if to appease him, not as the kind of condescension I'd expect from Bernie.

"Sure."

"Another night," I lied.

"Sure."

I looked at Jason again. Being naked suited him. Nudity didn't make him look vulnerable at all. He wore his body the way Bernie and I wore our leather, as an extension of himself. Jason looked back at me with a new expression, not respect exactly, but one that acknowledged me as someone to be dealt with differently than the rest.

I let our eyes lock for a moment, holding my stare. For the first time Jason gave himself away. He averted his eyes from mine, as any cat would.

*   *   *

Gene and I were hot that night. Gene was never the kind of guy to play games. He gave all he had, and somehow that was always more than his Master or Mistress expected. He was popular with the crowd I hung out with at the Cell. He had the right amount of arrogance as he begged to be put in his place, an attitude a lot of tops find hard to resist. Not that he was a pushy bottom, just a good one who expected the best because he was the best. And he always did a top proud.

That night I was crueler than I'd ever been before. With one booted foot, I pushed his face into my other boot. Gene, never presumptuous, waited for permission to lick my boots. His boot fetish was famous; I denied him the pleasure. Instead I kept my boots just within his reach and forbade him to touch them as I whipped him, watched him squirm and made him beg.

But mostly I thought of Jason. This was what Bernie wanted to do to Jason but didn't dare, what I wanted Jason to do to me.

When I finally shot my load down Gene's throat for the fifth and last time that night, I thought I'd died.

*   *   *

Then Max died.

Will mentioned it to me over beers at the Eagle a couple weeks later. The cause of death, he said, was uncertain.

I ran over to see Bernie early the next day. Jason answered the door wearing only a slave collar. His beard had almost grown in and he looked sexier than hell. I made a brief hello and ran back to the kitchen and Bernie who, as I expected him to be, was sitting over a cup of cold coffee.

I sat next to him, took his hand and was silent. We sat together a while before he said anything.

"It's so strange, Jimmy. The animal control people say he was killed by another animal but... He was such a gentle dog..."

I squeezed his hand.

"He'd broken his neck when he tried jumping over the fence to get away. His collar got caught..."

"I'm sorry, Bernie."

Jason came into the kitchen and poured himself a glass of milk. He moved with the same grace as before. Nothing in his movements or face indicated that he cared about Max or how Bernie might feel. He stopped and looked at me.

Bernie continued: "There were claw marks, but too big for a cat. So they think maybe it was a rabid raccoon or something. But no one saw anything. Neighbors just heard a lot of noise and called the cops."

"Where were you and Jason, Bernie?"

"I was at the Black and Blue with Jack. Jason was chained up in the basement being punished."

I saw Jason, standing behind Bernie, suppress a smile.

"Did *you* hear anything, Jason?"

"In the basement? Bernie sound–proofed it. You should know

that."

He did smile this time, and left the kitchen.

"Want some coffee?" asked Bernie.

"No, thanks. I'm okay."

I walked slowly down the steps to the front door, Jason trailing behind me. I held the door open a moment and looked back at him.

"What are you thinking?" he asked.

"I know better than to think, Jason. I already think I know more than I want to."

"That scares you?" he only half–asked.

"It scares the shit out of me."

Jason suddenly looked very alert, cocking his head as if he'd heard something. Then I heard it, the sound of Bernie's heavy footsteps above us. Jason looked back to me and gave me a strange smile, a smile that spoke secrets.

"Jason!" Bernie bellowed.

"Yes, Sir."

"Where the hell are you?"

"Down here letting your friend out."

I broke our stare this time, stepping out on to the front porch as Jason closed the door behind me. I heard Bernie's raised voice again, the sound of flesh hitting flesh, and Jason's cry of pain followed by a scuffle.

I walked away fast. I refused to be a witness.

*   *   *

I avoided Bernie and Jason after that, was always "too busy" to talk when he called, unavailable when he wanted to see me. Bernie must have known I was avoiding him, and I'm sure he was hurt. But what could I do? I wanted no part in the drama being played out in that house. So I kept my distance.

Bernie, I knew, was unreachable when he was in love. He couldn't hear the truth so there was no point in telling him. I was glad that he'd become my big brother instead of my lover.

*   *   *

Gene and I were walking home in the rain from Hamburger Mary's one Sunday morning a few weeks later. We were heading for our respective beds after we'd played most of the night, then gone to breakfast because we knew we were too wired from a sex high to sleep. We were exhausted but happy.

I'd gotten more back from Gene than I'd given — and any Top will tell you how rare that is! I was light–headed from the long night and no sleep, but it didn't hinder my mood. I kissed Gene goodbye at his front door and walked up our little street to my place.

When I got to my front door I saw two guys (who didn't look like they were from the neighborhood) looking over the neighbor's fence, calling, "Here, kitty, kitty, kitty!"

I wondered if one of my own cats had gotten out while I was gone, so I went over and asked them what was up. They checked me over a second, me in my leather, looking bedraggled and wet on a rainy Sunday morning.

"We thought we saw our cat," one guy said.

"What does it look like?"

"Sorta like a burmese," the other one said. "But real big."

"Yeah," said the first guy. "We found him up at the River a few months ago and brought him home. He ran away a few weeks later."

"Guess he heard he was getting his balls cut off!" He laughed at his own joke.

"I haven't seen a Burmese around here," I said.

"You know what one looks like?" asked the second guy, apparently skeptical that a leatherman should know one kind of cat from another.

Fucking queen, I thought. Go back to your own neighborhood.

"Yes," I said aloud. "I have cats of my own. Give me your

number and I'll call you if I see it."

One of them handed me a business card.

"And the cat's name is Jason."

I shuddered, not knowing if it was because I was cold and wet or because of the name.

They thanked me and walked off under their single umbrella as I stood sweating in my leathers. I shook off the uneasiness I felt and walked up the few steps to my apartment.

Fucking amateurs, I thought. Probably call themselves "cat owner." Dickheads in designer jeans. I'd run away from them, too.

I stripped off my leathers the moment I got into the door, and tumbled into bed, promising myself I'd give them a proper oiling when I woke up.

* * *

I don't know how long it took me to realize that the pounding in my head was really someone pounding at the front door. I looked at my clock; I'd slept an hour. After another five minutes of pounding I stomped down the hall, still naked, not giving a fuck who was at the door, messing with my sleep.

"Yeah?"

It was Jason. He stood there naked and wet, dishevelled but proud, with only his arms wrapped around himself to keep warm. He nodded a greeting as I pulled him indoors and into the warmth of my apartment. I stood him in front of the heater and grabbed a towel from the usual pile of unfolded laundry.

"Here, Jason. Let me dry you off."

He was so beautiful. I wanted to lick him dry. He rubbed his body against the towel as I dried his hair. Then I heard it, very distinctly: Jason was purring.

I was shivering again.

I pulled a pair of extra blankets from under the pile of laundry and wrapped myself in one as I handed the other to Jason. I pushed the laundry onto the floor and sat on the couch. The purring had stopped. I hoped it had been my imagination, and prayed it hadn't.

We were silent for a while. I avoided his eyes, half out of respect and half out of fear. Finally he spoke. His voice was deep and quiet, different than it had sounded before.

"Thanks."

"For which?"

"Getting rid of them." He paused and watched my cats enter the room. "They were the last people I expected to meet."

"They were assholes, Jason. I'd leave them, too."

Jason made a deep half–growl towards the cats. They stared at him a moment, then nosed each other as if verifying their impression. Then they sat, albeit cautiously, near the door and watched us through half–closed eyes.

The four of us sat together in the quiet of the rainy afternoon, as cats sit together with each other, demanding and expecting nothing more than each other's company.

Finally I blurted it out, what I'd been afraid to say before, even to myself.

"I love you, Jason."

I was sure I sounded like a fool.

I expected him to laugh, but he didn't. He only shrugged his shoulders and said, "I know."

A few minutes later, as if it were part of a conversation we'd been having for some time, he spoke.

"I tried to love Bernie. Only I don't know how. Not the way Max loved him, or Bernie loved me. I wanted to belong the way that they belong." He motioned to the cats in the corner.

"What are you going to do?"

"Go home. Be with the others."

"Home?" I asked. Others? I thought.

"I only came to say goodbye. Because you're my friend. Because you love me."

He came close to me now. My blood ran cold. He was

changing. His eyes first, then his face. The soft, silky black body hair increased into fur.

He leaned towards me, to kiss me. I leaned away, but he pulled me towards him

"Jimmy," he growled. "It's what you wanted."

Our mouths met in a kiss. I felt the sharpness of his teeth against my lips, the roughness of his tongue against mine.

Everything went black.

*   *   *

I woke up on the floor, my body spread out in a nest of unfolded laundry. Jason was curled next to me, licking me with his large, rough tongue, caressing me with large, padded paws.

I looked into his face and saw the softness of his beard, grown to cover most of his face now. I reached out to stroke the half–human face without thinking. He rubbed his face into my hand, took it into his mouth and chewed it gently as a kitten does when it plays. Then he bit down hard and drew blood. I cried out and pulled my hand away.

His face was more human for a moment.

"Sorry," he said with a low, guttural purr. Then he licked away the blood.

He purred again and kissed me. I felt his hard cock jab against my thighs with some urgency. I felt his teeth grow sharper and I struggled to get free of the kiss. He held me down and chewed on my nipples, his teeth like tiny needles piercing the hardened flesh. He drew blood again, purred with satisfaction and licked it way, like before, with his rough tongue. Then he paused to look at me with cool curiosity.

I had the sense that I was prey, to be played with between two gigantic paws. I tried to beg him to let me go but couldn't because I hoped he'd never leave me.

Suddenly I was thrown over on my stomach. He held me down as his nose found my asshole, then his tongue, and finally his dick. I screamed louder than I thought possible. I'd been fucked with just spit before, been fucked by cocks bigger than his, and enjoyed it. But I'd forgotten, until I felt his cock pierce my guts, that a cat's dick is barbed.

I felt his body grow furrier as it thrashed on top of mine, felt the disproportionate strength of a cat as he pounded inside of me, tearing me up. He was getting close, I could tell. His sharp, feline teeth bit into the nape of my neck. I screamed again as I felt my flesh tear between his teeth.

Then I wasn't screaming. I succumbed to the blackness surrounding me. I knew Death was fucking me.

It was over.

*   *   *

I woke up in my bed the next morning aching all over, my back crusted with blood, tiny scabs covering my tits. I wanted to believe that it had been a dream, but my body was the evidence that said it had been real.

I crawled out of bed and shut the window. The rain had stopped, but a puddle remained from the night before. Jason, I supposed, had gone out the window and over the rooftops.

As I looked out the window, studying the rooftops for a sign of him, I realized that he had put me to bed before he'd left, even tucked me in under the covers. I wanted to believe it was an act of love. All the pain running through my body, pain that would continue for weeks to come, was unimportant now: he loved me.

I called in sick for the entire week, not wanting to explain why I winced each time I stood up, sat down, or took a step. But I savored each pain as it shot through me. Every ache reminded me of Jason, forced another surge of blood into my cock, keeping it erect.

I wallowed in Jason's single act of tenderness. It was my meditation, his name my mantra. And every time I cried out in some sudden reminder of the pain I felt, I loved him more.

When I went to bed that night, and for every night for some time to come, I left the window open, hoping he'd return.

OTHER EXPLICIT GAY FICTION
FROM GLB PUBLISHERS

ROGUES TO REMEMBER   (No. 1 in Rogues Series)
Short Story Collection by **Bill Lee**   US $ 10.95   _____

> *The masculine characters are hot and the wall-to-wall sexual activity is hard to resist.*
> — Stan Leventhal

LEATHER ROGUES   (No. 2 in Rogues Series)
Short Story Collection by **Bill Lee**   US $ 10.95   _____

> *These are accounts of hot leather encounters in the classic styles... run the gamut of leather experience.*
> — Anthony F. DeBlase

BI RANCHERS BI MATES
Bisexual Novel by **Bill Lee**   US $ 9.95   _____

> *Hot, erotic, genuine bisexual sex on every page... Bill Lee outs and ratifies the bisexual lifestyle.*
> — EIDOS

SECRET BUDDIES
Gay Romantic Novel by **Mike Newman**   US $ 11.95   _____

> *Equal parts longing and sex, nostalgia and innocence — pure gay Americana.*
> — Aaron Travis

ADD $2.00 PER BOOK FOR SHIPPING AND HANDLING (US only)   _____
(We pay the sales tax)

Check or money order to: **TOTAL**

                                             _____

GLB PUBLISHERS
P.O. Box 78212, San Francisco, CA 94107

OTHER CONTEMPORARY GAY FICTION
FROM G|L|B PUBLISHERS

THE DEVIL IN MEN'S DREAMS
Short Story collection by **Tom Scott**   US $11.95   _____

> *Touches on sentiments, from ironic humor to painful remorse, which many gay men have experienced...*
> – Lambda Book Report

White **Sambo**
Novel by **Robert Burdette Sweet**   US $12.95   _____

> *Sweet manages to imbue his characters with human credibility and their situations with utterly recognizable tensions... for me this book was a find.*
> – Shelby Steele

SOME DANCE TO REMEMBER
San Francisco novel by **Jack Fritscher**   US $11.00   _____

> *Jack Fritscher didn't invent the Castro, he just made it mythical. Heady, erotic, comic... the first comprehensive fictional chronicle of the best of times.*
> – The Advocate

ADD $2.00 PER BOOK FOR SHIPPING AND HANDLING (US only)
(We pay the sales tax)   _____

Check or money order to: **TOTAL**

_____

G|L|B PUBLISHERS
P.O. Box 78212, San Francisco, CA 94107

Are <u>YOU</u> a G L B Writer?

G L B
A E I
Y S S
   B E
   I X
   A U
   N A
      L

If you have faith in your manuscript and want to see it in print, maybe we can help. We are cooperative "contributory" publishers, meaning that the author shares the cost of printing and promotion but earns a much greater royalty. We are especially interested in advancing gay, lesbian, and bisexual fiction, non-fiction, and poetry.

For more information, write to:

The Editor
GLB Publishers
P.O. Box 78212
San Francisco, CA 94107